NEW RECRUITS

THE SHADOW PATRIOTS
BOOK TWO

WARREN RAY

The limits of tyrants are prescribed by the endurance of those whom they oppress."

Fredrick Douglas

"There are no extraordinary men…just extraordinary circumstances that ordinary men are forced to deal with."

Admiral William (Bull) Halsey Jr.

ACKNOWLEDGMENTS

My thanks to my editor, Dave Nixon, who tirelessly spent many hours of his time going through this novel. He had the patience of a saint and the honesty that this type of work requires.

CHAPTER 1

A strong wind howled across the road blowing Meeks' unruly blonde hair in his face. He and Scar stood observing the plumes of smoke rising in the direction of Decatur, Michigan. They headed there to check out the last Patriot Center. Meeks tucked his hair back under his "Hawkeye" hat and got back in the black Mustang they'd picked up the day before. They found it at the Ohio Center, it had a full tank of gas, and it was a Mustang. Meeks had always wanted one, but with a wife and three kids, he could never justify it.

The two looked at each other and without saying a word, Meeks pushed down on the pedal and picked up speed as they drove on Highway 51 outside of Dowagiac. The faster he went the more adrenaline he could feel surging through his body.

The billows of smoke grew wider the closer they got to Decatur. They entered the town and saw a haze hovering in the air emitting a putrid smell. Houses up and down the main road were all burned down, some with small flames still shooting out. They both had seen this type of destruction before back in Victor, Iowa and Brainerd, Minnesota, but they hadn't seen it anywhere else.

They slowly reached the bend in the road on Delaware Street and turned into the dirt parking lot of two smoldering buildings.

Scar turned to his friend. "We can assume the Patriot Center is gone as well."

"Why in the hell would somebody do this?"

"I don't know. Maybe the workers at the Center were pissed they were being put out of business."

"Seems like a lot of work to set every house on fire. Heck, it had to have taken all damn day to do it," said Meeks.

"Whoever did it must have been pretty pissed off about something."

"What do you want to do?" asked Meeks.

"I don't know. See if anyone's around."

"Doubt we'll find anybody."

Meeks put the car in drive, and spun it around in the dirt. He took a right on Edgar Bergen Boulevard. He drove slowly as they observed the destroyed houses, while looking to see if they could spot anyone. The road went through a cemetery, where headstones sat on either side of them. As they came to an intersection, Meeks was the first to notice a group of vehicles in the parking lot of a closed-down school. There were people standing around them.

"Check it out. We got some guys over there," he said pointing to the school.

"Yes we do. That's weird."

"What's weird?"

"It's the only building not burned down."

Meeks kept his foot on the brake and watched the men turn their attention towards them.

"You think they're friendly?" asked Meeks.

"I'm not sure, but I'm..." Scar stopped mid-sentence when some of the men scrambled to their vehicles and a couple of others raised their weapons and fired at them.

"Oh boy," said Meeks.

"Back it up! Back it up!" yelled Scar.

Meeks threw the car in reverse and jammed the accelerator down, spinning the tires. White smoke from the tires blew past them as the Mustang rocketed backwards.

"Brace yourself," Meeks ordered.

Meeks pushed his left foot to the floorboard to steady himself, found a clear spot in the rearview mirror, whipped the wheel hard letting it go, and then grabbing back ahold. The car spun around in a 180, as Meeks slammed the gearshift in drive, and the Mustang shot forward like a cannonball.

Scar turned in his seat. "Here they come."

Meeks took a stiff turn to the right screeching the tires as the nimble car attacked the corner. The tight turn pushed Scar into Meeks forcing him to hang on. The street was straight and he smashed the pedal down unleashing the four hundred horses under the hood.

"Up ahead."

"I see em," said Meeks as he took another right and then a left. He threaded the car through the neighborhood trying to lose their pursuers, who were coming hard on their tail. Meeks needed to find his way out of the small town so he could call on the big V-8 once again. His knuckles turned white from gripping the steering wheel and a bead of sweat dropped from his eyebrow.

Scar pulled his Kimber .45 out, chambered a round, and clicked the safety off all in one motion. He pushed the window button and lowered the glass. A strong blast of air threatened to blow his Marine emblem hat off his head. He removed it before sticking his head out the window. He pointed the pistol at the SUV that was following them and fired off a couple of shots. The SUV slowed down, but then Scar saw a gun pointing at them and then the powder flash from the barrel. He emptied his magazine as he returned fire and moved back inside just in time to see a car coming straight at them.

Meeks slammed on the brakes with both feet and steered into a gravel lot of a grain elevator. He once again floored the pedal and had to wrestle for control as the car kicked up gravel and dust. The pursuing SUV followed them into the lot. Meeks went into a 360-degree turn, steering with it to maintain the controlled skid. The spinning tires created a dust cloud giving them cover.

Meeks swerved the car back onto the pavement, and the wheels bit instantly. He had to tangle with the wheel again for control. The low-built, heavy Mustang held the road like a magnet and they shot down St George Street, which led them out of town.

"Finally. Now, aren't you glad we picked up this bad boy yesterday?" asked Meeks with a slight grin.

"Nice to see you're enjoying yourself," said Scar shaking his head.

The car hugged a curve without as much as a tire squeal. They came to a turn off to the left. Meeks slowed down and took it. Trees canopied the road as he eased ahead. He looked to the left at a small path leading into the woods. He stopped the car.

"What are you doing?" asked Scar.

"Hiding. Better than trying to lose them. No telling if there's anyone ahead of us."

He turned the car and drove it onto a small trail running through more trees. It was bumpy as he guided the car further up the path, which wound to the left out of sight of the road.

They both got out and stuck close to the trees as they ran back down the path. After reaching the end, they hid in the trees and waited.

They heard vehicles in the distance.

Both stood silently.

Moments later, a truck and a car sped by them.

"Suckers," smiled Meeks.

"We better wait a bit."

Within minutes another truck passed.

Thirty minutes passed before they felt safe to move out. They both double timed it back to the Mustang and slid into the supple, black leather seats. Meeks turned the key and revved the engine. He put the car in reverse and began backing it up. As he got to the end of the path, a car passed by and came to an abrupt halt.

CHAPTER 2

In St. Paul, Minnesota, Harry Olson slumped on a bar stool sipping a vodka tonic with no ice. He kept his ball cap tilted back on his gray head. The place had the usual neon beer signs hanging on the walls, but to save on power, the owner kept them all off. The late afternoon light poured through the big windows by the entrance.

Olson had been the first one there when the bar opened at noon. A few others filtered in over the next couple of hours. He hadn't had a drink in many weeks, having only recently gotten back from Canada with the Shadow Patriots. He had been hesitant in getting involved, but his old friend, Bill Taylor, insisted it was his duty. After being chased up into Canada and fighting in Detroit Lakes, he was worn out and needed to come home to St. Paul to see what remained of his family.

A stranger came up next to him and offered to buy him a drink.

"You say you were with the Shadow Patriots?" asked the man with an east coast accent.

"Yeah, I was with them. Traveled with them all the way into Canada and back."

"So where are they now?"

"I don't know. I left them over a week ago."

"Well, how can I meet up with them?"

"Hell if I know," he said, annoyed with the stranger.

"You must have some idea where their camp is?"

"I just told you, I've no idea. Hell, for all I know they've disbanded."

"Disbanded? You can't be serious."

"A lot of us left. Why do you want to know all this anyhow?" asked Olson.

"I want to join up with them," responded the man.

"You do, huh?" Olson eyed him cautiously.

"Yep, want to join in on all the fun."

"Fun, eh?" It was a rhetorical question. "You think it'd be all fun and games."

The stranger didn't respond. He wondered if the man might not be as drunk as he thought. He didn't want to arouse any suspicions and decided to back off a little bit. He gave Olson a rousing patriotic line.

"Hey, anytime I can kill off some government pukes, then yeah, I'd say that's some fun," he said, trying to sound sincere.

"You ain't from around here, are ya?"

"From Chicago."

"That's a funny accent you got for being from Chicago. Sounds like you're from the East Coast."

The stranger hadn't thought about what he sounded like. "Yeah, I get that a lot. I spent quite a bit of time working back east. I pick up accents easily."

Olson didn't respond. He signaled the bartender for another round.

"I got this round. Make it two shots. Jack, if you've got it."

The bartender came back setting the shot glasses down.

They picked up their drinks.

"To better times in the good ol' USA."

Olson nodded, tilted his head back and swallowed the whisky.

"So, if I find these guys who should I ask for? Who's in charge?"

"Cole Winters, a good man."

"Cole Winters, huh? Where's he from?"

"Somewhere in Iowa, I think. I didn't really get to know him all that well."

The stranger finished his drink, slapped him on the back, and turned around to leave the bar.

CHAPTER 3

SOUTH BEND INDIANA

Winters walked up to Elliott asking if Scar and Meeks were back yet. The two of them had gone to check the last of the Patriot Centers. Since the death of Colonel Nunn, the capture of Commandant Boxer, and the elimination of the terrorists, the Shadow Patriots had very little to do. In fact, in the past couple of weeks more than half of their members had left the group for various reasons. Some were bored with the lack of action. Others wanted to see their families to safety and some were just plain afraid of being caught.

Elliott had also gone back to Iowa to check on his wife, Amy, and their two daughters. Knowing what was really happening, he wanted to move his family south before he continued with the Shadow Patriots. Like most folks from small towns, he had extended family living in the area. After relaying the news about what was going on, most everyone, including his mother who was in her seventies, decided to pack up and move to Oklahoma where they had relatives.

For Elliott it had been a good trip home, knowing his family would be safe, but at the same time, sad. His daughters didn't want him to leave and tried to convince him to stay. It had been a tearful farewell for him and he was still in the process of getting over it, having been back for only a few days.

With most everyone else going their own way, Winters had reservations for the future of their group. He would have liked to go south and looked for his nineteen-year-old daughter, Cara, who had run off with her boyfriend. He had a cousin in Florida and thought that perhaps she had sought out his assistance. For now though, he would put that on hold until he knew all the Centers were closed down.

Winters and Nate had led a small group down to Illinois and into Indiana, while Scar and Meeks went to investigate one in Ohio and another in Michigan.

Their operators had abandoned both the Illinois and Indiana Centers. They probably heard what happened with the others and decided to skip town.

They were all to meet back in South Bend, Indiana, at the closed down Catholic university. The once majestic campus with its golden dome was overgrown with grass and looked like an abandoned movie lot. Like all the schools in the Midwest, it had closed once the power grid failed and winter set in. The student population had already thinned with most joining the war effort, and the rest going back to their families.

Winters looked down at the sitting Elliott. "They're running late."

"Oh, they probably ran into some good ol' boys and are goofing off with them."

"I'll feel a lot better when I see them back here."

"You think them centers are closed down?" asked Elliott.

"If they aren't, I'm sure they'll take it upon themselves to shut em down."

Elliott chuckled. "Yeah, no doubt about that. Question is, what are we going to do next?"

"I don't know. I don't know what else we can do. Most everyone is gone anyways."

"Yeah, but we still have more than we started out with. Remember that day, when you came out of the train station shooting at those drivers. Heck, we all thought you were a crazy man."

"For a while, I wondered about that myself. I kept wondering if I was a Dr. Jekyll and Mr. Hyde type of guy. You know a little on the bi-polar side."

"Did you really?"

"Oh, yeah. I had done things I couldn't have imagined in my wildest dreams. I was really worried about myself."

"I had no idea, Cole."

"I was the Captain. Who was I supposed to confide in? I mean I had to keep up the appearance of strength."

"Well, you had me fooled."

"Don't mean to freak you out or anything. It's just kind of nice to get this off my chest. I'm much more confident about things now, but boy, at the beginning I was pretty scared and really unsure of myself."

"We all were, Cole. I gotta tell ya though, you put on a good front, cause we all looked up to you, for having done what you did at the train station."

"I'll tell you a secret, just as long as you don't tell the others."

Elliott nodded.

"I puked my guts out after I killed those men. Before that, in the woods, when they came looking for me, my legs were like rubber and I was literally crawling on my hands and knees."

Elliott started laughing.

"Some tough guy, huh," said Winters chuckling.

"Well, I about peed my pants when we went back to the first Patriot Center."

"I remember you shaking like a leaf. Oh, how jaded we've become."

"I suppose we can get back to a little normalcy if there's nothing left for us to do. What will you do?"

Winters didn't hesitate for a minute. "I'm going to go look for my kid."

"Where?"

"Start in Florida. We've got some distant family there. I'm thinking she might have reached out to them."

"How old is she again?"

"She's nineteen now and headstrong. We didn't always see eye-to-eye on everything. Actually, we almost never agreed on anything. She rebelled big time in high school. It was all I could do to get her to even graduate. Once she did, off she went with her boyfriend. Haven't seen or heard from her since."

"Must have been hard on your wife," said Elliott in a concerned tone.

"Worried Ellie to no end. It consumed her, especially when everything went to Hell. It didn't help when she got diagnosed with the cancer. The one thing she wanted before she died was to see her daughter again. I think she died more of a broken heart than cancer. I'm certain, it sped up the process."

"So, she doesn't even know her mom is dead?"

Winters shook his head.

"What are you going to say to her?"

"Ask her to forgive me. I was probably a little too hard on her. With everything that's gone on, the things we've done here have given me a different perspective."

"Yeah, I know just whatcha mean."

"I was really angry at her for not being there for her mom. I was very resentful, but now, not so much. I feel sorry for her, knowing she missed out on saying her goodbyes."

"Yeah, that is sad."

"Well, chances are, I might never see her again."

"You'll find her Cole, don't ever give up. Family is all that matters."

Winters nodded in agreement.

"Hey, if you want some company, I'll be more than happy to go with you."

"You'd do that?"

"You betcha."

"What about your family?"

"They're mostly in Oklahoma now. I've got some cousins who decided to stay put, but other than them, everyone's safe."

"Couldn't have been easy to leave them again?"

"No, it wasn't. My two girls, bless their hearts, didn't want me to go. I sat them down and reminded them how important it was for us to be fighting."

"How'd they take it?"

"They understood, but you know, it's hard knowing your daddy is putting himself in harm's way."

"What about your wife?"

"Amy puts up a good front, but she'd rather have me here, with you, than out West."

"I take it you didn't tell her everything we've gone through."

Elliott looked at Winters with a slight smile. "Oh, hell no, you know I didn't."

"Who'd believe it."

"Yeah, no kidding."

Winters was glad to have Elliott as his friend. He missed his old friends a lot, but was comforted to know he had gained the friendships of Elliott and the others. They had all gone through a lot in the past couple of months and their experiences bonded them together like nothing else could.

CHAPTER 4

DECATUR MICHIGAN

Meeks backed the car down the pathway, but stopped when he spotted a compact car blocking the exit. The two occupants were pointing at them.

He turned to Scar. "Hang on brother."

Meeks punched the gas. The car zoomed backwards, bounced up onto the road, and plowed into the compact. Scar jumped out first, followed by Meeks, each grabbing their pistols and firing as they stormed the car.

Bullets ripped through the open windows. The two men inside tried desperately to escape. Scar stopped firing and pulled open the passenger door to see a dead Middle Eastern man.

"Looks like we got ourselves a Jiji here."

Jiji was a nickname Scar had come up with for Jihadis.

Meeks looked inside and saw the driver slumped in his seat. He was a white man in his late twenties.

Scar started digging around, looking for anything that might tell them who these two were. He found a map and unfolded it.

"Whatcha got?" asked Meeks.

"A map."

Meeks came around to the passenger side.

They both looked down at the map of Michigan, which had several towns circled. Some of them, including Decatur, had an "X" through the circle.

"What do you think those markings mean?" asked Meeks.

12

"Not sure, but it doesn't look good."

"It's got a lot of towns circled."

"We need to get out of here, don't want any of their friends showing up. You think this dream car of yours will make it?"

Meeks walked around it. "It doesn't look too bad. I think ol' Betsey is good."

"Betsey huh?"

"Every hot car needs a name."

Meeks cranked the engine on. He pulled the damaged car forward and turned onto the pavement. He got out, walked around to the rear and inspected it.

"I think we're good. Such a shame, ruining this beauty."

Scar grabbed the two dead men's weapons and hustled back over to the Mustang.

Meeks stepped on the gas. Despite a scraping noise coming from the back, it was running fine. He forced a couple of turns of the steering wheel just to make sure.

Scar pulled out the map. "We should go check out some of these towns that are crossed off."

"Whatcha thinking?"

"I have a bad feeling about this, but if they're anything like this last town."

"We got ourselves more bad guys."

"Yep."

"Where to?"

"Paw Paw is not too far north of here," said Scar as he looked down at the map.

Scott Scarborough studied the map with the mindset of a Marine. He had spent four years in the Corps and had seen action in Grenada. It wasn't a long engagement, but the experience of combat had changed him. He came away with a different perspective on life. No longer did he view the world through a boy's eyes, but with the eyes of a mature man.

He had joined right out of high school, not knowing what to do in life. He enjoyed the experience and made lifelong friends. Once he received his honorable discharge, he went back home and married his high school sweetheart, Tera, who was two years younger than him. He got a job in construction and learned how to build houses. This skill prepared him to start his own company and with his wife's business savvy, they were able to prosper and grow into a successful firm. He took pride in building their first and only home, and he built it big enough for a large family. Unfortunately, after several miscarriages, they were only able to have one child, whom they named Scott, after him.

The boy took after his father, growing into a tall broad shouldered man with the same sense of humor. Scar was proud when his son joined the Corps three years ago, and qualified for fixed wing flight training. He was worried about him though, because he was flying EA-6B Prowlers in the war. This aircraft pinpointed and neutralized the enemy's fire control radar, which meant, he was in the thick of it. He hadn't heard from him in sometime. When he did, Scott insisted he was safe. As a former Marine, he knew this was a lie fabricated to not worry the parents. He had done the same thing for his parents.

Scar's parents were both still alive and once Scar made the decision to join the war effort, they had taken Tera and her parents to Texas to his parent's summer home on the Gulf. This comforted him, knowing this was probably the safest place in the country.

CHAPTER 5

PAW PAW MICHIGAN

Before Meeks and Scar reached the town of Paw Paw, they could smell the burnt embers. They passed farmhouses, which hadn't been touched, but as soon as they rounded the curve into the town, they could see every structure had been set on fire.

It looked like it had been a couple of days ago. Some of the homes were still smoldering, but most were not. It had the same weird feeling as Decatur had when they passed through there. Dead silence, no one around, not even a corpse.

"Where in the hell could everyone be?" asked Meeks.

Scar shook his head. "This is the strangest thing, it's just like the last town."

"At least we know what the X's mean."

"Yeah, that's what I'm afraid of. Look at how many there are."

Meeks slowed to a stop and took another look at the map.

Scar pointed at it. "From Cheboygan, all the way down the west side of the state is crossed off, including bigger towns like Kalamazoo."

"Notice Detroit isn't circled," said Meeks.

"Well, it's right next to Canada."

"Hell, probably nothing left there anyways."

Scar gave Meeks a serious look. "We need to get back and tell the Captain."

Meeks gave the steering wheel a hard turn, but before he stepped on the gas, he noticed a figure staring at them from around the corner of a hedgerow.

"Look over there."

"Where?" asked Scar turning his head.

"Behind those hedges, someone is staring at us."

"I don't see em."

"Cover me," said Meeks getting out of the car.

As Meeks walked over to the hedges, Scar grabbed his sidearm and got out of the car. Meeks called out, but no one answered. He walked around the corner of the hedgerow but didn't see anyone.

He called out again. "Is there anyone there?"

A figure ran behind some evergreen trees. Meeks took off and ran around the back of a destroyed home. He caught a glimpse of the figure running through the doorway of a metal shed. Meeks turned to wave Scar over and waited for him.

"He ran into that shed."

They approached the shed slowly with guns drawn. Meeks reached for the handle, and gave it a quick yank.

A little girl with blond hair stared at them with big blue blank eyes. She had a button nose on her frightened face with black soot hiding her fair complexion. At four-foot-four, and weighing no more than sixty-five pounds, she looked to be ten or eleven years old. Her movements were slow and weak, like she hadn't eaten in days. She wore a pink and white windbreaker that needed washing along with her blue jeans and gym shoes.

"Well, hello there," said Meeks putting his sidearm away. "We're not going to hurt ya. What's your name?"

Meeks knelt down. "My name is Meeks and this big goofball is Mr. Scarborough. You can call him Scar for short."

Scar tucked his gun behind his waistband and gave her a wave. "How are you doing, hon? Where's your mom and dad?"

She shrugged her shoulders.

"Well, come on out of there. Maybe we can help you out," said Meeks getting up.

She walked out of the shed and they headed back toward the Mustang. Scar looked at Meeks, who gave him a half smile.

"Are you hungry?" asked Scar reaching into his backpack. He pulled out a sleeve of peanut butter crackers and handed them to her. He also found a bottle of water and set it on the hood.

She eagerly grabbed the crackers and started to gobble them down.

Scar gave her a smile. "Those are almost my favorite, but I prefer the cheese ones."

She looked up at the tall man and returned the smile.

After she ate all the crackers, Meeks tried, once again, to get her to tell them her name.

"Now that you've devoured those crackers, you ready to tell us your name."

She nodded. "I'm Sadie Allen."

"Well, that's a great name, Sadie. How old are you?"

"Ten."

"Where are you're parents."

"My daddy's fighting in the war."

"What about your mom?"

"I don't know. She was taken by those men."

Meeks looked over at Scar, then back at Sadie. "What men?"

"The men who came here. The ones who burned all our houses down."

Scar knelt his big frame down and looked Sadie in the eye. "You saw these men then?"

She nodded.

"Do you know who they were?"

She shook her head.

"Did they have uniforms on?"

Sadie looked at the ground and then back up at Scar. "Some did."

"What color were the uniforms?"

"Black."

Scar looked over to Meeks. "Sounds like the National Police."

"Some of them talked funny."

"Talked funny how?"

"Some of them only talked to each other and I didn't know what they were saying."

Scar looked up at Meeks. "Jijis."

Meeks gave him a nod.

"So, you said your mom was taken. Was everyone else taken too?"

"Yes. They had lots of big trucks here and everyone had to get in them."

"How did you get away?" asked Scar.

"My mom told me to run away and hide."

"Do you know why she told you that?"

"At first the men were friendly, but then they got angry with us when my friend Emma's, grandpa said he wasn't going. So they pushed him to the ground and said we had to go."

"I'll bet you were pretty scared."

Sadie nodded.

"It's going to be okay," said Scar.

"When did they set fire to the houses?"

"After everyone left." She pointed to the burned down structure across from them. "I was watching from my house. They went up and down the street with this thing that shot flames out of a long stick like thing."

"A flamethrower? These guys had flamethrowers? Unbelievable," said Meeks.

She nodded. "I was upstairs in my room. I was really scared when the smoke started coming into my room. So I ran downstairs and ran through the backyard to our shed."

Meeks turned to Scar. "Well, doesn't that sound familiar?"

Sadie looked puzzled.

"Meeks and I had a similar thing happen to us."

"How long ago did this happen?" asked Meeks.

"Two days."

"You've been here all by yourself for two days?

She nodded.

"Do you know if there's been anyone else through here?"

She shook her head.

"Well, Sadie, you're a brave little girl. Do you think you'd like to come with us till we find your mom?" asked Scar.

She smiled. "You'll find her?"

"Of course we will," said Meeks as he raised one eyebrow to Scar.

"Well, let's get out of here," said Scar.

Scar opened the passenger door and pulled the seat forward. Sadie hopped in the back. Meeks started the car and turned to Sadie. "You like going fast?"

Her face lit up.

Meeks returned the smile. "Good, cause I love going fast, so buckle yourself in little lady. There's nothing like not having to worry about getting a speeding ticket."

He put the car in low drive, kept his left foot on the brake and stomped on the gas pedal. The back wheels started spinning, enveloping them in white smoke. When he let off the brakes, the car shot forward. Sadie screamed in delight. Meeks turned to Scar and flickered his eyebrows. Scar rolled his eyes and let out a hardy laugh at his friend Meeks, whom he had known since grade school.

Meeks loved sports, especially football, which is why he coached the local youth football program, in addition to coaching the high school team. It was a big commitment, but he enjoyed every minute of it. He never wanted to be too far away from the game. After setting a couple of school records as a running back at Iowa, he came home and got hired as an assistant coach for his hometown high school, where he eventually became the head coach.

Once the economy started to slip, budgets became tight and the school district discontinued all the sports programs, which effectively put him out of a job. He then worked with Scar for a little while before the construction business took a nosedive and Scar's business went under. He and Scar had both decided to join the war effort together. Meeks moved his wife and three teenaged boys to Florida with her parents.

Meeks was grateful when Winters had discovered the murders at the Patriot Centers. Figuring he should already be dead, he was thus very loyal to him and wanted to see an end to what they were doing. Meeks loved history and realized what they were doing would someday be written down for generations to come - provided they were successful.

CHAPTER 6

WASHINGTON D.C.

Major John Green pulled out onto Eisenhower Drive and headed toward Washington Boulevard leaving Arlington National Cemetery behind. He pointed his car west toward his mother's home.

It had been a month since his friend Lieutenant David Crick was killed in action by terrorists in Detroit Lakes. He wasn't able to make the funeral and had needed to visit with Crick's parents. He had spent most of the day with them relaying the details of their son's death and talking about old times.

Green had known the Cricks since he was a child. His parents were old friends. The two fathers had met in basic training and served together, both making a career of the Army.

The visit had been both sad and joyous at the same time. They went through old photos, laughing and crying together. As much as he wanted to, he didn't give them the full details of the death. He didn't think it to be in their best interest, at least not right now. If they knew that Colonel Nunn had set them up to be killed by the terrorists and did so with the blessing of the government, then no telling what might happen to them, if they should mention it to the wrong person.

Green drove in the bustling city with wonderment as to how it appeared as normal as before the war. It was in stark contrast to the Midwest where he had been stationed for the past nine months. People there struggled for food and keeping themselves warm through the long winter. Here in the District, it didn't look at all like the country was at war with China, and that it was being waged on the West Coast. Cars crowded the interstate as folks left work to head home or went to restaurants for social meetings with colleagues and lobbyists. He wondered if these people had an inkling of how bad, it really was outside the nation's capital.

It had been a long and exhausting day. He looked forward to getting back home with his mom who would spoil him, and yet knew when to leave him alone. He needed a good night's sleep before his morning meeting with Lawrence Reed.

Reed was in charge of the Patriot Center Program and had requested a meeting with him while he was in Washington. Green was apprehensive and wondered what was on the agenda. No doubt, he wanted to question him down to every little detail on the Shadow Patriots and on Colonel Nunn's unfortunate "accidental" death. Green would have to again go through the whole set of lies in his mind before he felt comfortable enough to repeat them to Reed's face. He figured the man would question him in various ways trying to expose any lies. Since his own commanding officer, Colonel Nunn, had set him up to be killed in Detroit Lakes at the hands of Al Quada, after which he discovered the truth about what was going on, he had no problem lying to Reed. Green would have to act as if he cared about the death of Colonel Nunn. This was his greatest lie, because Nunn's death had been at his own hands, when Nunn had tried to kill him in his office. This duel between Nunn and himself played out like a low budget kung fu movie. The arrogant old man, was too cocksure when trying to best his protégé, all the while thinking he had a move not shown to his young student. The elder had been quick, but not quick enough for Green who was enraged by Nunn's actions. He let out all his anger on the old man and violently took him out with powerful swings to the head.

Traffic thinned out as he entered Alexandria, where his mom lived. He'd be back home in just a few more minutes. He was confident dinner would be waiting for him when he got there.

He turned onto her street. Dogwoods lined the streets, with their pink and white flowers in full bloom, sprinkling petals on the well-manicured lawns. The walkways had pink and red azaleas. It was a late spring, just as it had been in the Midwest. The difference here was the pall of doom didn't spoil the beauty.

Green pulled into the driveway and noticed his mom out in the front yard wearing gardening gloves. A tray of seedlings was beside her as she worked the soil. Soon she would get them into the ground.

As the car pulled in, Sarah Green turned her head and smiled. She was fifty-eight years old and in as good a shape as she had always been. She was originally from the D.C. area. Being the daughter of a former diplomat, she had spent a good portion of her childhood in Europe. She had attended the University of Virginia where she met her husband at a football game. After graduating, she married him at twenty-one and had her only child at twenty-three. She had let her hair go gray rather than fight the never ending battle of coloring it. It was easier, and as a widow of an Army Colonel, she was too busy with charity work to bother with it.

She raised her small frame up and took her gloves off as she walked over to greet her son.

"How did it go, John?"

Green closed the door. "As well as could be expected."

"I've got a roast in the oven. Should be about ready."

"Sounds good. I'm starving."

"Come in then."

They both walked into the white two-story colonial, which had high ceilings and white trim. The walls were a deep yellow in the living room and were off set by an Oriental pattern rug that lay centered on the hardwood floor, which ran throughout the home. In the living room, a fireplace stood between windows that had long white curtains hanging to the floor.

Green breathed in the aroma of roast beef, and it instantly made his mouth water, making him even hungrier. He took his shoes off and followed his mother into the kitchen.

There was a war and food shortages all around the country. However, these problems had not come to roost in Washington, especially if your family had money.

She put on oven mitts, opened the oven door, and pulled out their meal. The thermometer read 160 degrees. It was ready and they sat down to the dinner table. Both were entertaining their own thoughts, so there wasn't much conversation, but they enjoyed each other's company. After dinner, Green went into the living room and sat down to read the newspaper, while his mother did the dishes.

The front-page lead heading said it all.

SHADOW PATRIOTS STILL ON KILLING RAMPAGE.

Green put the paper down after reading about the Shadow Patriots. The media had dutifully reported the misrepresentation of the facts, which had been had been spoon-fed to them by the National Government. The

Shadow Patriots were a bunch of sadistic thugs, guilty of raping women and killing innocent children.

Mrs. Green walked in and sat down. "Is it true what they say about that gang?"

Green hesitated before he answered her. He wasn't sure if he should tell her, but at the same time, he wanted to defend the Shadow Patriots. After all, they had rescued him and his men from an ambush in Detroit Lakes. It was there that he had lost his friend, David, in a gunfight with the terrorists. Had it not been for the Shadow Patriots showing up, he himself would not be alive today.

He shook his head. "No. There's not a grain of truth in that article."

"Do you know these men?" she asked.

"I do." He paused before going on. "Had it not been for these men, I would not be here."

Mrs. Green looked surprised.

"Those men, those Shadow Patriots, saved my life and the lives of my men. They weren't the ones who killed David. I don't know how much to tell you because it may be better if you don't know. The ones responsible are still a threat and they're unaware that I know their identities."

"You're talking about the new government, aren't you?"

Green gave her a surprised look.

"Oh, don't look so surprised. I've been around D.C. long enough to know what goes on in here. I know there are things going on behind the scenes. So much has happened in this country in the last six months that nothing would shock me."

"Don't be so sure."

"That bad is it?"

"I'm having to meet with the one in charge tomorrow. He's going to question me every which way to try to determine if I know more than I'm letting on."

"How much do you know?"

"Enough to know that I'm a danger to them."

"I see. Are you prepared?"

"I think so. I've been going over it in my head for the past week. My biggest concern is that my body language might give me away."

"I wouldn't worry too much about that. You'll do fine."

23

CHAPTER 7

Winters and Elliott sat at a long table discussing the future of the Shadow Patriots and what their intentions actually were. Nate came walking up to them interrupting their conversation.

"Scar and Meeks are back, and you're not going to believe what they've got with them."

Winters looked at Nate with a confused curiosity. "Ok, I'll bite, what?"

"No, no, you'll need to come and see."

The three of them walked out of the room and into their makeshift cafeteria where Scar and Meeks were sitting down with a child.

Scar gave Winters a nod of his head. "Captain."

Winters reached the table. "Hey, guys. So, who do we have here?"

"Captain, this here is our new friend, Sadie," said Scar. "Sadie, this is the man I've been telling you about."

Sadie put down her sandwich, stood up, and extended her hand. "It's a pleasure to meet you, sir."

"Well, it's nice to meet you too, Sadie." Winters was immediately taken with the girl's politeness. "You look really hungry, so don't let me interrupt you."

"Yeah, if you're not careful, Meeks might snag some food right off your plate," said Scar.

"Guilty as charged," said Meeks, giving Sadie a friendly bump.

"Got some things to tell you, Captain," said Scar.

"Why don't you finish eating and meet me outside," said Winters tilting his head toward the girl. Since Winters didn't know Sadie's background, he didn't want to talk about things in front of her. Coming here as an orphan, her story couldn't be good.

Elliott and Nate accompanied Winters outside where they found the black Mustang with a mangled rear end.

"Wonder what they did to this badboy," said Nate as he walked over to inspect the damage.

Nate was a car buff and could fix anything. He had restored several cars over the years as a hobby and it had turned out to be a great way to make extra money. He opened the hood of the Mustang and admired the big engine. He had owned several Mustangs in the past preferring them to any other sports car. He liked them because they were easy to work on and they looked good, which helped him pick up girls when he was younger. A good-looking car always impressed the girls, at least the ones that were attracted to him. Rock and Roll and hot cars were what Nate was all about in his youth, and to this day, not much had changed.

"Something tells me they've got quite a story to tell," said Nate.

Ten minutes later, Scar came outside and the three of them stood in apt silence as Scar filled them in on everything that had happened to them including the circumstances where they found Sadie.

Scar unfolded the map he found on the dead Jiji. "We only checked out two of them, but all the crossed out ones look to be destroyed."

"So, this is their next move," said Winters thoughtfully.

They all nodded to each other.

The moment made him think of the old man, they had met at a closed down gas station in Minnesota. He remembered him saying not to worry about the why, instead, concentrate on stopping it.

"What are ya gonna do with that kid?" asked Nate.

"We should get her up to Canada," replied Winters.

"Don't think she'd like that," Scar quickly answered. "Meeks and I kind of promised her we'd find her mother."

Winters was about to respond harshly to him, but then remembered his own daughter. He had been tough with her and didn't want to make the same mistake with a frightened little girl.

"Then we'll just have to find her."

Scar's face lit up. Sadie had already endeared herself to him and Meeks and didn't want her to leave.

"First thing we need to do is put the word out as to where we are. We need everyone back here."

"We going to go kick some ass, Captain?" asked Nate.

He put his hand on his shoulder. "As much as we can."

Later that evening, Winters sat alone in the dorm's common study room. It had a couple of couches, an easy chair, and several long tables. He was looking at the map with Arabic writing on the side, wondering what it said. When he heard a light tap at the entrance, he looked up and saw Sadie standing there.

"May I come in?"

He waved her in. "How polite," thought Winters.

"I see you got yourself all cleaned up. You're looking much better."

"Glad to get that smoke off of me."

"Did they find you a place to sleep?" Winters asked her.

"Yes, I'm in room 220."

"Well, then we're neighbors, cause I'm right next door. Did you get enough to eat?"

She nodded her head.

"What's your mom's name?"

"Elizabeth."

"That's a pretty name."

"My daddy calls her Lizzy."

"And what's his name?"

"Sam Allen."

"How long has he been gone?"

"He left in the fall."

"I'm sure you miss him."

She nodded solemnly. "Do you have kids?"

"Yes I do. I have a daughter, her name is Cara."

"I like that name. How old is she?"

"She's nineteen."

"Where is she?"

Winters decided to be honest with her.

"Well, I don't exactly know."

"How come?"

"She ran off with her boyfriend."

"You miss her lots, don't ya?"

"Yes I do."

"What about her mom?"

Winters paused for a moment. "She died a little while ago."

"I'm sorry."

"There's no need to be."

There was an awkward silence.

She looked up from the floor and into Winters eyes. "We both have something to be sad about."

Winters met her gaze.

"We've both lost our families."

Winters smiled at her.

Sadie got up, moving next to Winters on the couch and pulled out a string. "You want to play Cat's Cradle?"

Winters gave her a smile. "Absolutely."

Her face lit up.

They began to tug on the string. Winters was getting a kick out of it. He had played the game with Cara when she was younger. It had always been a fun bonding experience. Sadie was quite good making The Soldier's Bed, Candles and The Manger.

CHAPTER 8

ALEXANDRIA VIRGINIA

Green woke early and went for a morning run. He got back to the house to find his mother up and making breakfast. He decided to shower and dress before sitting down to eat.

He came down the stairs in full Class A uniform, which made his mother look twice. She met him in the kitchen and immediately went to work straightening his jacket and medals. She had done the same for her husband over the years and was as good as any in knowing what needed fixed.

"You look so much like your father," she said smiling proudly.

"I wish he was here. I could use his advice."

"He taught you everything you need to know. You just need to trust yourself. Come and sit down. You've got a big day ahead, and that requires a big breakfast."

Thirty minutes later, he was out the door and headed to his meeting with Director Lawrence Reed.

Major Green walked into the plush Lafayette Office Building. Reed's secretary greeted him and asked him to wait.

He sat down and mentally prepared himself. He had never met Reed and didn't know what to expect. He figured he was crafty, which was the only way to survive and thrive in politics, especially in the District.

After a few minutes, the secretary led Green into Reed's office. It was as lavish as the reception area. Oil paintings hung on the walls, a Remington statue of a cowboy on a horse sat on his desk. A large salt-water tank filled with exotic fish stood by the wall near his desk.

He noticed another man sitting on a couch in the far corner of the large office. The man was busy looking at some papers he held in his hands. He didn't get up and made no attempt to acknowledge Green's presence.

A short heavyset man came over to greet him. "Major Green, it's a pleasure to finally meet you."

"It's nice to meet you too, sir," said Green, putting out his hand.

Green noticed a weak grip. It was more like a handshake you'd expect from a child. He wondered if that was a way to throw people off his real character. He kept his composure as Reed offered him a seat. He was curious why Reed didn't introduce him to the other man.

"I understand you're a family friend of the Cricks. I'm assuming you visited with them?" he asked.

"Yes, I am and yes I visited them yesterday."

"I hope all went well for you."

"It did sir, thank you."

Reed sat at his desk. "Major Green I hope we can be of assistance to each other. I'm sure you want to find these men who call themselves the Shadow Patriots, these murdering rebels, and bring them to justice."

"I would, sir. I can think of nothing more satisfying than that."

"Well good, good."

The two sat in awkward silence for a few moments.

"I've read all your reports on the matter, your capture by the rebels and subsequent engagement with them. I've no doubt that you've left nothing out, Major."

Reed stared at Green before continuing.

Green wondered if he was testing him. Reed wasn't going to question him like he thought he would. Rather, he would gage his responses to seemingly innocent questions and statements. He had to put in his mind that he was angry at Winters and wanted revenge. He didn't want to sound defensive to any innocent remarks made by Reed.

"Thank you, sir. I spent considerable time on the final report, to make sure I didn't leave anything out."

"Excellent, Major. It's been quite a journey for you and your men." He paused for a few moments. "You'd probably like to know the name of this man?"

"Yes sir, I would."

Reed took his time.

Green shifted in his seat.

"We have the name of the rebel leader."

Green stiffened his body.

"His name is Cole Winters."

Green was shocked that Reed knew Winters' name. He wondered how they were able to discover this and what they were going to do now. He knew it was only a matter of time before they would be able to ascertain where he came from and what he looked like.

"Cole Winters, huh," said Green trying to sound surprised.

"That's our man."

"How did you get this information?"

"We sent a man to St. Paul to snoop around. He ran into a former member and after some drinks gave him up."

"And are you sure of this?" asked Green.

"Nothing is certain, until we have a visual confirmation, but it has pointed us in a right direction. We think we know where he's from and where he worked. It's just a matter of time before we come up with some pictures." He paused for a moment, studying Green's demeanor. "This where you can help us, Major."

Green leaned forward in his chair.

"We want you to confirm his identity, Major."

So, this is where all of this was leading. This is what they wanted from him. They wanted him to betray his friend.

"Won't be a problem, sir."

"Good, good. It's why we're having you reassigned here."

This took Green by surprise. He had always wanted an assignment in D.C., but after what had happened, and knowing the kind of people he'd be dealing with, he no longer felt the same way. He wanted to be back with his men.

"What about my men, sir?"

"They'll all be sent out to the war."

"I would rather be with them, sir."

"I understand that, but you're too valuable to us."

"What will my responsibilities entail?"

"I'll need you to help coordinate the capture of this Winters fellow."

Green knew there was no way he was going to change Reed's mind. He did some quick thinking and decided he wanted at least one of his men with him. Someone he could trust and would understand his situation.

"If I could have one request."

"Yes, of course, Major."

"I'd like one of my men here with me."

"I'm sure we could arrange that," said Reed as he stood, signaling the meeting was over.

Green stood up and Reed escorted him to the door. He glanced over at the strange man in the corner as he walked out of the office. Reed told him his secretary would handle all the particulars. The door closed and he stood alone in the reception area.

CHAPTER 9

SOUTH BEND INDIANA

Winters got up before sunrise and went outside for an early morning walk, as was his new habit since arriving at the catholic campus. He appreciated the fact that no one felt the need to join him and enjoyed the solitude the empty grounds offered. He couldn't get enough of staring at the majestic buildings and wondering what it must have been like to attend such an amazing institution. He imagined the thousands of students walking the halls, cramming for exams, making friends, and partying, all while getting an education and preparing for life. It was sad to see the university no longer fulfilling its mission.

It was a strange and unexpected twist of fate for the school, and for him, this past year. A year ago, he was still employed at the plant in the small town where he had worked and lived for the last twenty-five years. Then everything he had taken for granted and counted on changed in mere months. The economy tanked, bombs exploded, the government fell and war broke out. Everybody's life changed overnight. Misery was all around as people panicked not knowing what to do or whom to turn to for help. Many of his friends and neighbors, including his own daughter, pulled up roots and moved to where ever they thought it would be safer for them. He and his wife Ellie decided to stay and tough out a harsh Midwestern winter. They held out hope that Cara would come back and they needed to be home when she did. That hope faded over the many months.

Thankfully, they had adequate food storage to survive the winter but some of their neighbors did not. They helped several, but there wasn't enough for everyone and many died of starvation or from a lack of needed medication.

Now, here he was standing in the tall dew covered grass of a neglected quad admiring a once great school. Now just a cluster of buildings where he and his men had taken up residence. They came here because of its close proximity to the neighboring states they had not yet investigated. He wanted to make sure the rest of the Patriot Centers were closed down. However, after learning about the burned towns in Michigan, he sensed fate had dealt him another ugly hand. There was more to do and he accepted the fact he was right where he was supposed to be. He had a new foreign enemy to fight. The symbolism of this Catholic school, versus his new Islamic enemy was not lost on him.

He thought about the coming days. He didn't know what they were up against or where to engage them. He wasn't sure if he could rally up enough men or how many they would need. The only thing he knew for sure was death would follow him wherever he went. After watching his friends die beside him, he assumed death was a certainty.

His thoughts turned to how killing had almost become second nature for him. He had taken many lives and it had changed him into a hardened man. He was a man no longer afraid. It was a new side that he started to embrace. However, he wanted to be careful and not allow his Mr. Hyde personality to take over completely. Meeting Sadie last night, had actually mitigated that fear. She opened a window releasing memories of his softer side. He had not been around children in a long time and had forgotten the joy they brought. Sadie reminded him so much of his own daughter when she was that age, innocent and full of hope. It was unfortunate to meet under such circumstances, but she seemed to be handling the situation very well. That was the magic of being an age, where you thought everything would always work out.

He wondered if the Spirit prompted Sadie's mom to have her daughter run away. She must have sensed an impending danger. It was definitely not a normal reaction to tell your child to run away. Normally, you'd want your children close to you, so you could protect them.

Winters tried to wrap his mind around it. Surely, the National Police were forcing people to move south into the camps for their own safety. He only hoped that they would be able to find her. However, in the back of his mind, he knew he was fooling himself. Perhaps Sadie had already rubbed off on him by thinking there was still a chance of hope for a bright future.

CHAPTER 10

Winters came back inside to the cafeteria where he found Scar and Elliott eating breakfast. He grabbed a chair and sat down with them.

"So what's the game plan, Captain?" asked Elliott.

"Figure out what we're up against."

"Where's the map?" asked Scar.

Winters pulled it out. "Notice the circles are in three different colors."

"They probably got three different groups running around."

"That's what I was thinking," said Winters.

"Might explain why all the circles aren't crossed out. They might not be communicating with each other. At least not frequently anyways."

Winters nodded in agreement.

"These red circles are around smaller towns than the blue ones."

Winters looked up at Scar. "What do ya think it means?"

"Smaller forces, I'd say."

"If that's the case, then we should try and find the red group first."

"That would be my recommendation."

"It looks like they started at the top of the state and have been moving south, so they shouldn't be too far from where we are."

"Eau Claire might be a place to start," said Scar pointing on the map.

"It's as good of a place as any," said Winters.

Elliott looked over to Scar. "How many guys ya think they got?"

"All together, I'd say at minimum, several hundred and if they got flamethrowers like Sadie said she saw, then they're well-funded too."

"Okay, let's go and scope it out," said Winters as he stood up.

Winters went outside and waited for the rest of his inner circle. They would take two SUV's, with him, Elliott, Scar and Meeks in one and Nate, Burns and Murphy in the other.

As he waited, he heard someone calling out to him. "Captain."

Winters turned to see Sadie skipping his way.

"Good morning, Sadie. Did you sleep well?"

"Yes, I did."

"You know, instead of calling me Captain, why don't you call me Cole."

"Doesn't everyone call you Captain?"

"They do, but you don't need to. I'd like it better if you called me by my first name."

"Okay Cole," she replied with a smile.

"Listen, we're going to go and see if we can find those bad guys that took your mom, okay."

"Can I come?"

"No, I don't think that'd be a good idea. You stay here and see if they can put you to work somewhere. We'll be back later tonight."

"What if something happens to you?" she asked in a somber tone.

"Nothing's going to happen to us. We're just going to go and take a look, okay?"

They both watched as Meeks and Scar walked outside carrying rifles.

"Just going to go look, huh?" she stated.

"Always need to be prepared, hon."

"Check you out," said Meeks. You look a whole lot better cleaned up and fed."

"I do?"

"You looked like a drowned rat yesterday and now you look more like a little princess."

Sadie put her hands on her hips and gave Meeks a half smile.

"No? Don't like the princess look? How about a ballerina?"

She gave Meeks a love pat on his arm.

"Well, maybe a sporty girl."

Ten minutes later, everybody was loaded up in the SUV's and had said their goodbyes to Sadie. Meeks, sitting in the back, turned his head to see Sadie still watching them and then run inside.

"I sure do hope we can find her mom," said Meeks.

"What if we don't?" asked Scar.

"I don't know," answered Winters.

Elliott drove the lead vehicle and headed toward Eau Claire on Highway 31.

Scar looked up from the map. "Captain, we should go through Berrien Springs and check things out before we go over to Eau Claire."

Winters turned around to Scar. "Where's it at?"

Scar extended the map to him. "Right here. It's on the way."

"Go east on Snow Road," said Winters to Elliott.

Winters grabbed the handheld radio. "Nate, we're going to stop in Berrien Springs, over."

"Ten-four," came the reply.

They arrive in Berrien Springs and drove through town before hitting the business center. A few people were milling around, staring at them as they drove in. The two SUV's took a left on Main Street and parked. They all got out and walked over to a coffee shop. The seven of them entered the shop and just like in a movie, everyone stopped what they were doing and looked at the strangers.

It was a small shop and there was a group of four old men sitting at a table to the left with another two at the lunch counter. A middle-aged woman was behind the counter. She wore an off white apron around her shirt and jeans.

Scar walked up to the counter. "Are you still serving?"

"We are," she looked at him cautiously. "We don't have much though."

"Well, we don't need much," he responded to her smiling.

Another man came out from the kitchen. He also wore a dirty white apron over a t-shirt. He appeared to be the boss as the lady behind the counter showed him deference.

"Where you guys from?"

"Most of us are from Iowa."

"Why are you here?"

"We're just passing through is all."

36

"You here to cause trouble?"

"Not at all. Why do you ask?"

"Whenever strangers come into town, it's usually to cause trouble and you guys are not from around here. So, we'd all be happy if you left."

Nate had heard enough and started to move forward. Elliott grabbed his arm and held him back.

"Sir, we're not here to cause any trouble, in fact we think there's trouble coming here soon," said Winters.

All the patrons kept still with their eyes on Winters.

"Why do you say that?" asked the man wearing the apron.

"We've been through some towns where all the houses were burned down and we believe this might be the next one."

"Really. How do we know you're not the ones doing it?"

"Well…we'd certainly not announce it."

"Hmm maybe. What's your name?"

Winters extended his hand out. "I'm Cole Winters."

The man leaned back. His eyes opened wider.

Winters drew back his hand. "What's the matter?"

The man twisted around and opened a draw. He pulled out a .38 revolver, turned back and pointed the snub-nosed gun at Winters.

"Hey, what are doing?" shouted Winters putting his hands up.

"Get the hell out of here."

"What are you doing that for?"

"You said your name is Cole Winters. You're the ones that have been on a murdering rampage. We know all about you."

"Sir, I can assure you what you've heard was all lies."

"Really, so you didn't murder your wife huh?"

"What?" Winters voice started to quiver. This news hit him fast and hard. "No, no, that's not true. My wife died of cancer."

"I just heard it on my satellite radio this morning."

"Sir, if you'd please put the gun down. We can explain everything. We don't want any trouble here. We came through to warn people is all."

Winters could see the man was unconvinced, but didn't know what to do next. He decided to get his men out of the coffee shop.

"Listen, we're going to leave okay. Like I said we don't want any trouble." Winters turned his head. "Guys, let's just back up and get out of here."

All the Shadow Patriots started to back up. Burns and Murphy hit the door first, followed by Elliott and Nate. Scar kept a smile on his face as he grabbed Winters by the shoulder and guided him backwards. They made their way to the entrance, where Meeks held the door. Before shutting the door, Meeks looked at the people in the coffee shop and said, "Don't say we didn't warn ya."

Outside, Nate was extremely angry. He wanted nothing more than to go in there and beat the hell out of the man with the apron. "I just want to knock some sense into that dumb-ass."

Elliott put his hand on his shoulder. "Let it go, Nate. They can't know, what they don't know. It's not their fault."

Winters silently walked away to the SUV. The rest of the men followed him. They knew hearing about his wife that way was a punch in the gut. He reached the passenger side of the vehicle and before he got in, he heard a man come out of the coffee shop.

"Excuse me."

Everyone turned around and waited as the man came jogging up to them.

"I'm really sorry about what happened. My name is Jim."

He walked up to Winters and shook his hand. Jim was in late sixties. He wore a ball cap over his white hair. His blue jean overalls covered his long sleeved multi-colored flannel shirt.

"Don't worry about it," said Winters. "You don't know who to trust these days."

"Well, it's just that Henry in there tends to believe everything he hears on the radio.

"Like I said, I don't blame him."

"So, it's not true what the news said about you guys, huh?

Winters shook his head.

"I knew it all to be lies anyways. It's just so hard to know what's what anymore."

"I can assure you, we've been doing nothing but saving people."

"Your wife, you said she died of cancer? I'm real sorry to hear about that. It's sickening that they'd say that about you."

Winters looked at his men and noticed they were all giving him a sympathetic look. This was the last thing he wanted from anyone. Winters needed to change the subject and spent the next five minutes giving Jim a brief synopsis of their story.

The news shocked him and he promised to share the story to everyone in town. He then told them all of the news concerning the Shadow Patriots, and what the media was saying about them. He shook everyone's hand and scooted back into the coffee shop.

The Shadow Patriots loaded back up into the two SUV's and took off for Eau Claire. Winters noticed right away that no one was saying anything, which was unusual for this bunch. He turned in his seat to face Scar and Meeks. "Something tells me we need better PR."

This broke the tension.

"Maybe we can hire a D.C. firm, maybe one of those K Street ones," quipped Meeks.

"I'm sure they'd love the challenge," added Scar.

"Might have to pay a premium," said Meeks.

Scar grabbed Meeks' arm. "Yeah, and all of it up front."

CHAPTER 11

EAU CLAIRE MICHIGAN

The two SUV's were on Hochberger Rd when they saw a car coming toward them from the North. Elliott looked at Winters. It was unusual for a car to be on the road, so they knew something wasn't right.

"See if they'll stop," ordered Winters.

Elliott put his foot on the brake and flashed his lights off and on. The approaching vehicle didn't appear it was going to stop, but then it slowed down so as to get a look at the two SUV's. Scar rolled down the window and stuck his head out. He smiled and waved for them to stop. The minivan stopped just past them and then backed up.

The driver of the van was an older man who had what looked like his wife next to him and his grandchildren in the back. The driver rolled down his window.

"Don't mean to rude, but I wasn't sure if you were government folks."

"We're not. I'm Scarborough and this is Elliott."

Elliott nodded his head and said hello.

Scar continued. "You look like you're in a hurry, is there anything wrong?"

"Oh you could say that, alright. The damn National Police pulled into town about two hours ago and started ordering people around. They told us there's a gang of terrorists coming this way and they needed to get us all to safety."

Elliott turned to Winters. "So that's how they're doing it."

Winters got out of the vehicle and walked over to the mini van.

"What did everyone do?" asked Winters.

"Hell, they weren't giving us much choice. A buddy of mine came to our house and told us. They've got all the roads blocked off. Nobody can get in or out of town."

Winters shot Scar a concerned glance.

Scar look back at the driver. "How did you get out?"

"Oh please, you can block off all the roads you want, but this here is farm country. I took off through the fields."

"How many men you think they have?" asked Winters.

"My buddy said at least a hundred, maybe more."

"Did they say where they were taking you?"

"No, only that it was somewhere safe."

"Where are you headed to?"

"Berrien Springs. Say, who are you guys? I don't recognize any of you."

Winters didn't want to introduce himself in case the man also heard about him on the radio. "We're not from around here. Listen, when you get to Berrien Springs, warn everyone there what you saw and tell them to get out town right away. These men, these National Police, are not our friends. They're not here to help anyone but themselves. They're rounding people up and taking them somewhere, and they've been burning down all the houses. We've seen them do this in other places."

"Damn friggen government!" the driver replied hitting the steering wheel with both hands.

"How can we get into town without being seen?"

"Why? What the hell are you going to do?"

"Try and stop them."

"Well...alrighty then. Best thing I could tell you is to get out into the fields right now. Go over there," the driver said pointing west. "You'll run into some woods, get out and start walking. It'll take you right up to Main Street, which is where they've got all their trucks parked."

"Thanks."

"Good luck and God bless you."

The minivan pulled away from the Shadow Patriots. Winters walked back to Nate who had been behind them. He told him to follow him to the tree line, and then he hurried back to his SUV and got in. Elliott slowly pulled down into the ditch and up on the field, where he picked up the pace. He had been a farmer and was used to driving through fields.

Winters turned to Scar and Meeks. "What do you guys think?"

"Not sure what we can do Captain, but recon it and plan as we go," said Scar.

"We need to see how they operate before we do anything," said Meeks.

"Yeah, kind of what I was thinking," said Winters.

"Sly little bastards, coming in pretending to be saviors and helping everyone," said Meeks.

"No kidding," said Scar.

"Question is, where are they taking them?" asked Winters, as he leaned back in his seat. He wondered if they would be able to do anything to help the people of Eau Claire. They didn't have enough men or firepower to be able to do much, but find out where the cops were taking them. This would be a big help in figuring out what they were up to and perhaps allow him to find Sadie's mom.

After crossing through a baseball field, the two SUV's came to the tree line that had been described to them. Elliott pulled in as far as he could and parked it. Nate came in next to him. Everyone got out, grabbed their rifles and without saying anything, the seven of them started through the woods. Ten minutes later, they found themselves on Staley Road, which led to Main Street. They crossed the street to another small set of trees and hustled behind houses to get further into town. As they got closer, they saw transport trucks parked in the road all up and down Main Street. They also saw the National Police ordering the townspeople around. The citizens didn't look happy with what was happening. The scene was chaotic, with children crying, and everyone scrambling to avoid having their families separated. The cops were barking out orders. Police dogs pulled on their leashes.

They sat silently watching the scene unfold. They were anxious because there was little they could do. The National Police had a much larger force and were scattered everywhere.

"Captain, when they pull out, what do you want to do?" asked Scar.

Winters debated the question in his mind. Should they stay and take out the smaller force that would stay behind or follow the transports and see where they're taking everyone?

"To hell with the town. We need to see where they're going."

They started back, keeping out of sight and soon came up on Hochberger Road. Winters and Elliott came out of a patch of trees and started to hustle across the open backyard of a house. As soon as they reached the intersection, they heard a bullhorn crack.

"Stop, right where you are," came the voice.

The two were startled as a black car came racing toward them. Winters and Elliott stopped dead in their tracks. The rest of the team returned to the cover of the trees.

The car stopped in front of them, and two cops got out keeping themselves behind the doors. They ordered them to drop their weapons.

"Don't shoot us," yelled Elliott.

"Drop your weapons old man," shouted a cop with sergeant strips on his sleeve.

Winters and Elliott slowly removed the rifle slings from their shoulders, dropped the weapons to the ground and raised their hands.

Another police car came racing to the scene. Two more cops got out and the four of them came rushing in on Winters and Elliott, knocking them to the ground.

"Where in hell you two going?" asked the sergeant as he place handcuffs on them.

"We don't want any trouble," said Winters.

"Trouble is what you got, old man."

The cops kept them on the ground as the sergeant radioed his commander. "Got a couple of loose ones here, over."

"You got it under control, over," came the response.

"Ten-four. We'll bring em down."

"Where are you taking us?" asked Winters.

"Somewhere safe, old man."

"Why?"

"For your own protection."

The sergeant looked at his men with a slight smile on his face and gave them a nod. The four cops then went for their batons, pulled them out and started to give their captives a beating.

Winters looked up to see a baton swinging down at him. The cop wound up for another blow, when Winters heard the crackle of gunfire. Blood spurted out of the man's head as he fell backwards. Two more dropped beside him, while the sergeant looked up and then down as a bullet knocked him over backwards. His bullet proof vest prevented the bullet from penetrating, but it knocked the air out of him.

Nate came running up to him and held his rifle to the sergeant's head. He looked down at the frightened cop. "Here's for screwing with a bunch of old men." He pulled the trigger.

Scar helped Winters up. "You guys alright?"

Burns reached into the cop's pockets, grabbed the handcuff key and took off the cuffs.

Winters rubbed his arm. The baton hit him right at the place where Johnny-Boy, back at the train station, had shot him. His arm throbbed with pain.

"Sorry that took so long," said Scar.

"Yeah, we sure as hell weren't expecting them to give you guys a beating," said Meeks.

"Nor was I," said Winters.

"What about these guys?" asked Meeks.

"Let's move em over to the trees and get their cars out of here, no sense in making them too easy to find."

After moving the bodies, they hopped in the cop cars and took them up Staley Road. They drove down a long driveway and parked it behind a house. They jumped out and trampled back through the trees to their SUV's.

"What now?" asked Elliott.

Winters turned to Nate. "Let's split up. As soon as we figure out the direction they're headed, we'll hook back up."

Elliott pulled out, and headed back though the field. As he crossed Hochberger Road, he spotted a farmhouse with multiple outbuildings and headed toward it. He pulled up to a large red barn.

"Think we can get on the roof?" asked Winters.

"Meeks can," said Scar with a slight grin on his face.

Meeks gave him a dubious look.

"I know how much you like heights, buddy."

They walked into the barn and found a ladder. Scar and Meeks grabbed it, carried it outside, and leaned it against the barn. Meeks scurried up the ladder and was quickly out of sight. Moments later he called down. "Got a good line of sight here guys, come on up."

Winters ascended the ladder. "This is perfect."

Scar held the binoculars up. "They look like they're about done."

Winters got on the handheld radio. "Nate."

"What's up?"

"We're up on a barn roof. Got a good view here."

"Yeah, us too, we're on top of some warehouse."

Twenty minutes later, they heard the roar of engines. Winters and company all waited in anticipation for them to leave. They didn't have to wait too long before the trucks started heading east. The convoy consisted of twenty military transports. Two police cars led the convoy with two bringing up the rear.

"Let's give them a minute, guys," said Winters. He got on the radio and repeated the order to Nate.

As the convoy pulled out of town, Winters could see a large majority of the cops staying behind. He knew that they would be the ones to torch the town. The thought of this angered him so much, that he was tempted to take them on, but knew it was more important to find out where they were taking everyone.

Scar stood and pressed the binoculars to his eyes. "Captain, they're headed north."

Winters grabbed his radio. "Nate, you seeing this."

"We see him alright."

"Meeks, get your map out."

Meeks reached into his jacket, and pulled out the map. "They're turning onto 140, which will take them to Interstate 94."

"Okay, then let's go." Winters repeated the order to Nate.

They made their way down from the rooftop and piled into the SUV. Excitement filled the cab as they all thought about what was to come. They desperately wanted to know what was happening to their fellow Americans.

Elliott kicked dirt up as he pulled out and across the field. As he got onto 140, Nate came up behind them.

Not wanting to alert the cops, they kept their distance from the convoy. The road was a straight shot with no turns and had weed filled fields on either side.

After a few minutes, Elliott noticed the convoy slowing down.

"Are they stopping?" asked a nervous Elliott.

"Is that the interstate up there?" asked Winters.

Meeks looked at the map. "It should be."

They came to a complete stop.

Winters grabbed the binoculars "Doesn't look like they're going anywhere."

He couldn't believe they had already reached their destination. "Is there a town up ahead?"

Meeks looked back at the map. "Yeah, Waterviliet but it's one that's already been crossed off."

"This can't be their destination," said Scar.

"I don't like this," said Winters. "Something's not right."

Nate walked up to Elliott's window. "Whatcha guys thinking?"

"Not sure, thinking maybe they got engine problems," said Elliott.

Scar put his hand forth. "Hand me those binoculars, Captain."

Scar got out of the vehicle and climbed on the roof of the SUV for a better view. He scanned up ahead noticed the transports were moving. "They're turning left."

Winters stepped out and looked up at Scar. "What's over there?"

"I don't know. I can't see over the trees."

Scar was just about to climb back down when he noticed one transport take a right and head towards the interstate. "Captain, one's headed east onto the interstate."

Scar jumped down. "What do you want to do?"

Winters thought for a moment. "Let's go see what's up to the left."

Everyone scrambled back in. Elliott put the SUV in gear and took off. They came to where the transports had taken a left.

"This is a sandpit," said Elliott with a concerned tone.

"Pull it in Elliott, everyone get ready, I don't like the looks of this."

Elliott swung the truck onto the dirt road. He came to a fork in the road with tire tracks veering to the left. Once around the bend, the road became wider, and the tracks went around a big sand dune. He came to an abrupt halt.

Winters thought about what to do next then a sickening feeling overwhelmed him.

"Everyone out!" ordered Winters.

CHAPTER 12

WASHINGTON D.C.

Green drove away from the Lafayette building with his mind racing faster than he could comprehend. He needed time to think about what all this meant and how to access his options. He could hand in his resignation, but wasn't sure if it might not raise suspicion. They might question him more and maybe even interrogate his mother. If he stayed, he'd have to continue to promote the lie about his loyalties to the National Government.

On the other hand, this position would allow him to see firsthand what they were up to. He might even be able to get messages to Winters. This is why he wanted one of his men with him. He would choose Josh Bassett, his young corporal. He was someone he knew he could count on. Bassett had already met with Scott Scarborough, on several occasions passing messages back and forth. He was devoted to Green and loved his country.

The more he thought about it, the more certain he became, knowing he might be able to discover their endgame and maybe even be able to stop it or at the very least expose it.

He turned off H St, merged onto I-395 and headed home. He looked forward to another meal with his mother. She would be interested in how things went with Reed, and though she wouldn't ask, he knew she'd want to know all the details. Pulling into the driveway, he got out and found her in the kitchen making lunch.

Sarah Green smiled at her son. "How'd did it go?"

"Well…on one hand it went easier than I thought."

"And on the other?"

"They're reassigning me here in D.C."

She looked surprised. "To the Pentagon?"

"No, not the Pentagon. The Lafayette building, it's where Reed has his offices and he's the one I'll be working for."

"Isn't that where they do international banking?"

Green nodded.

"Strange place to have an office for someone like him. What's your assignment?"

"They want me to coordinate the capture of the Shadow Patriots."

"Sounds like they want to keep an eye on you."

"I don't think so. They're still hot on catching them and I'm the only one who has met Winters in person and knows what he looks like."

She didn't respond.

"They know who he is now."

"How?"

"They sent someone out there snooping around asking questions."

"So, what are you going to do about it?"

"Help my friends anyway I can."

"You'll be putting yourself in danger, John."

He paused. "I know, but I have to help them."

"If the situation escalates, John, at some point you're going to have to make a decision, which will expose you. You need to be ready for that."

"If that happens, there's a good possibility they'll come after you."

"There are other options we can consider."

Green stood there impressed with his mother.

CHAPTER 13

EAU CLAIRE MICHIGAN

As soon as the Shadow Patriots bolted out of the SUV's, they heard machine gun fire echoing throughout the sand pit. They stopped and looked at each other.

Scar pointed to a small hill. "Up there," he yelled.

They all ran toward it and started to climb up the sand. It was slow going up the hill. Gunfire kept crackling. As they got closer to the top, they could hear screaming echoing through the sandpit.

Winters mind flashed back to the train station where he had heard that same type of rapid firing.

They all reached the top of the hill and stopped in horror.

The National Police and what looked to be Jijis had lined up close to two hundred women, children and old folks. Executioners stood behind them. Spent cartridges flew out of their automatic weapons as they swung them back and forth firing at their victims.

Winters was the first to bolt down the hill. He swung his AR-15 off his shoulder and threw the bolt back. He raised the rifle and started firing.

The others fell in behind him. All were firing now in mid-stride.

The executioners didn't expect anyone to interrupt them and were surprised at the sudden attack from the rear. Their reaction was slow at first, and a couple of them fell dead on the sandy ground. Then they quickly scattered. Some ran toward the transports, others retreated in the opposite direction, all while trying to return fire. Their aim was rushed and not accurate.

Nate ran up and stopped. He held his M-16 to his side, pushed the switch to full auto and emptied the magazine in seconds. The barrage of rounds knocked over two bad guys and in one swift motion, he ejected the spent mag, slammed in another and pulled back the slide taking aim at two more with the same results.

"Over to the left guys," yelled Winters to Scar.

Scar and Meeks swung left to outflank a group trying to escape. They both fell to a kneeling position to take better aim at six fleeing killers. Meeks held his MP5, 9mm and flicked the switch to a three shot burst. He took aim, pulled the trigger once and dropped one and then another. Scar the better shooter, fired his AR-15 one at a time. He shot at one who fell against his friend tripping him.

"Meeks, go for the right side," ordered Scar.

"I got em."

Meeks shot another three shot burst and then another. Both hit their marks.

Scar aimed at the one who tripped by his fallen friend. The cop was on all fours struggling to get up. Scar fired into his backside. The cop screamed in pain. Meeks ran up to him and finished him off.

Burns and Murphy swung towards the transports trying to cut off an escape route.

Two Jijis knelt down and took aim at them.

Bullets flew by them.

"Get down Murphy," screamed Burns.

Both of the Army vets fell to the ground.

"Damn bastards," said Murphy.

"Go auto," ordered Burns.

They both pushed the switch on their MP5's.

"Now!" said Burns.

They lifted up and sprayed the ground in front of the two Jijis. Sand flew up around them as the lead found their marks. Burns stood up and emptied his mag.

"Over there," said Burns pointing to the right.

Three Jijis made it to their vehicles. One got into a squad car and two others into one of the transports.

Burns looked at Murphy. "I got the car, you go for the truck."

Murphy jumped up and sprinted towards the truck.

Burns threw in a full mag as the car peeled out. He raised his MP5 and emptied it into the driver's side as it spun around. Projectiles struck the whole side taking out the glass. The dead Jiji lost control and his foot jammed into the accelerator. The car crashed into a sand dune where its engine raced. Tires dug into the sand, but it went nowhere.

Murphy sprinted up behind the transport as it backed up. He swung to the driver's side, dropped his rifle and pulled out his Glock 30. He chambered a round as he rushed up to the driver's side, jumped on the running board and grabbed the mirror bracket for support. He raised the pistol and fired into the cab, killing the driver. Murphy looked up and could see the passenger trying to get control of the transport. He kicked back up, swinging from his arm on the bracket, and fired point-blank at the Jiji.

Winters turned to Elliott. "I've got the right."

Elliott was just behind Winters as they approached the five cops using the dead as cover. Bullets whizzed by him and he fell to the ground to take cover. He dropped his rifle and pulled out his Taurus 1911. He aimed at an exposed cop and fired three shots. The third hit the cop in the chest. The impact threw the man backwards.

Winters kept pushing forward with a crazed look on his face. Rounds flew by him as he fired his AR-15. He emptied the mag, taking out two who were hiding behind their victims. A panicked cop jumped up and threw his rifle as he tried to make a run for it. Winters took out his Colt and dropped the fleeing cop. He then swung right and aimed at the last Jiji. The Jiji put his hands up as if to surrender, but Winters didn't feel merciful. He exploded a round into the man's head. The Jiji jerked backwards.

Then it was over.

Scar and Meeks came up and checked to see if anyone was still alive. Meeks went to one side and Scar the other. They looked at each other and shook their heads.

Winters, breathing heavily, stood in silence looking at all the carnage. The enormity of the scene overtook his senses. Children lay dead in the embrace of their fallen mother's arms. Old ladies with their husbands lay holding hands. Some bodies lay sporadically in different angles. The scene reminded Winters of his friends being slaughtered back at the train station.

Memories poured through his mind of the screams as he had helplessly watched them die.

Winters' legs felt like rubber. Elliott came up to him and grabbed him around the shoulders. In an attempt to bring him back to reality, said, "Captain, we need to find that other transport."

Winters looked at him with a blank stare.

Elliott said in a reassuring tone. "Cole, there's nothing else we can do here. We need to go."

Winters nodded.

CHAPTER 14

The Shadow Patriots tore out of the sandpit and got on Interstate 94 heading east. Chasing a slow moving transport, Winters didn't think they would have much of a problem catching up to it and held out hope they'd be able to find them. He needed this. He needed some redemption for letting those innocent people die, while they stood around being cautious. He knew that decision would haunt him forever.

The atmosphere in the truck was of stark contrast to their usual friendly banter. Each was dealing with what had just happened. Instead, they focused on finding the transport as if it was the most important thing they had left to do in life.

As they passed the Hartford exit, Elliott slowed down and everyone leaned toward the windows to see if perhaps the transport had turned off. They spotted nothing. Elliott sped up, with Nate right behind him. They blew through another exit, but still hadn't caught up to them.

"We're coming up on Paw Paw," stated Scar matter-of-factly. "This is where we found Sadie."

"Doubt they'll stop there," said Elliott stoically.

"We'll be coming up on Kalamazoo," said Scar.

"Meeks is that one crossed off?" asked Winters.

Meeks unfolded the map Scar had taken from the Jiji they'd killed. "It is, and so are the rest till we get into the suburbs of Detroit."

"That's got to be where they're headed," said Scar.

"Captain, I see them," shouted Elliott.

Winters grabbed the binoculars from the dash. "It's them."

There was a noticeable change of attitude among them. They began to speak in a more excited but still reserved tone.

"How do you want to handle it?" asked Scar.

"We could try and flag em down."

"It worked before," said Scar, referencing the time they flagged a convoy down in Wisconsin.

Winters picked up the radio and told Nate to back off while they attempted to stop the truck.

Elliott soon caught up to the transport, pulled along side, while Winters rolled his window down and leaned out. He looked up to see the driver glaring down on him. Winters smiled and signaled him to pull over. The driver turned away and then looked back brandishing a gun.

Winters yelled to Elliott to stop.

Elliott jammed on the brakes as gunfire erupted.

"Not too friendly is he," Scar said moving forward in his seat.

"I don't want them to wreck," said Winters.

"Let's see if Nate can slow them down," said Scar.

Winters radioed Nate forward.

Nate passed them and charged ahead of the transport, just as the driver began firing at him. He kept firing but Nate zigzagged all over the road. The transport sped up trying to ram him. Elliott got up alongside the truck, which then swerved into their lane, forcing Elliott to the shoulder of the interstate.

Burns and Murphy rolled down their windows in Nate's truck, leaned out and started firing at the transport. Meeks joined in as Elliott pulled back up to the side of the big truck. The driver fired wildly at them. Meeks returned the fire.

"I think I got him," said Meeks.

"He's slowing down," said Winters. "Back off, Elliott."

The military transport swerved over into the medium and bounced a few times before coming to a stop. The passenger door flew open and out jumped a Jiji, shooting at them as he ran away.

Nate slammed on his brakes and swung his truck around, speeding the wrong way on the interstate toward the Jiji. Nate stopped short on the pavement. Burns and Murphy hopped out, and using the doors as cover and fired at the lone gunman. The man went down and didn't move. Burns cautiously made his way over to him, checked him and signaled he was dead.

Elliott pulled up behind the transport. Scar and Meeks jumped out, and ran to the driver's door. Meeks waited a moment before climbing up onto the running board. With his arm extended, holding his Sig Sauer 9mm, he looked into the side mirror for any movement. Then, taking a chance, he moved quickly to the window, and found the driver slumped over dead.

"He's a goner."

The two of them joined Winters and Elliott at the back of the transport. Winters, throwing caution to the wind, jumped up on the bumper and moved the canopy. Inside were six young girls looking petrified.

"I'm not here to hurt you, my name is Cole. Are you ladies alright?"

They all nodded their heads.

"Okay, well, why don't you guys come on out of there?"

Winters climbed down. Scar and Meeks undid the latches and dropped the tailgate. They each put their hand up and helped the girls down.

"Easy now," said Scar to a young blond.

Meeks offered them water, which they readily accepted and hastily drank from the bottles. The girls stared at the Shadow Patriots suspiciously, not knowing what to expect. Winters sensed their mistrust, so he introduced everyone to them, and then explained what happened to the others.

Upon hearing the news of their families, the girls broke down in tears.

Winters stood off to the side with Elliott and Scar. "You notice anything unusual about these girls?"

Scar looked at them. "Yeah. All six of them are drop dead gorgeous."

"And young," added Elliott.

"You guys thinking what I'm thinking?" asked Scar.

Winters took off his hat, and rubbed his forehead. "They were going to rape them."

Scar turned to Winters. "We might even have some kind of sex trade happening."

"Spoils of war," said Elliott.

"What do you want to do, Captain?" asked Scar.

"Let's get them out of here and then figure out what they want to do."

One of the girls came walking toward them. She was the oldest of them, late twenties, with long brown hair and brown eyes. Her dark gray windbreaker couldn't hide her figure. Even though she was considerably older than the others were, it was easy to see why they selected her along with the younger girls.

"Thank you for rescuing us. My name is Amber."

Winters acknowledged her, but despite him being years older than her, and what they had done to save her, he was nervous talking to such a beautiful women. He had never been comfortable talking to girls in high school, and still felt the same way.

"You're welcome, I'm just sorry we weren't able to save the others."

She nodded.

"May I ask you how all this happened?"

"It was awful. The police came into town and went house to house ordering us to come out onto Main Street for an important announcement." Amber paused for a moment. "Once we were all gathered together they told us we had to go with them. That it was for our own protection."

Winters shook his head.

"Some protection," said Scar.

"There wasn't anything we could do. All our men are out fighting in the war. We're just women, children and old people, so there was no one to stand up to them. What are we suppose to do now?"

"We can get you to safety," answered Winters.

"Where? Where is it safe anymore?" she asked haltingly.

"We have contacts in Canada," Winters offered.

"Canada? No, I'm not going to Canada, maybe they'll want to go," she said pointing to the other girls. "But not me. I want to hold whoever killed my mom and grandma responsible. Is it true what your friend Meeks said?"

Winters tilted his head.

"That you guys are fighting them?"

"Yes, it's true."

She extended her hand to Winters. "Well, consider me a new recruit."

Winters thought for a second about whether this was a good idea or not, but then thought, "who was he to keep someone else from taking revenge. No one stopped him." He grabbed her hand tightly and looked deep into her eyes. Winters could see the pain and hatred in them. "Welcome to the Shadow Patriots."

CHAPTER 15

The two SUV's easily had enough room for the additional passengers. Amber sat between Scar and Meeks, while another two girls sat in the back. Amber had attended Northwestern on a softball scholarship, which had allowed her to travel to California, Arizona and Florida, playing in tournaments. Coming from a small town, the experience was one she didn't want to leave. This is why, after graduating, she took a job in Chicago as a Pharmaceutical Representative. After seven years of making good money and five years of a bad marriage, she had decided to come home when the country took a turn for the worse. It was a decision that had saved her life, as the area where she worked was one of the many locations hit by a dirty bomb.

The two in the back were sisters. Neither said anything and only held each other's hands after Winters refused to take them to the sand pit. Winters told them the bad guys, were still in Eau Claire, and would no doubt want to find out what happened and go to investigate.

Winters knew it was cruel and harsh to turn them down. Not only was he concerned for their safety, but also, it was a horrific scene. If they'd witnessed it, they would never forget it. The dad in him was trying to shield them from such memories.

Winters wondered what these girls would want to do and where they'd want to go. He wouldn't push the subject. They would need some time to grieve the loss of their family and friends. Based on his own experience, watching his friends get murdered, he knew it'd take more than a few days.

Winters thoughts turned to the matter at hand. Just where were these girls being taken and for what purpose. The obvious purpose was to use them for the pleasure of the tyrants and terrorists, but a far deeper concern was the possibility of a sex trade.

Elliott drove the SUV south on Highway 131. They wanted to put as much distance as they could between them and the cops, who they figured would be somewhere on the interstate. They got back to the campus late in the evening. The only lights on, thanks to Nate hooking up a generator, were in the building they were using. The sisters in the back needed to be awakened when they pulled into the parking lot. Winters stepped out onto the pavement, but needed to stretch his legs before he could get them to move.

Nate pulled up beside the first vehicle and all of his passengers got out. There was just some small talk among the girls as they huddled together. The eldest, Amber, felt responsible for them. She had known all of them since they were little girls and walked them inside.

Winters stayed behind as the group went in where they'd be able to get some food. He wanted to take a few moments before having to deal with the situation at hand. It had been a difficult day. He would second-guess himself for the rest of his life, if he could have done more to save those poor people.

He turned when he heard light footsteps coming quickly toward him. He couldn't tell who it was until Sadie grabbed onto him.

"Cole, I was scared you weren't coming back," said Sadie.

"You needn't worry, Sadie." He patted her back a few times.

"Is it true what they're saying in there?" she asked still holding on to him.

"Well, if it's Meeks going on, then I'm sure the truth is being stretched a bit."

She let go of him. "But you saved those girls though, right?"

They walked over to a bench and sat down. He looked at her in the glow of the indoor lights flowing out onto her face. Sadie wasn't as innocent as she should have been. She'd been through a lot and now, here she was, worrying about him. He had told himself he'd be honest with her. She deserved the truth, though, perhaps, not all the details.

"Yes, we saved those girls, but we weren't able to save their families."

"I'm sorry you're sad."

Sadie's perception took Winters off guard.

"But you're still a hero for saving those girls," she said smiling up at him.

He shrugged his shoulders. He didn't feel like a hero, but she was being sincere.

"Yes, I suppose you're right."

She jumped up and took his hand. Winters stood up and followed her lead into the building. Everyone turned their heads as they entered the makeshift cafeteria. Sadie led Winters to where Amber and the other girls sat.

Winters introduced Sadie to them. She let go of his hand and politely went to each of them to ask their names. Amber looked up at Winters and smiled. He then made his way over to the table where his lieutenants were sitting.

"Sadie is really taken with you, Captain," smiled Elliott.

Winters sat down. "Yeah, she is."

"Sorry if she heard us blabbering on about what happened."

"It'll be nice that there's some other girls here for her," said Winters looking over at them. Sadie had all of their attention, and talked a mile a minute. It gave him a little comfort. "She wasn't shy, that was for sure," he thought. He was glad the girls had taken a liking to her. Perhaps, she could relieve the newcomers of some of their sadness.

He turned his attention back to the men. They didn't look dejected but he knew they all felt bad about failing to save those poor souls back at the sandpit. Saving the girls from the transport was certainly a win for them, and they could hang their hat on that accomplishment. As a group, they didn't dwell too much on what went wrong, but rather looked into what needed to be done next. Focusing on the future was more productive than wallowing in self-pity. He knew each would use today's event as another weapon in their determination to stand tall and fight with even more bravado.

"So, gentlemen," Winters began, "now that we know what the cops are doing, we need to figure out what we're going to do next."

They all nodded their heads.

"Something tells me our answers are in Detroit," said Elliott.

"Or Dearborn, Captain," suggested Meeks. "Besides those cops, we killed ourselves some Jijis."

"It's a likely area, big Muslim population there," added Elliott.

"It'd certainly make sense," said Winters. "When the Brits interrogated Boxer, he told them it took months to train and import those terrorists into the country. And since we killed them all, they must have wanted a closer supply."

"Plenty of angry young minds to be hired there," said Elliott.

"It seems weird. Cops working side-by-side with terrorists," said Meeks.

"No kidding. Especially when there's girls involved, I wonder how they divide them up," said Scar.

"If they're dividing them. Maybe they're sharing them," said Meeks.

"I don't give a rat's ass how their doing it. All I know is, that it's up to us to stop them and kill the sons-of-bitches," said Nate.

Everyone nodded.

"Okay, first things first," said Winters. "We need to find out where they were taking these girls and then try to determine their next move."

"Got to be Detroit or Dearborn," said Elliott.

Burns spoke up. "I'm pretty familiar with Detroit, Captain. Murphy and I can go do a recon, and see if anything comes up."

"Okay, then we'll concentrate on their next move," said Winters.

"Don't forget, Captain. We've got their map," said Scar. "It should give us a pretty good idea of any pattern they're following."

"Then it's settled."

.

CHAPTER 16

WASHINGTON D.C.

Reed sat in his seat at the Four Season's restaurant with his "boss" the billionaire Gerald Perozzi. Reed looked forward to ordering some appetizers to go along with his drinks. It was their favorite hangout for happy hour. The food was excellent as well as the service. One of the better benefits was that everyone knew who they were and there was always a table waiting for them.

Perozzi especially liked the young waitresses that worked there. He'd had modest success in picking up some of the ladies, despite the fact he was in his seventies. He did maintain a strict workout regimen, which helped him appear younger. In reality, his money is what attracted the ladies.

"So, Major Green seemed a bit vague."

"It went about as expected. He wasn't going to give up any more than what was in his report, so I didn't bother pressing him."

"Do you think he knows more than he's letting on?"

"I'm sure he does."

"Still, we should keep an eye on him."

"Oh, of course. I'll initiate the usual bugging of his computer and phones."

"You can never be too careful with the help."

"Find out anymore on this Winters fella?"

"Indeed we have." He pulled out a file from his briefcase and handed it to Perozzi. "I just got this in today."

Perozzi began to read the report. "Says his wife just died and he's got a kid somewhere. Call our media friends. Tell them who Cole Winters is and that besides being the leader of the rebels, he is wanted for murdering his wife."

Reeds snickered. "Already did that, it's today's headline."

Perozzi gave him an approving nod. "I need for you to go to New York tomorrow."

Reed didn't respond.

"I want you to meet with Mordulfah. I know you're not fond of this guy, but we need to kiss his ass for the time being. At least till we get what we want, after that, who knows."

CHAPTER 17

G reen arrived at his new office. It was a nice plush one, wood trim, with wall-to-wall deep pile burgundy carpet. A large walnut desk sat between two windows overlooking the city.

He didn't think this was permanent and wondered how long he'd be welcomed here. He had a secretary, named Grace, who greeted him and showed him around the building. After getting the grand tour, he went to his office and sat down, not knowing exactly what he was supposed to be doing.

After an hour, Grace rang him and informed him Lawrence Reed wanted a meeting. Green thanked her and quickly recapped his situation. He would have to make sure he had their trust and not say, or do, anything that might give him away. He got up and walked to the elevator in the hall. He stood and waited for it to arrive.

He was ushered into Reed's domain. "Come in. Come in, Major. I hope you like your new office and it suits your taste."

"Yes, it's fine, thank you."

"I wanted a quick meeting with you."

Green sat down.

"We got a new report in today and I want you to handle this while I'm gone."

"What kind of report?"

"Well, it's right up your alley. We think those rebels attacked some National Police out in Michigan."

Green tried to contain himself. "Oh, really?"

"Yes, our forces were in Eau Claire on routine patrol and were attacked. These rebels killed all the police officers."

"How can I help?"

"Scour the report, look at the photos, and see if this appears to be the gang's usual handiwork. Try to figure out where they might attack next, and where they might be hiding. Something tells me this won't be the last time we hear from them."

"Yes sir, I'll get on this right away."

"They burned down that town, Major."

"Any other towns?" asked Green.

"We think so. I've got a report coming in from the National Police later today, my office will forward you a copy."

Reed got up and Green recognized the cue, their meeting was over. He shook Reed's hand and left. He felt anxious as he went back to his office. His mind raced, knowing what he had just been told was completely fabricated propaganda. The only correct information was that Winters and his men likely killed those cops.

Question was, "Why did they do it?"

Why was Winters even in Michigan? Green knew the rest of the Patriots Centers were closed down. So, why was he there? Winters had to have a good reason for going because he wouldn't have risked his men's lives for nothing.

He sat down, flipped the folder open, and started reading the report. It stated the Shadow Patriots were in Eau Claire and shot up the place. The National Police were on a routine check of the town and the rebels ambushed them. The cops lost eleven men during the shoot-out.

Green went through the pictures. Knowing the truth about the government, allowed him to have a different perspective as he looked through the photos. He concluded that someone moved and staged the dead. They simple didn't look right to him and only contained a smidgeon of the truth.

Green sat back in his chair thinking about what really happened. He thought it more than likely the National Police were the aggressors and Winters had stumbled upon them and gotten into a firefight.

Green read the report again and noticed there was no mention of the population, even though their town was burned to the ground. So, how many were killed and how many had survived. Were there any survivors and if so, where were they? He would have to fill in the factual details.

Corporal Bassett arrived in D.C. tomorrow. He'd have to send him to Michigan to get to the truth.

CHAPTER 18

SALINE MICHIGAN

Burns and Murphy headed to Detroit, driving across the deserted Highway 12 in the early morning. It was a drizzly day with the wind whipping through the trees. Burns was at the wheel of an old Ford Taurus, comfortable and not bad on gas. Finding fuel was always an issue and they needed to conserve that special commodity whenever possible. Thankfully, they could always count on siphoning enough gas out of an abandoned car to go another hundred miles.

They left before sunrise so they would have enough time to look around the Detroit area. They had no illusions about the dangers of traveling in that area and knew they would stick out like a sore thumb.

Burns, a ten-year Army vet, didn't wear a ball cap and his salt and pepper hair was in need of some serious grooming as it had started to grow over his ears, and his beard had grown along with it. His job as a pneumatic parts sales representative had taken him to Detroit on several occasions. He had to come into the city every so often to meet with various plant managers.

Burns had met Murphy when he came to work for Exacta Pneumatics, which was located outside of Chicago in Oak Park. Murphy was a design engineer and worked closely with Burns on customer specs. The two formed a bond when they discovered each served in Desert Storm. They shared a same love of country and a desire to see it get back to basic values.

Murphy, like most of the others in the Shadow Patriots, liked wearing a ball cap. His cap boasted of his service in Desert Storm. He had a sergeant's pin attached to the side along with an American flag pin. Although Murphy had tired looking bags under his blue eyes, he had an energetic personality, which Burns loved. They often got in trouble in company meetings. Neither could keep quiet about the stupid ideas, their bosses would implement. Their time in the military instilled common sense in them, something the corporate world seemed to lack.

Murphy had inherited a large sum of money and they had plans to open their own manufacturing company. They had started to put the plans together, when the economy collapsed.

Both were divorced and their families were already in the south. This made it easy for them to pull up stakes as soon as the first dirty bomb blew up in downtown Chicago. With everything that was going on, they figured more would go off in the city. Once China invaded California, both knew they would have to volunteer their services once more for their country.

Burns motioned to his left. "Check out the sandpits. I wonder if any bodies are buried there?"

"Wouldn't surprise me," replied Murphy.

Thirty minutes later, the two passed through Saline, a small community south of Ann Arbor and an hour west of Detroit.

"Hmm, none of the houses are burned down here," said Murphy.

"Doesn't look like anyone is here."

"Let's take a look around," said Murphy.

"Yeah, why not."

Burns took a left on North Maple Road. Murphy kept looking for any signs of life, trampled grass, a stray pet, a light on in a home, or any smoke. Neither of them saw anything.

"Nice little town here," said Murphy.

"Wonder if everyone left on their own or were forced out."

After passing a middle school, they took a left on Woodland Drive and then headed back through town on Ann Arbor Street. They continued zigzagging the neighborhoods and found only a trash bag caught up in a tree, trapped from flight.

They came down Ann Arbor where tall shrubs and evergreen trees bordered the road to their right, hiding any buildings. As they passed a break in the shrubs, something caught Murphy's attention.

"Stop...stop."

Burns hit the brakes and came to a full stop.

"Back it up just to that paved pathway.

Burns put the car in reverse and crept backwards.

"Over there...see the cars?"

"I see em."

The two waited for a few moments looking at cars and the buildings trying to figure out what the purpose of the buildings was.

"What do you think this is?" asked Murphy.

"Offices maybe."

Burns pulled the gearshift into drive and let off the brake. The car idled slowly down the road until they came to the entrance.

"It's a retirement home," Murphy spoke up.

"Let's check it out," said Burns."

Burns passed a couple of houses before pulling into one where the driveway wound around to the back. He pulled in and made sure they were out of sight of the road.

They both grabbed their side arms and hid them under their jackets. They got out and Burns trotted up to the front door to make sure no one was home. He knocked a couple times before he was satisfied there was no one around. He jogged back to the car and found Murphy across the back yard close up to the tree line. They moved slowly through the small area of trees to the back of one of the buildings.

"Let's go to that white house over there and get to a second story window," whispered Burns.

They retreated to the car and retrieved their binoculars and rifles. Better prepared for surveillance, they used the shrubbery as cover to work their way to the front of the white two-story house. Burns again knocked on the door before breaking a window and going in. They climbed the stairs and found a bedroom overlooking the backyard. They could see some more cars in a cul-de-sac but still didn't see anybody.

"Something tells me we're going to be here awhile."

Murphy nodded.

Burns looked around the small bedroom. The bed had a white bedspread on but had a layer of dust, giving it a grayish appearance. He walked out of the room, and found a couple of folding chairs.

Burns sat on the folding chair staring out the window and thought about yesterday's events. As an Army veteran, he never had a problem with killing his enemy, it was something he had trained for and had used in the Gulf War. In all the action he had been involved in, either in the Middle East or even in the past few weeks, he had never witnessed the mass killing of innocent lives. He had seen death up close before, but never women and children. The experience was unsettling and shook him to his core. He couldn't get it out of his mind and had nightmares about it last night. The only thing that saved his sanity was rescuing the girls in the other transport. The looks on their faces once they realized they had been saved, had a lasting impact on him. It was a shame it was short-lived after they found out their families got murdered. Still, he took satisfaction in knowing they would be able to live their lives.

Burns thoughts turned to Winters and all the men. He couldn't have asked to be serving with better men. Each one of them was committed, loyal to each other and honorable. With everyone having a stake in the outcome, it made for a cooperation that was unusual, even by Army standards. There were no hidden agendas, no one shirked their duty, and there was an unwritten understanding on their goals. No money in the world could buy something like that.

"Got a couple," said Murphy looking through the binoculars.

"National Cops?" asked Burns

"Yep."

Murphy handed the glasses to Burns. He took them and observed the two standing outside. Two more cops, smoking cigarettes had also come on the scene.

"We're gonna have to find out what's in those buildings before we take off, but we'll have to wait till it gets dark."

CHAPTER 19

MANHATTAN NY

Reed, carrying a briefcase full of money, exited the Gulfstream G650 twin-engine jet at Teterboro airport in New Jersey. He ambled over to an awaiting limousine, where a chauffeur opened the door for him. Sliding into the car, he immediately grabbed a bottle of single malt scotch from the small, but fully stocked, bar and poured a drink. He swirled the caramel colored liquid for a moment allowing it to breath. He inhaled the contents deeply before taking a sip. He eased back in his seat thinking about his meeting with Mordulfah, a Saudi Prince in the royal family, and a true believer in Jihad. Perozzi asked Reed to meet with him in New York before the man headed back to Michigan.

Reed didn't necessarily like meeting with such men, but he knew the government required their services. Each side wanted something only the other could offer.

After a quick trip through the Lincoln tunnel, the limo pulled up to The Plaza Hotel. Reed didn't wait for the chauffeur and let himself out. The doorman recognized him from his many trips there and acknowledged him as Reed waddled toward the entrance. The hotel manger approached Reed and handed him the key to his room. Reed was accustomed to this service. He was too important to have to worry about trivial things, like checking in. The manager then escorted Reed to his meeting in the Royal Plaza Suite.

The private elevator door of the penthouse opened and a young man greeted Reed and led him to the living room. The man relieved Reed of the briefcase full of cash and offered him a drink. Another man came in and introduced himself as Wali. He wore a business suit and had the appearance of an educated man. He told Reed it would be a few minutes before the prince arrived.

"Typical of royalty, making someone wait," thought Reed. "Who the hell did this guy think he was, keeping him waiting? He may be a prince in his country, but he was in America, or what was left of it," snickered Reed to himself.

A minute later, Mordulfah, the Saudi Prince, entered the room. He was not a tall man, five foot eight, slight build, typical beard, but well maintained, it looked striking against his dark skin. His robes flowed around him as he entered the room. He walked up to Reed and shook his hand. Reed noticed the firm shake, but saw that his eyes spoke volumes. They were dark, and probed you like an MRI, missing nothing. Reed felt like the man was looking into his soul. The man had not smiled or changed his facial expression. Reed let go of his hand and moved a step back.

"Sit down, Mr. Reed," said Mordulfah. "Do you need your drink refreshed?"

Mordulfah's servant, the man who showed him in, came and grabbed Reed's glass before he had a chance to refuse him.

Mordulfah waited until Reed had his drink back in his hand before he continued. Reed noticed the prince didn't have a drink in front of him.

"Mr. Reed, I hope you had a comfortable flight. I sent you my best jet."

"Yes. It was quite nice."

"Good, good. Well, let us get down to business then."

Reed didn't respond.

"I trust you'll give me all the updates to the operation in the Midwest."

"Of course. We'll give them to you as they come in."

"I was looking through the file before you arrived. It seems to be lacking some crucial information."

Reed got annoyed. "Lacking?"

"Yes, it doesn't say anything about the ambush our forces suffered yesterday."

"Our forces," thought Reed. "More like my men and some of yours." Reed set his glass down. "We've not done a full investigation of the matter, but as soon as we do, it'll be forwarded to you."

"That's very kind of you Mr. Reed, however, I already know what happened."

Reed was starting to lose his tolerance of this guy's demeanor. Pompous jackass came to mind. If Perozzi didn't need his services so badly, he'd tell him to go to hell.

Mordulfah continued. "It would appear your band of rebels are the responsible ones. What do they call themselves?"

Wali took a document out of a file and handed it to Mordulfah.

"Ah yes, the Shadow Patriots. Why have you not dealt with them?"

Reed decided he needed to put things in perspective for the prince.

"They are nothing but a small band of old men. Can your forces not deal with such a nuisance? Surely, with what you're getting out of this deal, that shouldn't be a problem."

Mordulfah stared at Reed and didn't respond.

Reed didn't want to be the first to break eye contact or to say anything. However, the longer it went on the more nervous he felt. After a few more moments, he reached for his drink and picked it up, he noticed his hand shaking a little. He quickly took a drink and set the drink back down. "We'll give you an update in the next day or two."

Mordulfah didn't respond.

"Will you be here still?"

"No. I'm leaving to go back to Michigan in the morning. I have much to do before then, as I'm sure you do as well," said Mordulfah as his servant came in.

The servant nodded to Mordulfah.

Reed knew they finished counting the funds he had brought with him. He got up, "I see you've found everything in order. You'll find all the supplies and armor you requested will be waiting for you in Detroit."

Mordulfah didn't get up as Reed left the room. He turned to Wali, "Such arrogance for a fat little man. He needs to be careful how he treats people. One day he may find he cannot hide behind Perozzi."

Wali nodded his head in agreement.

Reed was glad to be done with the meeting. Though it hadn't been much of a meeting, hand him some cash, pretend you respected him, and act like you liked him. He hadn't felt so nervous around anyone since he was a kid getting beat up by bullies. Reed now understood why Perozzi had partnered with the man. Beneath Mordulfah's slight stature was a man who was as evil as they came. No doubt, he would fulfill his side of the bargain. The man had a commanding personality. He would be able to gather more forces in the Detroit area and make a Jihadist army out of them.

Reed headed to the lobby and then to his limousine for his next meeting with various diplomats from the UN. He needed to assure them everything was going as planned, and everybody would get what was coming to them.

CHAPTER 20

SOUTH BEND INDIANA

Winters noticed more men filtering in, some he knew, and others he did not. He wondered if they knew who he was. Since the battle at Detroit Lakes, their numbers had started to dwindle. Everyone thinking they had accomplished their mission. No one had any idea the Patriot Centers was just the beginning.

Winters certainly hadn't expected trouble like this. Even his friends in Canada, Colonel Brocket and General Standish, had no knowledge of anything like this. He needed to send word about what was happening so they could look into it further.

Winters thought about his wife and the lies the media was reporting about him. No doubt, Cara had heard it on the news. He held out hope she wouldn't believe what they were saying. However, it wouldn't surprise him if she did. She was a stubborn teenager and at an age where you naturally rebelled against your parents. However, some of the things she had learned in school were what seemed to push the rebellion further than normal. The country had been going through changes in the last decade and attitudes had been shifting as to what America stood for. There had always been a "Blame America" element in the school system, but recently it seemed to be more radicalized than ever.

Cara had always been vocal about her beliefs and was quite stubborn. She believed everything her teachers taught her, despite the counter arguments he and his wife Ellie had presented. Ellie had been more forgiving of her and said it was just a phase. Winters wasn't so sure, and never stopped trying to convince her that not everything she learned was correct. This only led to intense arguments and hurt feelings on both sides. Winters had become frustrated, not so much at her, but being powerless in making her recognize the truth. If she believed the news reports, it would be devastating to him. However, with no way of defending himself and the fact she left on less than ideal terms, he had to wonder.

Winters walked to the storage room where they kept their supplies. He checked their current supply of ammo and found they had more than enough. The Brits and Canadians had been such a blessing in that regard. Because of them, he didn't need to worry so much about supplies, although fuel was still a concern. Winters couldn't be thankful enough and wanted to pay them back for all their help. The only thing they requested was to help get America back as their number one ally. The world, they had said, needed her to be stronger than ever. Winters wasn't so sure it could come back from the grip of evil.

Winters walked into the commons area where Sadie was talking with some of the new arrivals from yesterday. She moved among the rescued girls, trying to comfort them. Sadie looked over at Winters, smiled and waved. He returned the wave and headed over to Nate and Elliott.

Winters sat down at the long table and turned to Nate. "How's our transport situation?"

"Good and bad. We got plenty of vehicles, but we don't have enough fuel for all of them."

"How many can go?"

"I'd say only four SUV's or five cars."

Winters jerked his head back. They needed more than that, many more than that.

"I've got guys out right now, siphoning gas wherever they can, so maybe in a day or so we could have more ready to go," Nate finished.

"Okay, well there it is then."

Elliott jumped in. "We should go pay Mr. Peterson a visit."

Winters thoughts went back to the time, when he first met Mr. Peterson. The Shadow Patriots had been on the run from the National Police and they had ended up on his farm. He was twenty years older than Winters, but despite losing some weight over the past couple of months, the older man was still in much better shape. He had been more than gracious in helping them, and after the cops discovered them, Winters had paid him back by losing the man's farm and everything he owned. They had all made their escape into Canada, where Mr. Peterson had stayed behind.

"Think those girls will want to go to Canada?" asked Nate.

"Haven't asked them yet, figured I'd wait a bit. I know Amber wants to stay and help us."

"Can she cook?" asked Nate.

"That's not what she was thinking. She wants to pick up a gun."

Nate raised an eyebrow. "I'm impressed."

"She used to target shoot with her Dad."

"Okay, okay. Nothing more exciting than seeing a girl with a gun."

Winters rolled his eyes. He got up from the table and started to walk outside, when Sadie ran up and grabbed his hand.

"Where you going?"

"Get some air."

"Can I come?"

Winters looked down at her. "Of course you can."

The two headed for the exit and stepped outside. The warmth of the morning sun felt good as they walked out onto the grass.

"How are your new friends doing?"

"They're still pretty sad. They want to go and bury their families."

Winters took in a deep breath.

"Don't you want to help them?" she asked earnestly.

"I do, but I'm not sure it's a good idea."

Winters stopped and sat down on the grass. Sadie dropped down beside him. He looked into her blue eyes. She had been through a lot, losing her mom and her home, but she didn't seem jaded. He envied what innocence remained. He didn't want to tell her it was too dangerous to go on a funeral detail. The enemy might be watching, but how could he turn her down. She was making the request for them wanting to help in any way she could.

"Let me think about it."

Her face beamed. "That will help them not be so sad anymore."

"What about you, Sadie? How are you holding up?"

She glanced out into the distance and then back to Winters. "I'm sad too, but I pray every night that I'll find my mom."

"We won't stop looking, I promise."

She held up her pinkie.

Winters held his up and grabbed on.

CHAPTER 21

SALINE MICHIGAN

Burns and Murphy had left early in the morning to scout Detroit. Keeping off the Interstate, they traveled on Highway 12, which went right through the small town of Saline. While checking out the town, they discovered some cops holed up in a retirement home, which was a curious thing. They needed to find out what was going on in there before they went on.

They had waited the rest of the day in the two-story white house, taking advantage of the beds. One stood by while the other caught some shut eye. The house had no power or running water, but it was better than waiting in their car.

Darkness couldn't have come slower as they both were growing restless. They were anxious to find out what the attraction inside was. As the evening came, more and more people started filtering in.

Finally, as it got dark, they stepped outside and crept across the backyard. A cool breeze wafted through the trees and the rising moon beamed through the cloudless sky.

They moved behind the first building and saw no lights on inside. They then went toward the parking lot.

"Hear that?" Murphy asked Burns.

In the distance, they could hear the whirl of an engine.

Burns strained to hear it before shrugging his shoulders.

They padded across the lawn to the trees that bordered the whole complex. Keeping to the cover of the woods, they kept going until they rounded another building where the parking lot was full of vehicles. The sound of the whirling engine got louder as they moved closer.

"It's got to be a generator, how else do they have any lights on," said Murphy.

Burns nodded.

They waited there for a while, watching a couple of cars pull in.

"Seems like a party," quipped Murphy.

Two men got out of one car and three from another. They were joking and laughing with each other as they made their way to the entrance. A few people came outside and engaged with them before the new arrivals went inside.

"What do ya want to do?" asked Murphy.

"Let's see if we can see inside."

They ran across the road to the building nearest them. They snuck up to the first window only to find the curtains closed. They found the same thing on the next set. They scooted down the long row of windows to find all of them closed off.

Burns came to a patio where lights sliced through the darkness. He heard voices and raised his fist. Murphy stopped dead in his tracks. Burns turned to Murphy and motioned him to back up. They slipped through the darkness, the way they had come and ran to the safety of the woods.

Burns gave Murphy a serious look. "Whatever is happening in there can't be good."

Murphy didn't respond.

"We can do one of two things. Neither one is going to be pleasant."

Murphy waited for Burns to continue.

"We can either walk in like we own the place or wait for one of them to come outside and knock him over."

"Then what?"

"Force him to talk."

"What if he doesn't?"

"Like I said, neither of these options are real appealing."

"I'd go with the first option if we had Scar here. He's good at improvising, me, not so much."

"Yeah, good point. We'll wait for one to come out alone."

"A small one if we can," laughed Murphy.

"Oh, gosh yes."

"So, should we water board the bastard?" asked Murphy slyly.

"We'll twist his arm and see what happens."

Murphy thought for a second. "I suppose we could give him a wedgie."

Burns rolled his eyes.

They sat, waiting for the next couple of hours and watched all the people move in and out of the party. They could see some were drunk inside and decided they wanted one who had been drinking. More than once they thought they had a chance only to have it spoiled by someone else coming into the parking lot. It was getting late and they were starting to lose patience when they finally spotted one coming out alone. He looked all around for his car, going in different directions before settling on a destination.

Burns and Murphy bolted out of the woods and across the parking lot. They split up and ran to either side of their unsuspecting victim. The man stopped at a car and reached for the door handle. Burns sprang up from behind. The cop thought he heard something and turned his head to see a fist come at him. The punch knocked him unconscious. His body collapsed to the ground.

Murphy came up behind Burns and looked to see if anyone might have noticed them. He gave the okay and opened the back door to the car. They picked him up and threw him in the backseat. Murphy climbed in with him and closed the door. Burns slid into the driver's seat and found the keys in the ignition. He thought it odd at first, but then thought who would have taken it.

Burns started the car, drove cautiously out of the parking lot, and turned north on Ann Arbor. He was nervous, but forced himself to keep cool, and took the first right on Harper Dr. Apartment buildings were to his left and he swung into the big parking lot. It was a large apartment complex and had windows busted out on several of the units, as if they had been ransacked.

Burns turned to Murphy. "Is he still out?"

WARREN RAY

"Yep. Did ya have to hit him so hard?"

"I barely touched him, he must be pretty hammered."

Burns drove to a secluded corner of the lot and shut the car off. He grabbed the canteen he had in his jacket, unscrewed the cap and handed it to Murphy.

Murphy poured water all over the man's face.

The cop woke up shaking his head back and forth. He was barely cognizant of his situation. He opened his eyes and stared at Murphy with a confused look.

"Hey, you all right?" asked Murphy.

"Who…what, what…where am I? Who are you?"

"Who am I? Dude you don't remember me?" asked a bemused Murphy.

"I… I know you?" he slurred.

"Yeah, I saved your butt that one time."

The man's eyes wondered around the backseat. "Yeah, yeah, you're huh."

"Carl, I'm Carl."

"Oh yeah…Carl."

"So tell me, what's going on back at that party?"

"You don't know?"

"If I knew, I wouldn't be asking you."

"Oh yeah…that makes sense…my head hurts what happened?"

"You tripped over yourself and fell backwards."

The cop rubbed the back of his head.

"So you were going to tell me what kind of party is going on."

"I was?"

Murphy nodded.

"Why don't you just go and find out yourself?"

"You know how bashful I am…always got to know before I go in. So you'd be helping me out."

"Oh, yeah. Well, you know it's the usual party…got plenty of booze and girls."

Murphy gave Burns a sideways glance. "Who are the girls?"

"You know."

"No, I don't know."

"The ones from the towns."

82

Murphy knew exactly what that meant. This is where they were bringing the girls. They were forcing the girls into slavery. He suddenly felt rage rifling through his body, he wanted to beat the hell out of this cop, but thought better of it. Better not to tip their hands.

"Hey Carl…I need another drink…you want to come to the party?"

"Depends how many girls are there?"

The man's eyes fluttered up and down trying to think. "I don't know for sure, there's a bunch though."

"Yeah…alright. Hey, how young are they?"

The cop smiled and snickered at Murphy. "They're not as young as what Mordulfah has."

Burns looked at Murphy. "Who's he?"

The man looked at Burns as if he was stupid.

"Mordulfah, come on you know he's that Saudi Prince. He's the one in charge."

"Where's he got his stash?"

"I don't know. Wherever he lives, I suppose."

Murphy had heard enough. He turned to Burns, tilted his head to the door, and they climbed out. Without saying a word, they took off back to their car, leaving their drunken friend to fend for himself.

CHAPTER 22

SOUTH BEND INDIANA

B urns and Murphy pulled in early the next morning. Although exhausted, they walked into the commons area and found Winters, Scar and Meeks sitting down eating breakfast. They walked directly over to them and sat down.

"You guys back already?" asked Meeks.

"Oh yeah, and we happened onto some really nasty things," said Burns.

Burns related what they had discovered.

After hearing their story, Winters leaned back to contemplate this revelation. The news didn't really surprise him too much. The existence of the "party house" was a logical conclusion to what they figured was happening to the girls. However, having it confirmed somehow made it different.

Hearing about this Mordulfah, character was the bigger surprise. He would need to find out who this person was, and how he fit into the government's grand scheme. Perhaps, Colonel Brocket would be able to find out.

"What do you want to do, Captain?" asked Scar.

"Rescue those girls as fast as we can."

"Yes, and at the same time, we need to stop these animals from kidnapping any more of them," said Scar.

Winters thought about that for a few moments. Scar was right, but they would have to prioritize their mission. The sooner they rescued the girls, the better. He couldn't allow anyone to remain a sex slave for even one day.

He looked at Scar. "We'll go to Saline today."

Scar nodded.

Winters turned to Burns and Murphy. "You guys go get some rest, we'll take care of this."

They both looked at each other. "We'll sleep in the car, Captain."

With that, they all got up and went to prepare for their day. Winters found Elliott and Nate and briefed them.

According to Burns, the "party house" only had a few people taking care of the place during the day, and since they would get there early, he didn't think they needed a large contingent to rescue the girls.

What he didn't know was how many girls there were and if they had enough vehicles to transport them. Nate was only able to fill five vehicles with fuel, which included a transport. With the exception of Burns and Murphy, who insisted on coming, he decided to just take just enough men to drive the vehicles.

Within an hour, they were ready to go. Everyone grabbed their gear and headed for the vehicles.

Amber approached Winters. "Captain, I think I should go with you."

Winters gave her a puzzled look.

"It would be comforting to those girls, if you had a female with you."

"It's going to be real dangerous."

"I should have been one of those girls, Captain. I'm not worried."

Winters shrugged his shoulders. "You can ride with Nate."

Winters had reached door of his vehicle when Sadie came running up. "Weren't you going to say goodbye?"

"Hey, you're up. I came by but you were still asleep."

"Is it true what they're saying, you found where they have more girls?"

"Yes we have."

"Can I come? My mom might be one of them."

"No, you stay here. If I find your mom I'll tell her where you're at."

"You don't know what she looks like."

"I'll look for the prettiest one, the one who looks like you."

Sadie smiled and gave Winters a big hug.

Winters pulled away and stared at her. After witnessing the slaughter in Eau Claire, he figured the cops were doing that in every town. He didn't have the heart to tell her, that her mom was probably dead. He would put that off for now. There was no sense in getting her upset.

Meeks turned and saw Amber walking over to the transport. "Amber's coming with?"

"She thought she could be helpful with the girls."

"She's going with Nate?" chuckled Meeks.

"Nate's going to love that, Captain," said Scar.

"Wonder if he'll ask her to cook him lunch," laughed Meeks.

"I'd like to see him ask her that," snickered Scar.

Winters turned to Elliott. "Nate's got more sense than that, right?"

Elliott gave Winters a grimaced look and shrugged his shoulders

They all walked over to their separate vehicles.

Winters got in and saw Sadie still standing there. He rolled down the window. "We shouldn't be too long, so don't worry."

"You know I will."

Winters grabbed onto the gearshift and threw it in drive. He pushed on the gas and led the small convoy out of the campus.

CHAPTER 23

Corporal Josh Bassett had gotten into Washington late last night and called Green at home. Green instructed him to come to his house in the morning. Bassett was a no nonsense soldier, and loyal to Green and to America. He was not afraid of much and took everything in stride. He stood six feet and had a muscular build he liked to keep in shape. He was a god-fearing man and believed the man up stairs had his back.

Bassett pulled into Mrs. Green's driveway, got out of his rental and headed to the door, where he gave it a hardy knock.

Green came to the door. "Corporal Bassett."

"Reporting for duty, sir."

"Come in, Corporal."

They walked into the kitchen, where Mrs. Green had left some breakfast for them. She had gone shopping to give them their privacy.

"Coffee?"

"Yes sir."

Green poured the coffee and instructed Bassett to help himself to the food. Bassett, with no hesitation, piled bacon and scrambled eggs onto a plate. He hadn't had bacon in quite a while and figured he wouldn't have another chance anytime soon.

"How did the men take the news of their deployment to the war?" Green asked.

"Most were pretty happy. They wanted to get into the fight. Others, not so much, especially knowing what they knew about what's going on in the Midwest."

"Yes, I can't blame them for that."

"They don't trust anyone in power anymore."

"They can trust their new field commander. I know him, he's a good man."

"They're disappointed you're not with them."

"As am I, Bassett."

"They're worried about you, we all think it's strange you're here."

"Yes, well, that's why you're here now. I need someone I can trust. You're going to be doing many things I can't ask anyone else to do."

"Are we going to be helping the Shadow Patriots?"

"As much as we can."

Bassett was pleased. "You can count on me, sir."

"Good, cause something tells me they're going to need our help. Have you heard, the government knows who Winters is now?"

"No sir, I didn't. How did they find out?"

"They sent a spy to St. Paul and he ran into someone with a big mouth. Once they got a name, the rest was easy. The media is blaming Winters for everything that Colonel Nunn was responsibly for and more."

"What are we going to do?"

"We're going to spy on the government, find out everything we can about what they're up to, and relay this info to Winters. The government still wants to find him, so we're going to feed them false info to throw them off track."

"How are we going to do that?"

"Oh, didn't I tell you? They put me in charge of finding the Shadow Patriots."

Bassett stopped eating, nodded his head, and gave Green a satisfying grin.

Green handed Bassett the report Reed had given him. "First thing I want you to do is go to Michigan. There's a report of the Shadow Patriots having a firefight with the cops in Eau Claire. I need you to find out what really happened. Also, look around see what else you can dig up. I'll get you official status by issuing you a Homeland Security badge."

"You can do that?"

"They're dead set on catching our friends and have given me a blank check. Hell, I'm even going to fly you out there on a military charter."

"A badge huh, I could use badge."

"This stays between you and me. You answer only to me." He handed him a slip of paper with an address on it. "They'll take your picture and get your credentials in order. You'll catch a plane out of Andrews to Detroit. Once you get there, check in with Captain Cox. He runs the National Police station there. Find out what you can, but don't push any subject too far. Remember, you're there to help catch the Shadow Patriots."

"You got it, Major," said Bassett, taking another strip of bacon.

CHAPTER 24

SALINE MICHIGAN

The Shadow Patriots pulled into the town of Saline from the south. They pulled into a parking lot on the corner of Ann Arbor and Henry St. The sun shone brightly and took the chill off the morning. Winters got out of his car and stretched his legs while he looked around the empty town. It looked like any normal town in America except there was no one around. No cars were parked on the streets and there was an eerie silence that wasn't normal. He lifted his head and noticed a water tower, wondering if it still held water.

Burns walked over to him holding a map. "Captain, that place is over there." He checked out the street sign and put his finger on the map. "And we're right here."

"Let's leave the transport here," announced Winters.

He walked over to Amber and handed her a Berretta .380. She took it and checked the magazine.

"What's our play, Captain?" asked Scar.

Winters turned to Burns. "Let's get to where you were watching them, so we can see what's up."

Five minutes later Burns and Murphy had them set up where they had been last night.

"This parking lot was full of cars last night, Captain," said Murphy.

"Hell, there's only three cars here, there can't be that many people inside," said Scar.

"Everyone must be working," said Murphy.

"Well duh, they're out looking for us," quipped Meeks.

Scar bumped Meeks' shoulder. "They're not very good are they?"

"Nooo they're not," snickered Meeks.

"I don't see any reason, we don't just walk right in there," said Scar. "Meeks and I will just go on in like we usually do."

"I like the sound of that, Captain," said Meeks.

Winters shrugged his shoulders. "We'll get to the rear entrance and wait for you."

Meeks thumped Scar on the shoulder smiling. "You ready partner? You got some wild story in your back pocket?"

"You know I don't, it's all spur of the moment for me, you just be ready."

Scar asked Elliott for the keys to the SUV and the two of them ran back to where they had hidden the vehicles. The rest would wait for them to enter the parking lot before they left the safety of the woods.

A couple of minutes later, Scar drove the SUV into the lot. He gave them a thumbs up. He parked and they stuffed pistols into the small of their backs.

As soon as they walked into the building, the rest of the Shadow Patriots ran out of the woods and headed to the back of the former retirement home.

A uniformed National Policeman looked up from his desk when he heard the door open. He immediately got up, grabbed his sidearm and pointed it at Scar and Meeks.

"Hey, hold the fort there, buddy," said Scar raising his hands.

"Stop where you are?" ordered the cop.

"I'm here on business. So put that thing away."

The cop didn't move. "Who are you?"

"We're here on the orders of Mordulfah. Now, do you want me to report just how rude you were to us?"

The cop lowered his weapon. "No, it's just that I wasn't notified of any visitors."

"That makes two of us. We weren't told to come here until the last minute, so don't worry about it."

The cop holstered his .45 and asked what they needed.

"You know Mordulfah, man's got an unquenchable thirst. So you can imagine what he wants," said Scar, astonished that this line of malarkey was working. "Where's everyone else?"

"Oh, they're bobbing around here somewhere."

"How many are you?"

"We're just three during the day. We'll have more later, when the party starts."

Scar gave Meeks a disgusted glance. "Why don't cha call them all up here so they don't think we're intruding."

The uniformed cop picked the phone up and hit a button to the intercom system. A few minutes later, the remaining two walked into the lobby. They all stared at Scar and Meeks who didn't bother introducing themselves. The uniformed cop stood up from his desk and told the others who sent them.

"Where's the bathroom?" asked Meeks.

"Down the hall," answered one the cops, who sported a goatee.

Meeks gave Scar a raised eyebrow then strolled down the hallway. He made it to the restroom, and turned to see if anyone had followed him. Scar was still holding their attention, so he hurried on down the hall. Reaching the backdoor, he unlocked it and found his brethren waiting. "There's just three of them, Scar's holding court with them right now."

Winters shook his head. "But of course he is."

"Man's got a way about him," laughed Meeks.

They all snuck back up the hallway with weapons raised, they moved to the unsuspecting cops and yelled at them to get their hands up.

Winters approached them. He looked at the three cops who did not look like the kind of cops he remembered as a kid. They were unkempt and looked more like third shift security guards. A year ago, before the war, there was no way they could have even passed the entrance exam.

"Now gentlemen, and I use that term loosely, where are all the girls?"

The cops looked at each other not knowing what to do. The goateed cop volunteered to show them. He led them through a door and down another hallway. As they came to the first door, the cop took out a master key and opened it. Nate grabbed the cop by the collar and yanked the man backwards. Winters peered in and found a girl chained to a bed covered with a dirty white sheet.

The girl's brown eyes opened. She jerked her head up. Winters turned his head and whispered for them to stay back. He then entered the room and approached the frightened girl.

"My name is Cole and we're here to rescue you."

The girl didn't answer.

"I'm not going to hurt you."

The girl stared at Winters. "That's what you all say."

Winters yelled out. "Bring that cop in here."

Nate grabbed the cop and pushed him through the crowd standing at the door. Nate held a gun to the cop's head as they came into the room.

Winters turned to the girl. "Do we look like the others?"

She shook her head.

Winters looked at the goateed cop. "Where's the key?"

The cop handed his key to Winters.

"Does this key work on all the locks?"

He nodded.

Winters reached for the lock, put the key in, and released their first captive. The girl rubbed her wrist, leaned towards the cop and spit in his face.

Nate chuckled, twisted the cop's arm, and escorted him out the door.

"What's your name?" asked Winters.

"Reese."

"Where you from?"

"Ithaca. It's a small town...well it was a small town before they came in and burned it down. Everybody's dead, they killed everyone except me and another girl. She's here, I think, at least she was. I don't even know where I am."

"You're in Saline."

She gave Winters a confused gesture.

"We're just south of Ann Arbor."

Reese nodded her head in recognition.

"How many girls are here?"

"I don't know. I've never been allowed to leave this room."

"How long have you been here?"

"Ten days." She looked right into Winters' eyes. "Ten days of hell."

Winters didn't respond. He turned to Elliott, who was standing in the doorway. "There has to be some kind of assemble room in this place. Let's bring everyone there."

He turned back to Reese. "What do ya say we get out of here?"

Reese moved out from under the covers and dangled her legs to the floor. When she got up, the dirty sheet fell back to the bed, exposing her naked body. She was twenty years old and had been a cheerleader in high school. She was blond haired, brown-eyed and stood at five-foot-five. She didn't bother covering herself and casually walked to the bathroom. Winters wondered what kind of hell she'd been through not to worry about her appearance. She came out of the bathroom wearing the clothes she'd come with. Dark blue jeans with a light blue tank top under a dark blue runners jacket. Winters gestured with his hand the door, and escorted her down the hall.

For the next thirty minutes, the Shadow Patriots released girl after girl and led them to the main assemble room. All the girls were in their late teens to early twenties and very pretty. They had dazed looks plastered on their faces. Some still without clothes wrapped themselves in blankets. Some were in poor health and needed medical attention. After talking to several of them, Winters discovered none of them had been there longer than a few weeks and all were there for the pleasure of the National Cops and various others, including a Middle Eastern variety.

Elliott walked up to Winters. "We've got seventy-five girls here, Captain."

Winters gave Elliott an astonished look. "Seventy-five? Is that all of them?"

"We've been in every room in this god forsaken place. Look at these poor things. Hell, my daughters are older than these girls."

Winters nodded, remembering his daughter, Cara. She was nineteen and could easily have qualified to be in one of these rooms. He stared at all the faces. Some had a look of relief, while others were noticeable anxious. A few were crying as they held each other for support. There wasn't much chatter among the girls, which made Winters wonder if any of them even knew each other. A couple of the girls looked like they were sick or possibly even drugged up. He wondered if they'd ever be able to recover from their days here. He was glad he had brought Amber with them. She was going around and checking on them, giving them words of encouragement.

Winters walked up to her as she was talking to two girls who were holding each other.

"How are we doing?"

"Some better than others. They're afraid and want to get out of here."

Amber turned to the two girls standing next to her. "This is Paige and her little sister Phoebe."

Paige was twenty and was two years older than Phoebe. Each girl had disheveled blond hair that didn't look like it had been washed in several days. The hair stuck together in strands as if it was wet. Their blue eyes had a vacant gaze as if they weren't paying attention. Neither one smiled as they said hello to Winters.

Winters, unsure what to say, asked where they were from.

"Harpor Springs," replied Paige in a soft voice.

"Where's that at?" asked Winters.

"Top of the state."

"How long have you been here?"

"Two weeks."

"They killed my mom," said Phoebe as tears welled up in her eyes. "They did it right in front of us."

"I'm so sorry," said Winters wanting to reach out to her. He didn't know if he should touch her after having a bunch of men raping her.

Thankfully, Amber knew what he was thinking and put her arm around Phoebe.

Paige looked at Winters. "We were just sitting at home when they came to our door. They ordered us outside and my mom refused. So, they just shot her right there. They dragged us outside and took us here."

Winters heart sank as he listened to their story. He had heard some of the same stories from Amber and the others they had rescued the other day. No matter how many times he heard them, he could never get used to it. Each had a story to tell and each had a tragic ending.

"We're going to get you guys to safety, okay."

They both nodded.

He gave Amber a reassuring look as Elliott approached him.

"Captain, a word."

They both turned and headed to the exit of the assemble room.

"How are we going to get them out of here, Captain?" asked Elliott. "We don't have enough room."

"We'll have to find some more vehicles or just cram everyone in. We need to hurry. We've been here too long as it is. Where's Nate?"

"He's out in the hall guarding the cops."

"Okay, get these girls organized."

Winters walked out into the hallway. He noticed Reese following him, so he turned to her and asked if she needed anything. She told him she just wanted some fresh air.

They both walked toward the entrance where Nate had the cops handcuffed with their backs to the wall.

"Nate we need more transportation," said Winters.

Nate turned to the goateed cop. "Where?"

The cop didn't answer, so Nate belted him in the stomach and asked him again.

He gasped for breath before answering. "Out back in the garage, couple of SUV's."

Nate grabbed the man's hair and yanked his head up. "Keys?"

"In the ignition."

"That wasn't so hard now was it," said Nate. He set his Mark 23 pistol down on the desk and swung his backpack off his shoulder.

He looked at Winters. "You want to go get someone to watch these raping bastards while I go check out our new wheels?"

Winters nodded and turned back to the assembly room.

While Nate busied himself opening his backpack, Reese floated over to the table and grabbed Nate's gun. She pointed it first at the goateed cop and started firing.

The cops screamed in agony as they fell to the ground dead.

Nate's reaction was quick, but once he saw what she was doing, he didn't care and let her finish. Winters was back to the assemble room when the gunshots echoed throughout the building. He sprang back down the hall to Reese and grabbed the gun from her. Her big brown eyes had a fleeting moment of satisfaction. It reminded him of his own struggle with Mr. Hyde and wondered if she'd have to battle the same urges. He was about to say something to her, but decided to let it go. He wouldn't judge her.

"Takes care of that problem," said Nate with a slight smile on his face as he turned and walked out the door.

Scar and Meeks, with their guns readied, sprinted down the hallway.

"Who shot em?" asked Scar.

Winters nodded his head toward Reese as she shuffled by them in a daze. Scar sensed what happened and turned to watch her leave the room.

"Guess she thought they deserved it," said Scar.

"Can't say I blame her," said Meeks as he knelt down to check the cops. "What do you want to do with them, Captain?"

"Just leave them. We need to get the hell out of here. Why don't you and Scar go get the transport?"

With seventy-five girls and eight Shadow Patriots, they had to commandeer the three cars from the parking lot besides two SUV's from the garage. They didn't have enough drivers and had to draft two of the older girls. This made Winters uneasy as he drove the lead car out of the parking lot. It would be a long trip and he wasn't sure if the two girls, having gone through such a traumatic experience would be able to handle it. Having Reese sitting beside him was a reminder on how any one of them could snap in an instant.

Winters took a left onto Highway 12 and watched his rear view mirror to ensure all the vehicles made the turn. With such a large, slow moving, convoy they were easy to spot. His mind was on high alert, causing his arm to pulse where he had gotten his wound from back at the train station. It hadn't bothered him in awhile, until he received a baton blow yesterday. He looked ahead at the desolate highway and prayed for safe passage.

He'd been driving in silence for what seemed an eternity and looked down at mileage. They'd only traveled thirty miles. The radio sitting on the dash came alive interrupting his concentration.

"Captain," said Scar who brought up the rear of the convoy.

Winters reached for the radio and answered.

"We've got company," said Scar.

CHAPTER 25

GROSSE POINTE MICHIGAN

Mordulfah entered the sprawling estate, which suited his needs well, and just happened to be the historical home of Edsel & Eleanor Ford. He, of course, was used to such surroundings, having grown up as a Saudi Prince. They were the chosen ones, the ones who led their followers and gave them instruction on how to live by Sharia law.

He had just gotten back from New York where he had met with Reed, the sniveling little fat man. Despite receiving another payment, he still fumed, wanting nothing more than to show the pompous Americans who was really in charge. He would have to bide his time before he would be able to accomplish his goals, but he was a long time planner and his patience would pay off in the end. Once he established himself here, he would engrain himself further into Washington politics, he could then concentrate his power. All his effort had been ten years in the making, paying people off, meeting important people and putting together deals with the infidels. He was still far from his ultimate goal of ruling this country and establishing Sharia law throughout the land for his people. He cared little for whoever survived. Either they converted to Islam or they'd killed them. It didn't mattered to him, which they chose.

Before doing any of this, he would have to muscle out that arrogant billionaire Perozzi, and separate him from his money. Perhaps an assassin's bullet would be the better way to go. No, he'd take greater pleasure in seeing the old man grovel at his feet, knowing he had outwitted him. Because Mordulfah pretended to be the puppet, Perozzi thought he could outsmart him. Perozzi, however, played a poor game of chess.

Mordulfah walked into his huge bedroom, turned to Wali, his faithful servant, and ordered him to bring a couple of girls. He needed to let off some steam. Not only was he out of sorts over his meeting with Reed, he was angry about the deaths of his men. These were men he knew personally, men who had come with him from their homeland. He took personal offense to their deaths and vowed to extract revenge from these so-called Shadow Patriots. They had also spoiled the arrival of fresh girls to his bed. He had looked forward to defiling fresh virgins, but now he'd have to suffice with the girls who had been here a couple of weeks. These girls gave into their fate, and were not nearly as pleasurable to bed.

Wali came back with two young blonde girls. Both were dressed in white and light blue silk garments. He gazed at them, trying to remember when he had them last. He liked blondes the best, as they were unattainable back home. Both were underage, which was one of two requirements, the other was that they had to be virgins. It was pointless to be in charge and not have the freshest girls.

He instructed the girls to go into the bathroom, telling them he needed a bath. They meekly slipped toward the tub and began to run the water. He admonished them not to make it too hot. Mordulfah ordered Wali to bring some food and drink. Wali walked out and Mordulfah moved into the bathroom where the girls proceeded to undress him. He smiled at them and thought to himself that it was good to be a Prince.

CHAPTER 26

SALINE MICHIGAN

The Shadow Patriots had been traveling just under an hour and were about thirty miles west of Saline. Winters and his men had just rescued seventy-five girls from the hell they had endured for the last ten days. The cops had taken the girls from their homes, and used them as sex slaves.

They were heading back to South Bend when Scar, who brought up the rear of the convoy, radioed Winters.

"What do we got, Scar?"

"We've got trouble, Captain. We got four, maybe five, cops trailing us."

Winters' face went flush as blood rushed to his head. His mind started racing as he contemplated what to do. He knew they would not be able to outrun them.

"What do you want to do, Captain?" asked Scar.

Winters raised the mic up to his mouth. He took a moment before speaking. He realized they were out in the open and had few options. "Any suggestions?"

"A good offense is a good defense," responded Scar the former Marine.

"What about that sandpit?" Meeks asked. "It can't be too far away."

Winters remembered they had past a large sandpit on their way to Saline. The pit reminded him of the shootout they had a couple of days ago, where the cops had murdered the citizens of Eau Claire. It was the first

100

sandpit he had seen since, and when they had passed by, he couldn't stop wondering if any bodies were buried there. He also remembered a couple of buildings at the front entrance and another across the street. Considering their slow moving convoy, this place was as good as any to make a stand. He didn't like the odds, but they would be better than trying to outrun a bunch of motivated cops who were in good position to knock them off one by one.

He spoke into the radio. "Meeks, I need you and Elliott to speed up. We need to get way ahead of them and make it to the sandpit. Scar, you think you, Burns and Murphy can block any attempt they try to make on Nate before we are in place?"

"Not a problem, Captain."

Both Burns and Murphy confirmed.

"Nate, when you get into the pit, find a good place to set up a defense. When those cops follow you in, we'll come in from behind them."

"What about the others?" Meeks asked.

Winters thought about Amber and the two girls who were driving. They had been through a lot already and he wanted them as far away as possible from the action. He would have Amber lead them back to South Bend while they handled the cops.

"Get them all up here with us."

Winters stepped on the gas and sped up. He looked in the rearview mirror at the five cars coming up fast behind him.

"I need you girls to be ready to get out of the car."

Reese turned to Winters. "I'm not leaving. You give me a gun and I'll shoot the bastards."

"This is not up for debate," said Winters trying not to shout at her.

"I don't care what you say, I'm not leaving. I think I've shown you what I can do, so I'm staying," she said defiantly.

Winters could not believe what he was hearing. He glanced at her. She had the same expression when she killed the cops back at the retirement home. Revenge coursed through her blood and she wanted to release it.

"Have it your way," responded Winters, knowing he had another new recruit.

Winters turned his head to the three wide-eyed girls in the back. "It's going to be alright," he said trying to sound convincing.

Once Winters reached the sandpit, he stopped the car in the middle of the road and got out. The other cars came up behind him.

Meeks and Elliott raced up to him. "Whatcha thinking, Captain?" asked Elliott.

Winters scanned the buildings adjacent to the entrance and the one across the street. The latter had a thick set of trees blocking the view from the east. That position offered a better vantage point should one of the cops happen to see through his plan and blow past them.

"I want the girls to keep going, we'll move my car behind this house here," Winters said pointing across the street. He then hurried the girls to the other cars and instructed Amber to head to South Bend. He slapped the top of her car and watched as she sped away.

Meeks turned to Winters and motioned at Reese.

"She wants to stay."

He shrugged his shoulders.

They all jumped into the car, with Elliott taking the driver role. He guided the car around the one-story yellow house and out of sight. Meeks, sitting in the back with Reese, took out his Sig 9mm and chambered a round. After some quick instructions he handed her the hot gun and two extra magazines.

Winters got on the radio and called out to Scar.

"How's it looking, Scar?"

He didn't respond.

"He's a little busy, Captain," responded Burns who was ahead of Scar.

"What's happening, Burns?"

"One of them is trying to run him off the road."

"Nate, how far away are you guys?"

"Not far, another minute I think."

"We're set up right across the street."

Winters checked the shotgun he had laying in his lap. It was a pump action 12-gage Mossberg 500 and was loaded with double aught buck.

Another agonizing minute later, the radio came back to life. "We're coming in now. We're here," shouted Nate

Winters spoke into the radio. "We hear you. Let me know where you go, Nate."

"I'm turning into the pit now."

Elliott put the car in drive and kept his foot on the brake.

"Not too far behind you, Nate," said Scar. "It's getting saucy back here guys. I've got five cars behind me."

"I'm taking the first right inside the pit," said Nate.

Winters held the radio to his mouth. "Let me know when you're in, Scar."

Moments later, "I'm in," yelled Scar.

Winters noticed his leg shaking a little bit in anticipation. He had been in many shootouts over the past couple of months and the experience had given him more confidence, but his anxiety mounted as he considered what they were about to do. They were going up against five carloads of cops who would have no problem killing their precious cargo. The only thing they had going for them was the element of surprise. He wasn't sure this was enough.

Elliott took his foot off the brake and stepped on the gas. He pulled around the yellow house and saw the cops up ahead in the sandpit. He floored the accelerator. Coming out of the tall grassy lawn, he passed a row of trees that kept them hidden. He hadn't noticed the last SUV lagging behind the others. As he pulled out to cross the highway, it slammed into the side of their vehicle. The violent crash shook all the passengers to the core.

Winters pushed himself off Elliott and grabbed the door handle, but the SUV blocked his exit.

"Get out Elliott."

Elliott opened the door, stepped out carrying his weapon and started firing into the SUV windshield.

Winters crawled out the driver's side. He kept low and reached the back door to pull Reese out followed by Meeks. The three of them ducked behind the car to take cover, as two cops emerged from their passenger side firing at them. Winters peered over the trunk of the car, raised his shotgun, and pulled the trigger. The weapon exploded with a booming roar splattering the paint off the driver's door. His second shot tore a hole through the side window taking out the driver who slumped in his seat.

Meeks advanced steadily to the driver's side of the SUV firing his AR-15 into the vehicle. Both cops in the front were dead. He squatted down to see another lying dead on the ground, and one more still on his feet. Meeks snuck around the back of the SUV and finished him off.

Winters grabbed Reese's arm and asked if she was all right. She shook her head in the affirmative. Just then, the radio came to life.

"Where are you guys?" yelled Scar.

Winters reached into the car and grabbed the radio. "We're coming."

Elliott looked at Winters. "This car ain't going anywhere."

"Meeks, what about the SUV?"

Meeks opened the driver's door and yanked the dead cop out. He got in, started it up, and threw it in reverse. The SUV creaked as he backed it up but was drivable.

Elliott pulled the other dead cop out and they all got in. Meeks floored the gas pedal, peeled into the sandpit, and took the first right. Their enemy stood behind their vehicles firing at the Shadow Patriots, who were using their vehicles as cover, but were parked in front of a large hill and had no place to go. Winters told Meeks to stop. He got on the radio. "Guys, we're coming in right now. We're in their SUV." He grabbed Meeks shoulder. "Pull up as close as you can behind them."

As Meeks moved in, Winters remembered that there were five cop cars, minus the one they were in, he only saw three of them. He began to panic. "Where was the other one?"

Meeks pulled in forty yards away from the cops and parked broadside to their enemy. Everyone got out the driver's side, took positions and opened fire.

The cops turned around and reacted immediately. One jumped into a squad car and angled it around to block the hail of bullets they were receiving.

Winters quickly realized the mistake the cops made. When they moved their car, they left their flank exposed. He got on the radio. "Scar, Scar. Backup one of the vehicles and flank them."

"Roger that, Captain."

Winters grabbed Elliott's arm. "Let's you and me get on top of that dune."

Elliott nodded.

"Meeks, you and Reese stay here, we're going up there," he said pointing to the dune.

Meeks acknowledged the command.

Winters put his hand on Reese's shoulder. "You okay?"

She looked at him wide eyed. He noticed her measured breathing and the determination she had when venting her anger. She held the gun with both hands and took careful aim as she pulled the trigger. The gun jerked back in her hands, but she held on and fired again.

Winters and Elliott backed away and made a dash to the dune to their right. The twenty-yard run seemed further as several bullets whizzed by them. They were just about there when Winters heard Elliott scream out in pain. He fell to the ground. Winters grabbed him under the arm, and pulled him along until they reached the safety of the dune.

"Where'd you get hit?"

"In the friggen leg. Damn bastards," he responded as blood poured out both sides of his left leg. Winters started swearing to himself, but remained calm as he took off his jacket. Buttons flew from his shirt as he tore it off leaving him in a white tee shirt. He tightly wrapped the makeshift tourniquet tightly around Elliott's leg.

"Can you move?"

Elliott nodded. Winters helped him up and they crawled to the top of the sand dune. Winters looked over the top and down at the cops below. He raised his Model 1911 Colt and took aim. He was about to fire when he noticed the cops, who were originally unaccounted for, on the top of the hill looking down on Burns and the others. The cops stood up with their weapons pointed toward the bottom of the hill.

A cold shiver shot up his spine as he realized his friends were exposed and had nowhere to go. They had only seconds to react. Winters grabbed his radio. "Burns, Murphy, behind you. They're up top...they're up top!"

Just then, the four cops opened fire with automatic rifles. Winters heard the echo of girls screaming mixed in with the booming gunfire, as it rained down on them. Winters aimed his Colt and fired, but they were too far away for it to be effective. Elliott turned over onto his stomach, raised his Winchester 30-30 and quickly fired off a couple of rounds. One of the cops fell and rolled down the hill. The other three ducked down and took cover.

Winters then took aim at the cops below and emptied his magazine on them. He threw in another magazine and pulled the trigger, while Elliott kept firing at the cops up on the hill, dropping another one.

All the cops below lay wounded on the sandy ground. Winters looked over to Elliott who kept searching the hilltop for the remaining two cops.

Winters grabbed onto the radio. "Burns we still got a couple behind you. How's it going over there?"

"Murphy's hit. Got a bunch of girls dead here, even more wounded."

Winters dropped the radio. He took a couple of deep breaths to slow his rapid breathing. He knew at that moment, after all they had done to rescue the girls, he had failed them.

He yelled down at Meeks to come up and help Elliott. He started taking long strides down the hill. He strode carefully to the cops lying on the ground. Holding his Colt, he walked up to them and found one still alive. He was young and looked up at Winters as if to plead for his life. For a moment, Winters thought about what to do. He had been in this position before and had made the decision long ago not to kill prisoners. However, knowing the wounded cop was responsible for the deaths of an untold number of girls, conflicted with Winters' morals. The cop made a move. It was all Winters needed. He tightened his grip on the big .45 and fired three shots into the hapless cop.

He was staring down at the dead man, when he heard the roar of an engine. He turned his head just in time to see the fifth police car tearing out of the sand pit.

Winters sprinted over to where Burns, Murphy and Nate were. When he came around the transport, the scene sent shock waves through his body.

During the past couple of months, he had been involved in many battles, and watched friends and innocent people die in front of him. Over time, he had gotten used to seeing the dead and bloodied bodies, but nothing had prepared him for the carnage that lay before him. Dead girls lay everywhere, some with their faces planted in the sand. Others were stacked on top of one and another in an obvious attempt to act as a shield. Blood was splattered everywhere. The moaning and crying overloaded his senses. Winters stared at them, not sure what to do first. Burns and Nate were already tending to some of the wounded when Scar approached.

"Captain, let's find some first aid kits.

Winters kept staring, unable to move.

"Captain," hollered Scar.

Scar's shout snapped him back to his senses.

With little time to spare before the cops came back with reinforcements, the Shadow Patriots quickly tended to the girls, and wrapped bandages around bullet wounds. With their military experience, Burns and Scar had the advantage of knowing what to do and willingly took charge of the care. Murphy was out of commission after taking a bullet to the shoulder. Elliott, past the adrenaline rush, was now in a good deal of pain, but he still managed to be of use. Reese had some medical training since she had been working on her RN degree. For the seriously wounded, they would have to wait until they got back to South Bend.

In total, eighteen of the girls lay dead, three more were dying and ten others had wounds of varying degrees. The dead include the two sisters, Paige and Phoebe. Having met them, Winters felt an extra burden with their deaths.

After loading everyone up and a quick burial, they headed back to South Bend. Winters drove, while Elliott, in a lot of pain, sat beside him. With the exception of a couple of girls in the back crying, they drove in silence. He gripped the steering wheel hard making his knuckles turn white as guilt crept through him. He could not stop thinking about the dead girls and whether he had made the right decision by pulling off into the sand pit.

Darkness enveloped them as they pulled onto the campus. Sadie ran outside excited to greet Winters and ran over to open his door. His ashen face startled her, and she took a couple of steps backwards to get out of his way.

Winters walked around to help Elliott. He got under Elliott's arm with his shoulder and escorted him inside. People poured out of the building and ran over to get everybody inside.

It was organized chaos as those who had medical experience hustled about making sure everyone got adequate attention. Winters stood and watched in earnest. He admired those who knew what they were doing. Sadie walked up to him and grabbed him around the waist. Winters looked down and put his arm around her. He felt comforted as she squeezed him. Neither spoke as they watched the others work.

A black squad car pulled out of South Bend and headed back east to Detroit. The two cops inside had seen enough. Having followed the convoy from the sand pit, they needed to get back to Detroit and report the whereabouts of the Shadow Patriots.

CHAPTER 27

DETROIT MICHIGAN

Landing in Detroit early in the morning, a cop met Corporal Bassett and drove him to the National Police Station. He introduced himself to Captain Cox, the station commander, an arrogant doughy man in his early thirties who didn't like someone from D.C. poking around in his territory. He wore his hair in a crew cut and had scruffy facial hair that needed shaving. The black tactical uniform had an extraordinary number of ribbons obviously revealing Cox's braggadocios character. Bassett sized him up immediately and recognized him to be insecure and a distrustful little weasel.

Cox didn't give him a warm reception and had only short and evasive answers to his questions. Bassett knew the man was trying to conceal info from him. Consequently, he ended the conversation and requested a vehicle so he could be on his way. Cox took his time, and reluctantly threw him a set of keys to a late model Ford Crown Vic.

Bassett laughed to himself after locating the car in the back parking lot of the station. With more than one dent, the car had seen its better days.

He got in and was surprised it even started. The fuel gage indicated a full tank. He wondered if it even worked as he pulled out of the parking lot and headed west toward Eau Claire.

Bassett was a farm boy, having been born and raised in the small town of Yoder, Indiana, just south of Fort Wayne. He liked the Midwest and felt fortunate to have served under Major Green there. It had been a nice break from his time fighting in Afghanistan, where he had done two tours. He knew that eventually he would end up fighting out West. For now though, he relished his duty in the Midwest. Racing through the barren landscape on an empty road, he felt back at home. He liked the loneliness the open road offered. His two days of crowded roads back in D.C. had been a shock. He had gotten the sense that the people there, weren't even aware the country was at war.

After speeding across the state on Interstate 94, he came to Highway 140 and noticed burned down buildings on his right. He decided to pull into the town of Watervliet. He drove along Main Street with his windows down. Thick rancid air assaulted his nostrils. He was amazed to find the whole town burned to the ground. It looked like old WWII pictures of Berlin after being bombed by Allied forces. The streets had an eeriness that was unsettling. He thought about what it took to do such a thing. It had to have taken a lot of men and time to wreak this kind of havoc. He shook his head in disgust wondering who had done this, and why. More importantly, he wondered where all the people were.

He stopped, pulled out a map and noticed that Eau Claire wasn't too far away. He took a pen out and circled Watervliet. After turning the car around, he continued south on Highway 140. Ten minutes later, he reached the small town of Eau Claire and found the same senseless destruction. He didn't waste any time there, but went on to the next town of Berrien Springs. Upon arrival, he witnessed the same. Pulling the map out, he circled both towns. He had a desire to go home to see if this happened to Yoder. However, since his family had all moved to Florida, and he needed to report to Major Green, he resisted the impulse.

He headed back to Detroit to question Captain Cox, though he didn't expect to get any straight answers from him. He thought about befriending some of the other cops in order to pry information from them.

A few hours later, he pulled into the parking lot of the National Police Station. He got out of the car and walked inside. He noticed the cops chatted in excited tones as he found his way to Cox's office.

He knocked on the door. "What's all the excitement?"

"Got ourselves a bead on the Shadow Patriots."

"Really? Where are they at?"

"They're on the campus in South Bend."

The news disheartened him. He hadn't been too far from them. "How'd you find that out?"

"Some of our men had a shootout with them late yesterday. They killed a bunch of my men, but two survived and were able to follow them to the campus."

Bassett tried to play it cool. "That's great news, so what are we going to do?"

"We?"

"Yes, we. I'm with Homeland Security and that's precisely why I'm here."

"Well, Mr. Homeland Security, you can stay here while we go round them up."

Bassett didn't respond. He, in fact, didn't want to go with them. He needed to get out of there ASAP and warn Winters.

"When are you leaving?"

"First thing in the morning."

Bassett left Cox's office and walked down the hall where a couple of cops sat at their desks. He approached them and asked for a telephone he could use. They pointed to a desk in the corner.

Bassett sat down and looked around before picking up the receiver. He had hoped for more privacy. He dialed Green's office. Grace, his secretary, answered and put him on hold.

"Major Green here."

"Sir, it's me."

"Corporal, how goes it?"

"Got great news, sir." He tried to sound as enthusiastic as possible since one of the cops was watching him. "The locals here found where the Shadow Patriots are holed up."

Green got up from his chair and moved to shut his office door. "That is great news, where are they?"

"South Bend, on the campus. Apparently, they were involved in a shootout with the cops yesterday."

"When are they going to go and get them?"

"First thing in the morning."

"Are you joining them?"

"No. The captain in charge here doesn't want my help."

"What are you going to do?"

Bassett paused a moment before answering. "I'll make myself useful to them."

Green knew what that meant. "You report in as soon as you get more good news."

"I will, sir."

"You be careful out there, Corporal. We've got a lot riding on this."

CHAPTER 28

SOUTH BEND INDIANA

The next morning Winters awoke feeling more aches and pains than usual throughout his weary body. The action yesterday was taking its toll. He reached for a bottle of aspirin and swallowed three to ease the discomfort. With everything he had done in the last couple of months, the running and fighting, he was losing his beer gut and was actually in the best shape he'd been in since he was a young man.

He had been restless all night and hadn't slept much, if at all. The only thing he could think about were the dead girls they had tried to save, but had let down. Over the course of the Shadow Patriot's short journey, he had seen a lot of death, and had become more hardened. However, he was not jaded enough to insulate what he felt when he saw those young girls dying, with blood everywhere and screaming helplessly. He would never forget their faces.

Winters made his way to the kitchen where Amber sat at a table eating a sandwich. Winters poured himself a cup of coffee and joined her. She was wearing her dark gray windbreaker over a black tank top that had blood smeared on it. She had her long brown hair pulled back in a ponytail. She wore no makeup, not that it mattered thought Winters.

"Have you been up all night?" he asked.

She nodded.

"How is everyone?"

She paused a moment before answering. "We lost one last night."

Winters put his coffee down and stared at the table.

"She had a lot of internal bleeding and there wasn't anything we could do."

The news stung Winters but he didn't want to show it. "What was her name?"

"Savannah."

Savannah, he said to himself. "How are the rest?"

"A couple more are serious but if we can get them some proper care, they should be alright. Everyone else just needs the rest."

"That's good to hear."

She looked at Winters in earnest. "You know, despite what happened, we still did a good thing."

"I know. I just can't help wondering if there was something different we could have done."

She reached out and took his hand. "Don't think that way. It wasn't your fault, there's nothing more you could have done."

Winters couldn't help but feel some comfort in her words and her touch. He hadn't felt a women's touch in quite a while and felt a little guilty for enjoying it. In all his twenty-five years of marriage, he'd never paid attention to another women, and here he was holding hands with one who was much younger than he was.

Scar approached them and Winters leaned back, pulling away from her grip.

"Morning, Captain, Amber."

"Scar."

He grabbed some coffee and sat down. "Well, we took one on the chin yesterday, but all in all, we were pretty lucky it wasn't all of us dead in that sand pit."

Winters looked at Amber. "Yes, it definitely could have been worse."

She gave him a slight smile.

113

"What are we going to do next?" asked Scar.

"Make arrangements to get the girls to Canada."

"We should get going on that today. Some of them need better doctoring than we can give them."

"Yeah, I was thinking the same thing. Elliott and Murphy definitely need to go. Who should we send?"

"Why don't we all go?" asked Scar.

"There wouldn't be enough room for everyone, besides we need to keep looking for more of these rape houses."

Scar nodded in agreement.

"You should go," Winters said to Amber.

She shook her head. "No, I can be of use here. I wouldn't feel right about leaving."

Scar cocked his head. "You might want to think carefully about that, we're a bunch of old men that seem to get ourselves into a lot of trouble."

"All the more reason to have a wise woman around," she said smiling.

Scar let out a laugh. "Well, I'll give you that. We are lacking in that department."

Winters waited for Scar to finish. "Let's have Nate, Burns and a few of the others drive them."

"What about Sadie?" asked Scar.

"Yes, her too."

"She's really attached to you, so I'll leave that one to you," said Scar.

Winters liked having her around. She was a great kid, unafraid and wise for her age. She reminded him of his own daughter, Cara. That is before she became a teenager. He had many regrets of how he had dealt with her. He blamed himself for pushing her away. Their arguments left them barely speaking and ultimately losing contact when she took off with her boyfriend. He felt guilty that Cara was not there when her mom became ill and died. He could see the pain in his wife's eyes knowing that her daughter wasn't around when she needed her the most. It was Ellie's dying wish, that he find her and make amends. One way or another he would fulfill this last request.

By midmorning, the Shadow Patriots had everyone loaded up and were ready for the long drive to Canada. The convoy would travel through Minnesota and cross the same way they had reentered the US en-route to Detroit Lakes a few weeks ago. Fuel would be a problem, as always, and they would need to make at least one stop to scavenge more. For now, this was a minor inconvenience, as there were enough abandoned vehicles to siphon fuel. Winters had faith in Nate to get them to safety.

Winters walked over to Sadie to give her the news he had been dreading for so long. He asked her to come inside so they could have a little privacy. They sat down at a table, sitting next to each other.

Winters took a hold of her hands. "Sadie, you're going to need to go with them."

She immediately shook her head. "No…No, I want to stay here with you."

Winters wasn't too surprised by her reaction. "That's not a good idea, hon."

She pulled away. "I don't care, I'm not leaving. I'm not going to leave without my mom."

"We'll keep looking for her, I promise," said Winters not wanting to tell her that he suspected she was dead.

Tears filled her blue eyes. "Scar and Meeks promised me."

Winters cringed at this. He wasn't very good at dealing with a girl when she started to cry. It always made him turned into to jelly. He remembered how Cara had done it on many occasions.

Winters put his hand on her shoulder. "It's dangerous for you to stay here."

"But you'll keep me safe, I know you will," she said between sobs.

Winters fell for the flattery for a moment.

"And you pinkie promised me. You can't break a pinkie promise."

Winters leaned back. This wasn't going as planned. Then he thought about how he'd had never forced anyone to stay or go. He always thought that as Americans, they should be able to make up their own mind. He was now debating that philosophy. She was an American, but she was a child who wanted nothing more, than to find her mother. It was a desire that resonated with him. He wished his own daughter had the same commitment. Against his better judgment, he decided to let her stay.

Upon hearing the news, she sprang toward him burying her head into his chest promising not to be in the way and be a big help. She kept crying, not out of sadness, but an overwhelming sense of joy. Winters held her, praying he had made the right decision.

CHAPTER 29

WASHINGTON D.C.

Green hung up the phone and sat back in his chair thinking about what Bassett told him. He worried that Bassett might be caught helping the Shadow Patriots. He knew what he was getting into when he decided to help Cole Winters. He owed him for saving his life back in Detroit Lakes, Minnesota. He also owed his country, a country that had lost its way and was now in freefall. This, he couldn't let happen, and would do everything in his power to stop it.

He had decided to update his mother, and get her prepared to leave her home. It wasn't something he looked forward to doing. He got up from his desk and walked out of the office, telling his secretary he was leaving for the day. He got in his car and headed home.

On the drive, he contemplated what he was doing and whether it was the right way to accomplish his mission. He didn't see a problem, but hadn't seen things escalating so quickly. He thought that perhaps he'd be able to throw Reed off track by giving him false information. Winters getting spotted threw a monkey wrench into the plan. Now Bassett would be in a precarious position and put his own life in danger.

He thought about what would happen if the cops catch Bassett and the possible consequences to him and his mother. He'd need a disclaimer for Bassett actions. He'd have to claim he went rogue. It would kill his soul, but if it worked, he could keep working behind the scenes. That is, if Winters escaped.

Green walked into his mother's home and found her in the kitchen. He smelled another fine meal she prepared. How lucky he was to still have her with him. He only wished his father, an Army Colonel, was still with them. He wanted and needed his counsel. The man had finished his career in the intelligence field and would have been able to give him sound advice.

His mother turned around. "You're home early. Wasn't expecting you for a couple of more hours."

"Well, I couldn't stay away," he said, smiling.

She stopped what she was doing. "John, when are you going to tell me what's really happening?"

Green was taken aback for a moment, but then realized her question wasn't too surprising. She had always known when something was wrong. He sat down at the kitchen table and she joined him.

"Remember when I said I was going to help Winters anyway I could."

She nodded.

"Well, I sent Corporal Bassett out to Michigan to snoop around, and he called me a little bit ago."

She sat silently waiting for him to continue.

"The local cops have located them."

"When will they go to take them down?"

"In the morning."

"And what about Corporal Bassett?"

"He'll go and warn them."

"And you're worried he might get caught."

Green nodded.

She didn't say anything and stared off in the distance. Then she came back around focusing on him. "So, you want me to be prepared to go?"

Green could never get used to his mother's intuition. He grabbed her hand and nodded in silence. He felt bad for putting her in this position but knew she understood the gravity of the situation. As the wife of a career

Army man, she had sacrificed a lot of stability in her life and here he was, doing the same to her as his father had done.

"You'll need to have a bug out bag packed and be ready to go at a moment's notice. Make sure you've got plenty of money in it and anything else you might be able to barter with. Keep the gas tank full and stash enough food and water for at least three days in the trunk."

She nodded. "I've already done all that."

Green slanted his head back. "Oh?"

"My dear, if there was anything your father taught me, it was to always be prepared."

Green smiled. "Yes, I guess I should have known better. I'm glad to hear you're prepared, and you should consider this conversation to be your heads up."

"Everything will work out, John. Have more faith in your young corporal."

"Yes, it's just that I have a bad feeling."

CHAPTER 30

GROSSE POINTE MICHIGAN

Mordulfah sat in a large room enjoying the sight of his new harem of young girls. He would not have had such a large selection back home in his native Saudi Arabia. There, he was a merely a minor prince and would never have been afforded such a luxury. Here, in Detroit, he had everything he could ever want, and soon he'd be Master of the whole region.

Wali entered the room and interrupted his thoughts.

"Your excellency, you have a call."

He looked up at Wali, expecting to be informed who was calling.

"It is Captain Cox."

Wali handed him the phone.

"Captain Cox, to what do I owe the pleasure of your phone call?" asked Mordulfah, not meaning a word of what he said.

"Prince Mordulfah, I hope I'm not interrupting anything important."

"Nothing so important that I can't speak to you, Captain."

"I have good news for you."

Mordulfah didn't respond and waited for the man to get on with it.

Cox felt nervous talking to the prince. He didn't like having to deal with him, but Mordulfah's man, Wali, had suggested they would reward him, if he kept them informed. Cox knew it was a way for them to be one step ahead of Washington, a government he no longer trusted. In these times, it was every man for himself.

"I've found out where the Shadow Patriots are."

Mordulfah instantly changed his mind about the phone call. "Where are they?"

"They're in Indiana," he responded not wanting to give up all the info.

Mordulfah didn't respond.

"We're going to round them up in the morning."

"Excellent news, Captain. Have you informed your superiors yet?"

"No, not yet, and I won't till I have them either killed or captured."

"Captain Cox, I want you to do me a great favor."

"What would that be?"

"I want you to bring me their leader, you can kill everyone else if you like, but I want their leader brought to me."

"I might be able to do that," responded Cox wanting something out of this.

Mordulfah sensed what the man wanted. "You do this service for me and I shall reward you greatly."

Cox smiled. "It won't be a problem, sir."

Mordulfah pressed the end key and handed the phone to Wali. He was pleased with the call. He wanted this rebel leader's head for taking the lives of his men, some of which were close to him. Before taking his head though, he'd make him suffer until the man begged for death. He would make an example out of him. This is what happens when you defy the will of Prince Mordulfah.

Mordulfah decided he needed to celebrate. He scanned the room from his chair, surveying all the girls and pointed to one. "The little blond one over there in the corner, bring her to my bed chamber."

Wali nodded.

CHAPTER 31

SOUTH BEND INDIANA

Winters sat in the cafeteria, eating lunch with Scar and Meeks. A few hours earlier, they had seen their friends off to Canada. Since then, all three had been taking it easy and getting some much needed rest. After yesterday's rescue, they needed some downtime to regain their strength. Winters would not stop worrying until those trucks came back. He hoped that both Elliott and Murphy would be in them, but it wouldn't surprise him if both stayed behind until they recovered from their wounds. Murphy was in much worse shape than Elliott was, and the body heals slower when you're up in age. His arm still throbbed on occasion from the wound he had received at the train station.

With Nate, Elliott, Burns and Murphy gone, he felt strangely uneasy. He always hated splitting his force, even though he knew it was necessary. He needed something to do to keep his mind off it. Perhaps a little time playing cat's cradle with Sadie would do the trick. He was both happy and anxious at having her here. He felt like a sucker for giving in to her. Then again, he was old enough to be more like a grandfather to her and that's what grandparents do, they spoil them.

"So, what's up next, Captain," asked Meeks.

"We should go back to Michigan, see if we can spot any more of these party houses."

Scar nodded. "Yeah, except this time we should take more men."

"Here, here," quipped Meeks.

Winters repositioned his hat. "Yeah, that would be a good idea."

"Even with the ones that came in today," said Scar. We've only got like sixty total."

"More should filter in the next few days," said Meeks. "Our buddy, Bill Taylor, said more were coming in from Minnesota. Should be here either today or tomorrow."

"Definitely need the band back together," chuckled Scar.

"We'll leave in the morning then, which means we need to scrounge up more supplies and fuel today," said Winters.

"I can get Bill on that. Some of them are a little restless anyways," said Meeks.

"So, what about Sadie?" asked Scar.

Winters responded a little defensively. "What about her?"

"Couldn't get her to go, huh?"

"She turned the waterworks on."

Scar laughed. "Yeah, I know how that works."

"Plus, you and Meeks made her a promise, if you remember."

Scar turned to Meeks. "Oh yeah, we did, didn't we?"

"Well, she looked at us with her sad puppy dog eyes. How could we say no?" said Meeks.

"Exactly, now you know why I gave in."

"She does have a way with us old guys," said Scar. "I got to say, I kind of like having her around. Reminds me why were here."

Everyone nodded in agreement.

"Which is why it's nice to have Amber here as well," said Meeks.

"And, don't forget Reese," said Scar.

Winters raised a finger up. "Yeah, she surprised me a little, after what happened yesterday. I didn't think she'd want to stick around."

"She held her own, Captain," said Meeks. "She stood right there with me, shooting pretty well at those cops. Give her a few lessons and I think she'll be alright."

"Well, I'll leave that up to you then."

"No problem, it'll give me something to do today."

"Don't want to scrounge with the boys?" asked Winters.

"Come on, Captain, you know Scar and I aren't all that good at that."

Winters looked at both of them with a smirk on his face.

Scar held up his hands in mock defense.

Later in the day, Winters bumped into Amber who was outside getting some fresh air. He strolled up to her and asked if she would like some company. They walked along the quad enjoying the beautiful sunshiny day. Stopping at the Memorial Fountain, they leaned against it.

Winters stared across the quad. "I was a little surprised you wanted to stay."

"I think I can be of use here."

Winters turned to her. Her beauty was making him tongue-tied and he struggled with what to say next. "Well, you've been an asset already." He cringed at his words, which he thought made him sound like a bookkeeper.

"I really believe in what you're doing, Cole."

He was surprised to hear her call him by his first name.

"I've talked to some of the guys about what you did at the Patriot Centers. The things you've done, all the people you've saved is so amazing. I can't even describe it well enough and give it justice. You're the bravest man I've ever met and I'm honored to be here with you."

Winters was shocked by her words. He'd never thought of himself as brave. If anything, he was someone who allowed his Mr. Hyde to take over at times.

"You shouldn't believe everything you hear, Amber."

"You're just trying to be modest."

Winters shook his head. "No, no I'm not. If you only knew how scared I've been, you'd think otherwise."

"Which says even more about you. Even soldiers get scared, Cole. It's not how you feel when you're fighting, but it's what you accomplish while doing it. I'd be more worried if you weren't afraid. You don't give yourself enough credit."

Winters thought about it. "Perhaps your right. I've never been one to brag, but truly, I couldn't have done any of this without the guys. They're all really incredible and they deserve much of the credit, cause without them, we wouldn't be here today."

"They all speak highly of you, Cole."

Winters was a little embarrassed and needed to change the subject. "What about you? How are you doing?"

"Tired of course, and sad about losing my mom and nana, but I'm angry too. I'm just so pissed that there are people out there who think they can do whatever the hell they want. I just don't understand it. None of the girls can either. Doesn't anyone know what's going on out here?"

Winters shook his head. "Not from what I can tell. They've been very good about keeping everything under the radar. Even with the Patriot Centers, and everyone they killed. They'll just say they died in the war. Who's going to question it? It's not as if we have any way of getting the word out. There's no postal service and very limited telephone service. Not that it matters much, who are we going to call, the media?"

"Yeah, right, the media," she said in a sneering tone.

"At some point, word will leak out. I know one of the guys, told a ham-radio operator friend of his, so there's some chatter out there. The problem is there's so much gossip, misinformation and disinformation, it's difficult to make anyone believe it, let alone the masses. I mean who would believe the government is purposely killing its own citizens."

Amber shook her head in disgust. "It's a hard one to swallow."

"Exactly, and every region of the country has its own problems to deal with."

"What about your British and Canadian friends?"

"With all the international politics and diplomacy involved, there's only so much they can do. Officially, they're not in this fight. Unofficially, they've been keeping tabs on what is going on. Everything they've done for us is under the table. Thank God for it though, cause I don't know where we'd be right now without them. They have an intel network, which is second to none and have been monitoring all communications trying to piece it together. Once they hear about this Mordulfah character, they'll be all over that as well."

"It's nice to know someone knows what's going on here."

Winters looked at her seriously. "Yes it is, and it's nice to have Canada as a friendly retreat, but we're mostly on our own.

CHAPTER 32

DETROIT MICHIGAN

Bassett set the phone down in the cradle and looked at the two cops sitting at their desks. He leaned back to figure out his next move. He needed to get out of there fast and travel to South Bend to warn Winters of the ensuing raid. He remembered that when he had pulled into the station the fuel gage in his car read empty. He would have to ask where he could fill up. He got up and walked over to one of the officers.

"Hey, how's it going? I'm Josh Bassett," he said putting out his hand.

The officer tilted his head up and grabbed his hand. "I'm Don Hadley."

Bassett sat down across from the man who was younger than him and had a southern accent. His crew cut made him look like he had just come out of high school. "Don, I'm with Homeland Security and am here to help get those Shadow Patriots."

"Yes, we all know who you are. Looks as though you're gonna be a happy camper after today."

"Right, very exciting to be finally getting these sons-of-bitches."

"Yeah, I can't wait to see the look on that guy's face. You know, he killed some of our guys."

"Sorry to hear."

"I'll bet Mordulfah will be happy as well."

Bassett raised an eyebrow. "Who's Mordulfah?"

Hadley answered in a low voice. "He's the guy who runs the Muslims here. They say he's some kind of Saudi Prince. Scary guy if you ask me. I've only seen him once and that was enough. I prefer to stay away from him."

"What's he doing here?"

Hadley didn't answer.

"Come on, man. This guy sounds interesting."

Hadley hesitated for a moment. "He's the one who's been helping us."

"Helping?"

Hadley seemed nervous and looked around again.

"Yeah, you know, help us move the population down south. We don't have enough people to do it by ourselves, so we've been relying on him."

Bassett's curiosity was peaked with anger. It was bad enough the government was forcing people out of their homes and relocating them. The reason for this baffled him in the first place, but to be using Muslims to help was beyond his comprehension. He tried to control his voice. "Oh, like contract workers?"

"Well, yeah, I guess that's one way of putting it."

"It sounds kind of strange though, when you think about it."

Hadley shrugged his shoulders. "I'm surprised you don't know about this. I mean you're from Washington, I would have thought you'd know."

Bassett rolled his eyes. "You know how the government is, one hand doesn't know what the other is doing."

"I hear ya. I can't say I know everything that goes on here either. I'm kind of on the low end of the totem pole. I hear stories though."

Bassett tried to play it cool and chuckled. "Man, I'm right with you. Hell, they told me to come out here and see if everyone's doing their job, and damned if I even know what anyone's supposed to be doing."

Hadley laughed.

Bassett leaned forward toward the desk. "So, what kind of stories."

"I don't know if I should be telling you this, but I hear that when they go to a town to help everyone move, sometimes they separate some of the girls."

Bassett clenched his fist and cocked his head back.

"Exactly," said Hadley. "Young girls too, and pretty."

"Are you saying what I think you're saying?"

Hadley nodded. "Disgusting isn't it?"

"Yeah, I'd say so."

"I can't confirm any of this, but I hear some of the guys talking."

"Where do they take them?"

Hadley shook his head. "Hell if I know. If it's true, and I think it is, I don't want any part of it. I mean, come on, I've got sisters that age. Thank God, they're in Texas. Wish I was with them."

"Yes, thank God for that."

"I wouldn't be telling you this if I didn't think you could maybe do something about it."

"Sounds like the spoils of war have hit our shores. I've seen this before in the Middle East."

"You were in the Army?"

Bassett nodded.

"Why aren't you out West fighting?"

"Got assigned to Washington by my former Commander."

"Better than being out West. Those damn Chinese are going to win this war and then what? They going to keep marching east? Hard to believe this is happening to our country. I mean, this isn't supposed to happen to us."

"I hear ya brother. I've got a lot of friends fighting out there. I haven't heard from any of them in a long time. I'm sure a lot of them are dead."

"Must be tough not knowing?"

Bassett sat back in his chair taking in everything the kid was telling him. It was a lot of information to process. He knew something bigger than just moving the population was going on here. It was obvious this Mordulfah character was at the center of it. Why would a Saudi Prince be here in Detroit, and why was the government asking for his help. If he is a prince, then he must have some deep connections in the government. The man must be getting something big in return for his services.

"Where is this Mordulfah guy at?"

"He took over the Ford Mansion in Grosse Point, I mean, can you believe it?"

"What's so special about it?"

"It is or was, an historical site. The place is huge."

"Where's it at?"

"Right on the water of Lake St. Clair."

"How long has he been there?"

"Not long at all, couple of weeks, I think."

"So he's been here?"

"Oh yeah. Cox is all up this guy's ass."

"Oh?"

"Yeah, even lets him sit at his desk and use his office. The man comes in with an entourage. He practically kicked Cox out of his own office, kind of funny to see Cox act like a little squirrel."

Bassett smirked. "Nothing like seeing the boss get his, right?"

Hadley returned the gesture.

"Hey, listen I need to get some more fuel for my car. Where can I do that?"

"You're going to have to ask Captain Cox. With the limited supply we get, he controls all of it."

Bassett didn't like what he heard. Cox didn't like him and he knew he'd have to come up with a good excuse. He got up from the desk and thanked Hadley for the information. He wanted to call Major Green again, but thought it might raise suspicions, plus he wasn't sure if it was a secure line. He'd have to wait to inform him about Mordulfah.

CHAPTER 33

SOUTH BEND INDIANA

Winters wandered into the cafeteria where Sadie was talking to Reese. She swung her head around and waved at him. He returned the wave and sat down after getting some coffee. She bounded over and sat next to him.

"How are you, Cole."

"Well, I'm doing much better now that you're here."

She beamed at the comment.

"I see that you've made a new friend."

"Reese, she's awesome, she's so pretty."

"How's she doing?"

"She's sad. She misses her mom."

"Well, we all miss our families, now don't we?"

She nodded. "She told me all about yesterday."

"Did she now?"

"Yep." She paused for a moment. "Weren't you scared?"

He looked at her and nodded.

"But you killed all those bad guys."

Winters hated having this conversation with a girl so young. How sad it was that she had to be a witness to all of this and not allowed to simply be a kid. To make matters worse, she didn't know where her mom was or if she'd ever see her again.

"Are you going to go and find more bad guys?"

"Yes, we're going back tomorrow."

"I hope you don't find anymore girls."

Winters gave her a puzzled look.

"If you don't find anymore then there aren't anymore."

"Yes, I suppose you're right about that." He didn't want to tell her that, in all likelihood, there were many more.

"If anyone can find them, it's you."

"Well, I appreciate your confidence in me."

"You'll find my mom too, I just know it."

He smiled at her. "Yes, we'll find your mom and when we do, we'll get you both to Canada so you can be safe with her."

She smiled again.

Winters took a sip of his coffee. He wanted nothing more than to find this girl's mom, but he wasn't holding out much hope.

"Tell me more about Cara."

Winters liked the change of conversation. "What do you want to know?"

"What was she like when she was my age?"

"Well, let me see if I can remember that far back."

She gave him a bump on the arm. "It wasn't that long ago."

"Seems like a lifetime ago."

"What did she like to do?"

"She liked sports. She played soccer and was quite good at it."

"I like soccer too, haven't been able to play for a while though. My team came in first place last year."

"Well, there you go, nothing like winning the championship."

"I even scored a goal."

"Sounds like you were pretty good."

"I got lucky."

He nudged her. "Oh, don't be modest now."

She laughed.

Winters was enjoying their time together. "She liked to dance. She took dance lessons for a long time."

"Oh, I took dance lessons too. Was she a ballerina?"

"No, it was hip-hop jazz kind of stuff."

"That's what I did too. I loved it. I love the dance recitals, being on stage in front of everyone."

"Oh yes, dance recitals are fun. They're even more fun for the parents."

"You're not just saying that, are you?"

"Not at all. Nothing like seeing your kid doing something special."

Winters noticed Meeks walking in. He was carrying a Winchester Model 94 lever action rifle. He approached the two of them.

"Hey guys."

Sadie greeted him.

"Whatcha guys up to?"

"We're just chatting," answered Winters. "What about you?"

"I thought I'd take Reese out and give her some shooting lessons."

Sadie perked up. "Can I come?"

Meeks looked at Winters.

"I don't see why not," replied Winters.

"Oh goodie, I've been wanting to learn."

"Well, you're in the right place for that, little lady," said Meeks.

"You up for it, Captain?"

"No, you go ahead. I've got some things I need to do."

Sadie got up and followed Meeks over to Reese who was sitting and reading a book. Winters watched her nod and put the book down. The three of them walked outside. Winters stayed and refreshed his coffee. He let out a sigh as he sat back down.

He pulled out the map Scar and Meeks had taken off the dead Jiji. He unfolded it and tried to figure out where more sex houses might be located. He took out a pen and put an x on the town of Saline where they found the first place. He looked at Eau Claire and the route that the transport was taking Amber and the others. That route would have easily taken them to Saline and then maybe Detroit. He leaned back in his chair and looked up at the ceiling. All roads lead to Detroit. That is where we'll find our answers

CHAPTER 34

DETROIT MICHIGAN

Bassett walked to Cox's office and saw him sitting at his desk. He gently knocked on the door and asked for a moment of his time. Cox waved him in and put down his pen.

"Captain, I need to get some fuel and I hear you're the man I need to ask."

"What do you need fuel for?"

"I need to go out and do some more inspections."

"Inspections? For what? From what I understood, you're here to see to it that we're doing our jobs. Well, Mister Washington, as you can see, we're doing our jobs. As I told you earlier, we'll have those Shadow Patriots rounded up by morning and you can go back to Washington with a fine report."

Bassett was afraid he'd say something like this. "Still, I need to make sure everything else is up to snuff."

"Snuff, what the hell is that suppose to mean?"

"That everything is in order."

Cox's demeanor turned even nastier. "I don't have a whole lot of fuel just to give it out willy-nilly. I gave you a car that was full of fuel and you used it all up. That was your allotment."

Bassett interrupted. "I understand, but..."

Cox cut him off in mid-sentence. "You apparently don't understand. I've got a whole parade of vehicles that have to run across the state in the morning so I'm going to need every drop I can muster up."

"No, you don't understand. I work for some powerful people, people who won't be happy with the way you're neglecting to co-operate with me."

"Are you threatening me?"

"No, it's just that…"

Cox stood up, cutting him off again. "You listen to me you son-of-a-bitch, I don't give a damn who you work for. I have full authority here and what I say goes."

Bassett wanted to get away from the man. "Okay, well if you're dead against it, then I'll leave it at that."

"Leave it at that? Really? And just what are you going to do for the rest of the day?"

"Well, I don't have much of a choice, so I'll keep myself busy till morning."

"You going to run and tell your mommy now? You going to call Washington and cry to them?"

"No, that's not my style."

Bassett could see that Cox was not satisfied with his answer. The yelling had attracted some attention. He turned to see a couple of cops at the door and didn't like the looks they were giving him.

Cox waved them in. "I want this man arrested."

Bassett's mouth dropped. He turned as one of the cops put a hand on his shoulder. Bassett grabbed it and twisted until the man dropped to the floor. He then threw his knee into the man's face. Blood spurted on the floor as the man yelled out in agony.

The other cop pulled out his nightstick and whipped it across the back of Bassett's neck. He stumbled into Cox's desk. More blows fell across his back. He then dropped backwards onto the floor. More cops rushed in and fell on him. They slapped handcuffs on him and pulled him up on his feet. He staggered between the two cops who held him. The blows hurt but he managed to put the pain out of his mind.

"That's how we do things around here, Mister Washington," said Cox.

They took him downstairs, threw him into a cell and slammed the door shut. They then bounded back up the stairs and locked that door as well.

He sat down on the bench and wondered if that was his bed as well. There was no mattress, but at least he had a toilet. He rubbed the back of his neck trying to work out the pain, which was now spreading. He considered himself lucky to have received only one blow on the neck. It could have been much worse. The blows to his muscular back were nothing and he soon forgot about them.

Bassett was pissed at himself for letting the conversation escalate the way it had. Words were never his forte. "Guess I'll never be a politician," he snickered aloud. Knowing he didn't have any options, he began wondering what the hell he was going to do.

He moved to the sink and turned on the water. A brown liquid came flowing out. Bassett gave it a minute, and watched it turn clear. He cupped his hands and splashed some on his face. He did that a couple of times trying to clear his thoughts. After a few more, he sat back down. As he sat there, he went through the conversation with Cox. The way it escalated so quickly led him to think that Cox did indeed have to answer to others. He thought back on what Hadley had told him regarding this Mordulfah character. With what he had witnessed in those burned out towns, he figured Cox and Mordulfah had to be behind it. Because of the news about Winters, he had forgotten to tell Green about the burning of the towns. It was definitely more important for him to know about Winters, but, learning about Mordulfah, and now Cox, he'd wished he told Green more.

CHAPTER 35

SOUTH BEND INDIANA

Dusk had settled on the campus. Winters saw Reese and Sadie come walking back inside with smiles on their faces after Meeks had finished with their shooting lessons. He also noticed Sadie had a holster hanging from her waist. He let out a deep breath at the sight. She came running up, excited to tell him all about their afternoon.

"That was so much fun," she said.

"Was it now?"

"Oh, yes, it was."

"I'm glad to see you enjoyed yourself."

"Meeks gave me my own gun," she said as she pulled it out, releasing the magazine, pulling back the slide, and emptying the chamber like an expert.

"It's a Ruger 22 an...SR22," she turned to Meeks for help.

Meeks nodded. "That's right, an SR22."

Winters looked up at Meeks.

"Don't give me that look, Captain. She got the hang of it real quick. Besides, you never know when she might need it."

Winters shook his head. He turned to Sadie pretending to be happy about it.

"I know it's not a toy, and I promise to be responsible," she said as she put up a pinkie.

Winters took a moment before grabbing onto the gun. It was a black two tone with silver on top. "Just remember, you don't pull that thing out unless you intend to use it."

"I'll remember, I promise."

He handed the gun back to her and she ran off to show Amber.

Meeks sat down with a slight smile on his face. "Hey, I had my own gun when I was her age."

"Can she handle it well enough?"

"Yeah, she can. It's a good gun for her, got a nice small handle on it, and fires real easy. I even taught her how to strip it down. You should have seen how she took to it."

"Well, I now wish I had joined you."

"Hmm, kind of glad you didn't, something tells me she wouldn't have it now."

Winters gave him an Hmph and a slight smile.

"Reese did a fine job as well. I think the lessons helped take her mind off of things for a while."

"I am glad for that. I'm a little surprised how she and Amber are handling things after losing their loved ones."

Meeks nodded. "Yeah, it's a hard reality for all of us for sure, but for them, I don't know how they're doing it."

Winters thought about it. "Given everything that's been happening, I guess it's not too much of a surprise. You just have to accept the reality of the situation and move on as best you can. I can see why they wanted to stay, gives them a sense of purpose."

"Mix in a little revenge with that."

Winters let out a breath. He knew all about that. Revenge did have its appeal, one he himself had enjoyed. However, the joy, if you could call it that, didn't last long. It was a dangerous thing, especially if you let it consume you. He had let that happen in the beginning, allowing his Mr. Hyde to surface at times. Teetering on that line was something he still had to remind himself. He hoped these girls wouldn't follow the wrong path.

He would keep a close eye on them, and would warn them if he noticed any changes in their attitude.

"Where's Scar at?" Winters asked.

"Seen him outside with Bill Taylor. Looks like Bill and his boys had a good day scavenging."

"Let's go see."

The two of them got up and walked outside. They walked over to the parking lot where Scar was chatting with Taylor. The two men were standing by a pickup full of boxes and fuel cans. Winters could see they really did have a good day scavenging.

"Captain, I think we did alright today," said Taylor. Bill Taylor was the man who had led the Shadow Patriots to Mr. Peterson's farm when they were on the run from the National Police in the Chippewa National Forest. He was also a bit on the crotchety side. He was the one who had given Major Green sass when he had attacked their camp killing many members of the Shadow Patriots.

Winters looked in the back of the truck and saw the boxes were full of dry goods, cans of meat and vegetables. "Very impressive, Bill, as always."

"After hearing about them girls, well let's just say me and the boys were very motivated."

Winters nodded approvingly.

"We'll all be ready to go hunting for them pedophiles in the morning."

"As are we, Bill," said Winters, looking at Scar and the others standing around nodding their heads.

They stood there conversing as the sun was setting, Winters enjoyed the camaraderie of the men, and was glad so many of them were back. Some he knew, but there were also a lot of new faces he got to know over the next hour as they shared stories of what had happened in their own home towns. Even though the many names and places were different, the stories of hardship were the same.

After the group broke up, they moved the supplies inside and got something to eat. Following dinner, Winters had Taylor set up a guard rotation for the night.

CHAPTER 36

DETROIT MICHIGAN

Bassett opened his eyes and stared at the ceiling. He was surprised to see his watch read midnight. He got up and moved to the sink to splash water on his face. Cupping his hands together, he drank some of the water, and then sat down rubbing his neck. The pain from the blow had mostly subsided, but the beating had taken more out of him than he'd expected. He wondered if anyone had come downstairs to check on him. Being a light sleeper, he thought he would have heard if someone had. He then began to wonder if they'd simply forgotten about him.

He heard a lot of movement upstairs and figured they were getting ready to leave for South Bend. He began to get frustrated as the movement increased over the next hour. He saw the failure to warn Winters as his fault, and his anxiety started to get the best of him. Why hadn't he just stolen some fuel and taken off rather than confront Cox the way he had?

As time went by, he heard less and less movement overhead, but vehicles were starting up and leaving the parking lot. He read his watch: 0100. The cops should be there around 0500. It would be an early morning raid.

Just as he had resigned himself to failure he heard the door at the top of the stairs unlock. Then a man came stomping down the stairs. He stood up to see that it was Hadley, who was approaching the cell as if he was on a mission.

"What's going on?" asked Bassett.

"Where were you really going today?"

Bassett stared into the young man's eyes and thought about what to tell him. He sensed that Hadley was not sympathetic to his unit's mission, and decided to go for broke and tell him the truth.

"I was going to go and warn the Shadow Patriots."

"You know them?"

"Yes, I do, and they're good men, they've been fighting the actual bad guys."

"What about all that stuff they've been saying about them?"

"It's all lies."

"Then they'll stop the raping?"

"I have a feeling they've already been doing that."

Hadley seemed relieved at Bassett's answers. He grabbed a key from his pocket and unlocked the door.

Bassett was both surprised and grateful. He held out his hand. Hadley grabbed it, giving him a firm handshake. "If we hurry we can still warn them."

"We?"

"I'm going with you, I've got my own car out front, fueled up and ready to go."

Bassett gave him a nod and ran up the stairs. The two hustled outside and jumped into the car. Bassett took ahold of the wheel, shoved the gearshift in drive, and floored the pedal. The car tore out of the parking lot.

"That convoy will be taking I-94. We can take Route 12 and should be able to get ahead of them."

"How many men do they have?"

"A couple of hundred, counting this unit and another that will be coming in from Minnesota."

"Did you pack us some weapons?"

Hadley reached into the back and grabbed a Colt M4 Carbine. "I've got two of these and a couple of nines."

Bassett nodded approvingly. "Ammo?" he asked.

"Got plenty." He reached back again for a paper bag. "I thought you might be hungry, so I grabbed some sandwiches."

"You're the man," said Bassett taking a hold of the bag and reached in for a ham and cheese.

They drove in silence as Bassett devoured the contents of the bag. Hadley handed him a jug of water. Bassett looked up and silently thanked God for the intervention. He only hoped that they would get there in time. Not only would they have to beat the cops, but they would also have to locate where the Patriots were staying. It was a big campus and he had no idea of their location. He thought about what their initial moves should be upon their arrival. He would have to be careful and be on the lookout for any cops that might already be keeping an eye on the situation. His other concern was how to best approach the Shadow Patriots to let them know who he was. If no one recognized him, it might present a problem.

CHAPTER 37

ox sat in the passenger seat of the lead vehicle. He was in a good mood. Not only was he going to capture the Shadow Patriots, which would give him some notoriety in the force, but Mordulfah would also pay him. He fantasized on just how much it would be. Besides a nice financial reward, perhaps he'd let him have his pick of the harem. He had been enjoying his time at the party houses, but he knew that Mordulfah was keeping the best girls for himself.

He turned to his driver, Alan Millsap, a man with whom he had grown up, and gotten into trouble with most of his life. Neither of them liked sports in high school, and had the same contempt for the jocks. They had also shared the same hobby, drinking and getting stoned. Barely graduating, they had both relied on Cox's uncle to get them on the force. Without his help, they would have ended up working crap jobs. He loved being a cop because the badge allowed him to continue his loose morals while affording protection from scrutiny. It also enabled him to get even with those he thought had wronged him. The list was quite long, and continued to grow as time passed.

Once the war started, young men by the thousands signed up to fight, quite a few of them came from the National Police. This left gaps in the force, and Cox, with no desire to put himself in harm's way, was more than happy to stay behind and take advantage of the situation. With the help of his uncle, he was promoted to be the commander of a station. Cox couldn't be happier than right now. He was about to increase his stature in the force, which would allow him to continue getting away with most anything he wanted to do.

"How much further?" he asked Millsap.

"We're an hour away, should be there by five."

"Good, should be close enough to radio those guys from Minnesota. What was that guy's name again?"

"Which guy?" asked Millsap.

"The douche bag that's bringing in the other forces."

"Oh that guy. It's Stiver, Lieutenant Stiver. If I remember right his men call him Junior."

"Junior, really? Yeah, he's a douche bag all right. Junior, who the hell would let themselves be called Junior?"

"Probably a faggot."

Cox laughed in agreement then keyed up the radio. "Lieutenant Stiver, Stiver come in, over."

After a moment, the radio crackled. "Stiver here, over."

"Stiver this is Captain Cox, where are you at, over."

"Not too far out, maybe thirty minutes, over."

"Don't be going in there without us,"

"We won't, we'll wait for you guys up on I-90. How far out are you? Over."

"About an hour, over."

"We'll see ya in a bit then, over and out."

Cox put the mic back in the cradle. Those bastards had better wait for us he thought to himself. No one was going to steal his thunder, and if anyone did, he'd take them out personally.

Stiver turned to his friend, Durbin, who sat in the passenger seat. "Who the hell does that guy think he is?"

"Someone who wants all the glory, that's for sure," said Durbin.

"With what we went through, we deserve it. Hell, we chased these guys all the way up into Canada."

"Hell yeah, we did."

"Those bastards belong to us."

"Man, they killed our buddies."

"You thinking what I'm thinking?"

"You mean go in there and grab the glory ourselves?"

"That's what I'm saying," said Stiver slapping the steering wheel.

"What if some of them escape."

"That's why I brought Jake and Elwood with us."

Stiver was referring to their two canines. The dogs were the ones who found the trail of the Shadow Patriots in the Chippewa forest and tracked them until a downpour washed away the scent. They lost the scent, but got the cops close enough for them to give them an idea the direction the Patriots were headed. Stiver regretted not bringing the dogs with them when they raided the Peterson farm. Had he done so, they would never have escaped. When he received word from Cox, he knew he wasn't going to make that mistake twice.

CHAPTER 38

Bassett and Hadley had been racing across the state of Michigan on Route 12, which was a more direct route to South Bend. Parts of the road were in dire need of repairs, but because Michigan ran out of money, they stopped maintaining them. Even so, Bassett liked not having to worry about construction zones or traffic as he flew down the road at over a hundred miles per hour. His passenger was nervous at the speed, but he didn't care at the moment. He was glad he had jumped in the driver's seat of Hadley's car. He didn't want to be disappointed by having a slow driver and have to tell him to pull over and switch.

During the drive, Bassett learned that Hadley was twenty years old. This was only three years younger than he was, but lacking his combat experience, the kid seemed much younger. Hadley was a transplant from Waco, Texas, and had the accent and manners to prove it. Three months after he joined the force, they transferred him to Michigan. He didn't like having to move, but didn't have much choice in the matter. They told him the National Police needed a larger presence in Michigan. He hadn't made any friends and his colleagues made fun of his accent, and called him a hick. They had given him desk duty and made him do all the paper work.

Having played soccer in high school, he suffered a severe knee injury, which required a replacement. The surgery had left him with a slight limp. This injury kept him from joining the military, despite their desperate need for men. Still, wanting to be of service to his country, he decided to join the National Police. They overlooked his injury because they also needed considerable personnel.

By making the decision to help him escape, Bassett knew Hadley's parents raised him to do the right thing, no matter the personal consequences. He admired the kid's courage.

Basset turned onto Route 23. They passed through Granger, Indiana, and then turned onto 331. Once they reached the campus, they began zigzagging through the streets looking for any signs of life. It was a daunting task because of the enormity of the place. They concentrated on looking for vehicles in empty parking lots but it was dark, which forced them to go slowly. Bassett was getting nervous. He knew locating them would be a challenge. He just didn't realize how much of a challenge until now.

Hadley yelled out. "Look over there to the left. I see some lights."

"I see em," he said as he made a left and inched forward.

"Look at all the cars," said Hadley.

"This is it," said a relieved Bassett.

He stopped the car and they got out. Bassett did a quick scan of the area, but didn't notice anyone. He whispered to Hadley. "Come on."

They started to the double doors when they heard the cocking of a rifle. They both froze.

CHAPTER 39

SOUTH BEND INDIANA

Stiver got on the radio and announced to his men that they would be going in without the help of Michigan's finest. The radio came alive with excited yelps from the Stiver's men. He put the mic back in its cradle and glanced over at Durbin who nodded with a smile on his face. They took a turn onto Business 31 and headed south. He looked at his watch and saw that he had an easy thirty minutes, if not more, before Cox would arrive. Stiver had a hundred men with him, which he thought was more than enough for a surprise attack. Thankfully, Cox had revealed the Shadow Patriots' location. What an idiot he thought to himself. After being briefed on Cox's plan of attack, he realized that his unit was to be utilized for support only. They would not be included in the actual assault. Little did Cox know how much capturing these men meant to him. The rebels had eluded him twice, once in the Chippewa and then the Peterson farm. He needed this more than that idiot from Michigan did. No longer would they remember him as the guy who allowed the Shadow Patriots to escape when they were right in his grasp. The rebels had been lucky. This is what he had been telling anyone who confronted him about it. Well, their luck was about to run out.

"Where do I turn?" asked Stiver.

Durbin extended the map and pointed to their location. "We're right here."

"Damn if you ain't taking us the long way around." Stiver studied the map of the campus for a few more moments. "To hell with that, we'll just take the damn bike path. Besides, then we can use these buildings as cover."

"We should send some of the others to flank their position so we can surround them," said Durbin.

Stiver gave that some thought before getting on the radio to order one squad to go to the left and a second one right to get behind the rebels in order to cut off any escape.

Stiver slammed the gearshift into drive and proceeded down the narrow path. It took them past the main building with its glorious golden dome. He grinned to himself at his genius as he turned to the right and followed the path. When Stiver saw a set of trees, he stopped and grabbed the map. "It's just up ahead. Get out and see if you see any one."

Durbin took off with a flashlight and came back after a few moments.

"Well?" asked Stiver.

"Lights are on and I see movement."

Stiver got on the radio to find out if the others were in place. After receiving confirmation, he told them what he wanted everyone to do.

CHAPTER 40

Bassett turned to the sound of the rifle and yelled out. "We're here to help."

"Who are you?" said a man emerging from around the corner.

"I'm Bassett, and this here is Hadley," he answered as he tried to make out who held him at gunpoint.

"Bassett? As in Corporal Bassett?"

Bassett was relieved. "Yes, yes, I'm Major Green's man. Who are you?"

The man walked up to him. "Well, well, young Corporal Bassett, it's me, Bill Taylor."

"Oh, Mr. Taylor, I'm so glad it's you," he said, shaking the man's hand.

"What are you doing here?"

"To warn you guys. You have a whole army of cops coming here any minute. Where's Captain Winters?"

Taylor took a moment to digest what Bassett was saying. "He's upstairs, come on I'll take you."

The three of them rushed inside.

"Get up, get up everybody." Taylor looked like a madman as he ran into the dining hall yelling out what was happening. Everyone immediately got up and scrambled to warn the others. Bassett and Hadley followed Taylor as the older man bounded up the stairs like a gazelle. He ran down the hall still yelling the warning. They reached Winters' door and Taylor pounded on it as he swung the door open.

"Captain, Captain, get up! We've got trouble."

Winters sprang up. "What's going on?" he asked in the darkness.

"Corporal Bassett is here."

"Bassett?"

"Yes sir, it's me. Your location has been compromised. You've got a couple of hundred cops coming any minute."

"Damn it," said Winters, as he jumped out of bed. "Taylor, go get Scar and Meeks and get everyone down to the dining hall. Corporal, I can't thank you enough."

"You can thank this guy. This is Don Hadley. He's a cop, and believe me, if it hadn't been for him, we wouldn't be here."

Winters looked at the young man as Sadie came running into the room. "What's happening?" she squeezed between Bassett and Hadley to reach Winters.

Winters felt her arms latch around him. He told Bassett he'd meet them downstairs. Bassett gave her a glance and then an affirmative nod to Winters as he and Hadley exited the room.

Winters squatted down. "We need to leave this place, and we need to leave right now, so let's get your stuff."

Sadie ran into her room and grabbed her jacket, gun holster and her string. She threw on her shoes and rushed back into the hallway. She grabbed Winters hand and followed him down the stairs.

They entered the dining hall and saw the men scurrying around with their weapons and backpacks. There was hardly any chatter among the men as they got themselves ready. Winters sensed their nervousness. Scar and Meeks came in and approached Winters.

"Captain, they're already here, we could hear trucks moving around."

Winters let out an anxious breath, thinking about what to do next. "Okay, we need to tell everyone." He jumped up on a table. "Guys, the cops are just now getting here. So we need to move fast before they can set up a perimeter."

Scar spoke up and suggested a rallying point.

Winters nodded in agreement. "Lets say we rally in Paw Paw. The place is already burned down. They'd never think to go there. Good luck and Godspeed."

Winters hopped down. "Meeks, get Amber and Reese with us." He grabbed Sadie's hand tightly and headed toward the exit. As he got to the door, he bumped into Bassett and Hadley. "Corporal, once again, I can't thank you enough."

"Wish we could have gotten here sooner."

"Where you going to go?"

Bassett looked at Hadley. "For now, we're with you."

Winters patted his shoulder.

They scrambled out the door into the darkness and ran across the parking lot. As Winters reached his SUV, gunfire rang out.

CHAPTER 41

As soon as Winters heard the first shots, he pushed Sadie down to the ground. He looked up and saw muzzle flashes coming from the corner of a building across the street. A second later, the Shadow Patriots returned fire. Ten men at first, then more poured out the dining hall and joined them laying down a barrage, taking out windows and small tree branches. They kept firing for close to a minute giving cover for everyone to get to their vehicles.

Winters ran with Sadie in tow and hopped into the SUV from the passenger side. Scar and Meeks arrived with Amber and Reese. Winters climbed over the console into the driver's seat, started the truck and threw it in drive. He bounced over the parking lot curb, floored the pedal, and shot up the street.

Winters kept his lights off and followed the two cars ahead of him. His left leg started to shake a little as he thought about what would happen if the cops were to catch them. He didn't care about himself as much as he cared about the three girls. The cops had used Reese once before and Winters had a feeling she'd go down shooting rather than go back to that hell. He didn't have any idea what Amber would do. She was certainly athletic and angry enough to put up a good fight. He was most concerned about Sadie. Her age and good looks made her an ideal target for the unscrupulous.

As he approached the intersection, he saw the lead car taking fire. Lights from a transport came on and Winters saw the cops had the exit blocked. He hit the brakes and swerved to the right entering a parking lot. The dark campus forced him to turn on his lights. It left them exposed and easy to spot.

"Take that bike path," yelled Scar who sat beside him.

Winters yanked the steering wheel to the left, jumped another curb, and headed down the bike path. He drove through the overgrown grass and steered the SUV between two stone buildings, which led them to a drive. Up ahead was another parking lot and he decided to make a dash for it. He maneuvered across the drive and two more bike paths before reaching the parking lot.

Meeks looked behind them. "Got one on our tail." He rolled down the window and moved his rifle to take aim. He fired a couple of shots.

Winters noticed another cop car ahead, coming in fast, trying to cut him off. He turned to the right heading south through another parking lot. Bullets pelted their vehicle. Sadie screamed as the back window exploded in a shower of glass. Amber was in the back with her, and they both got on the floor as they were now taking heavy fire.

Scar and Meeks both returned fire. Meeks turned to Reese and ordered her to open fire. She rolled her window down and took out the Sig Sauer P232 .380 ACP that Meeks had instructed her on and pulled the trigger.

Gunfire continued to erupt from inside the SUV as Winters tried to out run the two cars. He could hardly hear himself yell through the deafening reports of the gunfire.

Winters felt the SUV jerk right and sink low to the ground. The back tire had taken a bullet. Steering became impossible as the air bled rapidly out of the big tire. The two pursuing cars were right behind them.

"Take us over there," ordered Scar. "We need some kind of cover."

Winters drove the crippled SUV between two buildings and drove around back. He came to a stop. Meeks and Scar hopped out, ran around the side, and opened fire on the two approaching vehicles.

Winters pulled the girls out and took cover behind the SUV. He looked across the way to the football stadium, which gave him a general idea of where they were. He could hear more vehicles and gunfire in the distance.

Winters looked at the girls. "You guys stay right here."

Sadie grabbed his jacket. "Where're you going?"

"I just need to tell Scar that we're going to go around this building."

"Don't leave me."

Amber looked at her and volunteered to be the messenger.

Winters agreed and waited for her to get out of sight before ushering Reese and Sadie away from the firefight. Sadie grabbed Winters and Reese's hands tightly as they hurried to the other side of the building. They ran across a bike path to a set of trees and he told them to lie down on the ground.

They could hear the gunfire continue from where they had abandoned the SUV. Winters could hear bullets hit the building and ricochet. A window shattered. The sound echoed between the tall structures. He grew worried not knowing how long he should wait before getting the girls out of there. Why hadn't Amber come back yet? He wished he had grabbed the radio, but remembered they had only one with them. There was no way he could contact Scar or Meeks. He wanted to join them but didn't dare leave Sadie and Reese.

The gunfire began to slow down and then stopped. A horrible thought crossed his mind. Did the cops overtake them? He grew anxious waiting. It was all he could do to not go check on them.

"Why did it stop?" whispered Sadie.

"Well, I'm sure they scared them off," he said lying.

"Shouldn't we go find them then?"

"We'll give it a few more minutes."

The wait was agonizing for Winters as he lay in the tall grass trying to comfort the two girls. He felt helpless not being able to help his friends. Off in the distance, he heard whispers and muffled footsteps in the tall grass. The swishing of the grass became louder as the whispering came closer to them.

Was it his friends? Winters didn't know. He tightened his grip around his Colt as he waited for the figures to appear. A few more moments went by and then he saw them. Three figures, cloaked in the darkness, appeared. Sadie saw them too and stood up. Her movement caught the attention of the three figures. Then a flashlight turned on. It was then that Winters remembered, none of them had flashlights.

CHAPTER 42

The three figures moved in, pointing their weapons at Sadie as she got up to greet who she thought were her friends. The cops yelled out not to move and ordered them to put down their weapons. One of the cops grabbed Sadie, who immediately tried to pull away. She bit the man's hand and slid out from his grip. Winters made a move to help her, but stopped when another cop took ahold of her again and put a gun to her head. Winters didn't have any choice but to drop his pistol. He motioned to Reese to do the same. The other two cops grabbed their guns and handcuffed Winters. The cop holding Sadie holstered his gun and dragged her because she had started to squirm away again. The cop wrestled her to the ground, breaking her gun loose, which bounced away in the darkness.

"Look here, little girl, don't be trying that again, or I'll give you a good smacking."

"You like hitting little girls," she responded.

"Got yourself a smart mouth I see."

"Don't push it, Sadie," said Winters.

As the cops marched them to their car, Winters' mind began to race on what happened to Scar, Meeks and Amber. Did they kill them or capture them as well. His optimism of seeing them sitting in the squad car disappeared when they got there and found nobody in the backseat. He could only pray they were able to get away.

He heard more gunfire of various calibers coming from the north end of the campus. This gave him hope his men were still fighting. Some surely died tonight but not everyone.

Winters got in the back seat between the two girls and couldn't help but feel bad about their capture. The girls darted their heads from side to side with scared looks in their eyes as they tried to comprehend what was going on around them.

The cops took them back to the dormitory the Shadow Patriots had been using. He saw a cop standing at the entrance with two dogs sitting on either side of him. The dogs barked at Winters as he emerged from the squad car.

"Well, who do we have here?" asked Stiver.

"Don't know yet," said the one who had grabbed Sadie.

Stiver sauntered up closely to Winters. "Well, I'll be damned. Look at this. We've got him. We got ourselves the man himself."

Winters didn't respond.

"Mr. Cole Winters. I've been waiting for a long time for this moment."

Winters glared at the baldheaded man in the black tactical uniform. In the darkness, his shiny head appeared to be floating in air.

"We got him?" asked another.

"Oh yes, yes indeed. Ever since you escaped into Canada, I've been hungry for your head."

Winters let out a laugh. "Canada huh? You must be the dumb ass that let us slip through your fingers. That was a hell of day for us. Thank you. We really couldn't have done it without you."

Stiver's face grew red with anger. He wound up and belted Winters in the stomach.

Winters doubled over in pain trying to catch his breath. Having received a blow like this in high school, he knew the pain would subside in a bit. He raised his head up at Stiver and grinned. "Bet our escape didn't sit too well in the office."

"No, it didn't, but look who gets the last laugh."

"We'll see," said Winters who didn't want to show any weakness in front of the two girls. He wanted to give them some hope.

"So, who else do we have here?" asked Stiver staring at Reese and Sadie.

"I heard him call her Sadie, and she's got a smart mouth on her, Lieutenant."

"Does she, now?" Stiver looked at Sadie. "You're a little young to be running with these murderers."

"They're not murderers," she retorted back.

"Oh, I can assure you they are."

"You're the ones, killing innocent people."

"I've done nothing of the sort."

Winters stood back up. "Yeah, but you stood by and watched it happen. Or have you forgotten about Brainerd?" asked Winters, referring to the town of Brainerd, Minnesota, where the Jiji's had come in and shot the place up.

Stiver glared at Winters. "I had my orders."

"Yes, everyone has their orders, not the best of excuses, but hey, if that's what lets you sleep at night. By the way, how do you sleep at night?"

Stiver ignored him and began to focus on Reese. "And who is this beautiful little thing?"

Reese didn't answer.

"What's you name, girl," he asked, as he moved up close to her.

She hesitated a moment, then spit in his face.

Stiver wiped off the spittle, wound up and slapped her across the face. "You bitch."

She recovered from the blow and glared at him with a smirk on her face.

Durbin walked up to them. "Junior. Got a bunch rounded up."

"Good, we need to get out of here before Cox shows up."

Just as he said that, the sound of trucks rumbling toward them drew their attention to the street. A couple of SUV's turned into the parking lot while the rest parked in the street.

"Damn it," said Stiver.

Cox and seven of his men got out of their vehicles and approached Stiver. "What the hell were you thinking? I ran into a couple of your men up the street, and they told me what happened."

"And you are?" asked Stiver, knowing who he was.

"I'm Captain Cox. I'm assuming you're Stiver."

"That would be me."

"This was my operation. I invited you solely as a courtesy because of your troubles in Minnesota. You were here as backup. Why did you attack?"

"Well, we saw a couple of their vehicles leave the area in a hurry. Figured they knew we were coming, so I attacked. And, it's a good thing I did, cause they were all leaving. So, you must have a leak in your organization."

This put Cox on the defensive. "I have no such leak."

"Well, they knew we were coming," said Stiver in a condescending tone.

"They probably had lookouts and saw your dumb assess."

"Nice try, buddy."

"Who the hell do you think you are, Junior? Do you know who I am?"

Stiver raised an eyebrow and he glared at Cox. No one but Stiver's friends called him by his nickname. "I don't give a rat's ass who you are. All I know is that we busted up these rebels and I've got the prisoners to prove it."

Cox's face grimaced. "You think you're going to take the credit for this?"

"We are the ones who took him."

Winters listened, amused by the pissing contest, and wondered who was going to win out. He saw the anger grow in Cox's face and thought the man was about to explode.

Cox turned his attention to Winters. His eyes got wider as he walked toward him. He pulled a picture from his jacket, held it up to Winters' face, and smiled.

Winters looked deep into the man's eyes and saw determination in them. He could tell the man wanted him badly and he knew, at that moment, he would be going with Cox. He saw him reach down for his sidearm and pull it out as he turned around.

"This man will be going with us," yelled Cox pointing his gun at Stiver.

All seven of Cox's men raised their weapons and pointed them at Stivers men, who responded in kind. More of Cox's men then raced across the parking lot with their weapons ready. This action alerted Stiver's men who rushed in to help him. Jake and Elwood came to life barking at Cox.

They began pulling hard against their leashes, which caused their handler considerable trouble keeping them under control.

"He's my prisoner," Stiver screamed.

"I'm afraid I can't let you take him," returned Cox.

"The hell you say. You just want to take the credit for what we did."

"No, actually now that I know we have Winters as a prisoner, you can take all the damned credit for all I care."

This puzzled Stiver. "I don't believe you."

"Listen to me Stiver, we can either have an old fashioned Mexican standoff or you can let me take this man to Mordulfah."

That name had an immediate effect on Stiver. "Mordulfah?" He signaled his dogs to quit barking.

"You heard me. Mordulfah wants this man."

Stiver lowered his weapon. "Why didn't you just say so to begin with?"

"I didn't think it would be necessary."

Winters was surprised the mere mention of Mordulfah's name would cause such a change. Stiver's men glanced at each other with looks of resignation. He was obviously someone who instilled fear in these cops.

Stiver ordered his men to lower their weapons. "What about the two girls and the other prisoners we have."

Cox looked at them. "He'll be wanting the girls as well, especially the little one."

Stiver jerked his head back by that comment and grimaced. He'd heard about Mordulfah's fetish for young girls. It was something that didn't set well with him.

"You can have the other prisoners. That should be enough to put you back in the good graces of your superiors."

Stiver glared at him for moment and ordered his men back. A couple of them slid over to their car where Winters was standing, got in and pulled out of the parking lot.

Stiver and the rest of his men backed up cautiously.

Cox turned to Winters and snickered at having won the battle. He walked up to the only three prisoners he was interested in, and then moved closer to Sadie and smiled at her. "You, my dear, are an added bonus."

CHAPTER 43

Bassett and Scar kept in the shadow of the trees near where the prisoner negotiations had taken place. They watched Cox's men escort Winters and the two girls to their vehicle. Once the car left, the two of them got up and sprinted back to the statue of Moses, where Hadley waited with Amber and a wounded Meeks.

The five of them stole across the overgrown grass and got in Hadley's car. Scar grabbed the radio he had gone back for, after the firefight they had with the cops. After killing the cops, the three of them had gone to look for Winters, but found only the gun, Meeks had given to Sadie lying in the grass next to the sidewalk. After getting no response when they called out to them, they assumed Winters and the girls ended up prisoners. Scar and Amber, and the wounded Meeks, then headed toward the dormitory they would no longer call home. They figured that's where the cops would have taken Winters.

On the way, they ran into Bassett and Hadley who were not able to get off the campus either. The two of them had decided to hide and wait for everyone to leave.

"Who's got them?" asked Meeks, as they reached Hadley's car.

"Captain Cox. He's the station commander in Detroit," answered Bassett.

Meeks winced in pain as he put pressure on his right leg, where a bullet had grazed him. "Where are they going to take them?"

"I heard Cox yell out Mordulfah," said Scar.

"I keep hearing this Mordulfah's name and I'm about sick of it," replied Meeks.

Bassett turned to Hadley. "You said you know where this guy is?"

"Yes, over in Grosse Pointe, on the lake," answered Hadley.

"You think you can find it?" asked Scar.

"Won't be hard to find, it's the Ford mansion."

"What about this Stiver guy? Where's he from?"

"He's from St. Paul," said Hadley.

"Must be the guy who chased us up into Canada," said Scar to Meeks. Meeks nodded.

"Will he take our guys there?" he asked Hadley.

"More than likely. St. Paul is his area headquarters. Kind of like Detroit is for us."

Bassett turned to Scar. "These are your guys, what do you want to do first?"

Scar thought about that for a moment. "Let's go get our other guys first, then we'll go pay this Mordulfah character a visit." He turned to Meeks. "You going to make it buddy?"

"I'll manage, though this one's worse than the one I got a month ago."

"Your cat-like-reflexes are definitely slowing down."

"Yeah, no kidding."

Scar pressed the radio button. "This is Scar, anyone out there?"

He waited a moment before trying again.

Just as he was about to try it again, the radio came to life. "Taylor here."

Hearing Bill's voice gave Scar some relief. "Bill, where are you at?"

"I'm up by the interstate."

"How many men do you got with you?"

"There's six of us."

"Keep your eyes peeled for a couple of different convoys. Winters is in one of them and the rest of our guys are in the other."

"Which one is which?"

"I don't know yet, see which direction they go, we're on our way up there."

"Got it."

Bassett backed the car up, drove through the quad, and headed toward the Interstate.

A few minutes later, Taylor came back on the radio. "We got 'em, one's headed east, and the other west."

Scar responded. "Follow the one headed west. We're almost to the interstate. We'll catch up to you."

"You got it. So, who's in the one we're following?"

"The bulk of our guys. They'll be headed to St. Paul."

Scar put the handheld radio down and turned to Bassett. "Any suggestions?"

"No, not really, there's not enough of us to stop a convoy of a hundred men, and we're running low on fuel."

"How much we got left?"

"We're under a quarter tank."

Scar sat silent thinking about the situation trying to come up with a game plan. They would have to act quickly before they ran out of gas. Question was how can three cars pull over such a large number of cops and get away without being killed in the process. Scar was at a loss for what to do. A moment later, he grabbed the radio. "Taylor."

"I'm here."

"Where are you?"

"Passing Mile Marker 65."

"Okay, we're right behind you. How's your fuel?"

"Full tank. Why how much do you have?"

"We're under a quarter."

"Who's we?"

"I'm with Bassett and Hadley. We're in their car, and they came from Detroit, so we're not going to be able to keep following these guys for very long."

"Well, if you're running low, then so are they."

Scar hadn't considered that and thought perhaps it might present a chance to get their men back. "We'll follow them till they pull over."

"Got it."

Scar hoped it would be soon, and not in the Chicago area. He, like most everyone else, didn't want to get anywhere near Chicago, because the city had been hit with several dirty bombs. These bombs had destroyed large areas of the city, killing tens of thousands of people. The radiation forced everyone else out of the area, though he had heard of people going back in, ransacking and looting. He knew that those people would, sooner than later, pay for their stupidity and become ill with radiation poisoning.

CHAPTER 44

Winters sat between Reese and Sadie and tried to comfort them as much as possible. The handcuffs dug into his wrist, and made it difficult to get comfortable. They had been traveling for about an hour and during that time, Cox, who sat up front, hadn't said a word, and Winters wanted some answers.

"So, tell me, Mr. Cox, how much longer?"

Cox turned his head. "It's Captain Cox for starters, and we'll get there when we get there."

"Well, Captain Cox, tell me about this Mordulfah fellow, seems Stiver started to shake at the sound of his name."

"For good reason I can assure you."

"Oh, some kind of a boogie man?"

"He's more than a boogie man. You'll see soon enough."

"Paying good money for me is he?"

Cox didn't answer.

"Well, I'll take that as a yes. So, I wonder what I'm worth? I'm assuming I'm worth more alive than dead?"

Again, Cox didn't answer.

Winters looked over at Sadie and gave her a reassuring wink. She smiled slightly, not knowing what else to do. Winters decided to go for broke and try to irritate Cox as much as he could.

"So, Captain Cox, have you always been a rapist or is this something new for you?"

Cox turned in his seat. His eyes were as big as saucers.

"Were you just never good with the ladies?"

Cox continued to stare Winters down.

"Or is that the only way you can get it up?"

Reese let out a small laugh.

Winters could see blood rushing into Cox's face. He didn't think it would be this easy to get his goat. He wondered if he had hit too close to home. Winters was enjoying this and decided to go on.

"So, just how young do you like them?"

Cox pulled out his sidearm and pointed it at Winters face. "Shut up or I'll shoot you right now."

"I'm just curious how this all works. I've never raped a girl before. So, like I said, I'm just curious is all. Is it the power trip that helps you get it up?"

"Shut the hell up."

"You're not going to shoot me, you wouldn't get your prize money."

Cox pointed the gun at Sadie. "Then I'll do her."

Sadie jerked back into her seat. Her eyes grew bluer as they widened.

"Well then, when I meet Mordulfah, I'll be sure to tell him what a sweet young thing he missed out on," said Winters with a determined look.

Cox turned to his driver. "Pull over."

The car came to a stop and Cox got out, opened the back door, and yanked Sadie out to the ground. She got up screaming at him, and he pushed her back to the ground. He then grabbed Winters' arm, pulled him out, and shoved him to the back of the vehicle. He then leaned back and swung a haymaker, hitting Winters in the face. The force of the punch made Winters fall to the ground. Cox grabbed his arm pulling him to his feet. Winters' head hurt like hell, but seeing his chance, he head butted Cox in the nose. The nose splattered, throwing blood in all directions. Cox screamed in agony as he fell back.

"You broke my nose. I'm gonna kill you," he said pulling his sidearm out.

WARREN RAY

Millsap came up and got in front of Winters. "Captain, don't do it. He's not worth what Mordulfah will do to you when he finds out."

Cox breathed heavily trying to calm himself down. He ordered his man to take Winters to another vehicle. Sadie cried out, wanting to go with him.

Moments later, Reese and Sadie were brought to the back of the transport Winters was in.

Winters was pleased to see them both back with him and asked how that happened.

"I just started screaming like the little girl that I am," Sadie said laughing.

"Then we started calling him a molester," added Reese.

Winters let out a laugh.

Reese shook her head. "Yeah, Chester the Molester. He didn't take to that too well."

Winters looked at them. "I'm surprised he didn't gag you."

"I think his nose hurts too much to think straight," said Reese.

Winters leaned back proud of his two girls, especially Reese. He really liked the way she handled herself with Stiver and now Cox. He knew she was a fireball when she had killed the guards back in Saline, and then after participating in a firefight, sticking around, rather than go to Canada. He hoped that she'd be able to handle herself when Cox turned her over to Mordulfah.

The convoy started moving again. Sitting in the back of the transport reminded Winters of his initial trip to the train station with his friends back in Iowa. It was there a strong wind had blown the hat off his head, and he jumped out to chase it down. That action had saved his life and set him on his current path. There would be no jumping out the back of this transport, as there were three cops guarding them.

164

CHAPTER 45

GARY INDIANA

Bassett continued to drive Hadley's car down Interstate 90, following Taylor and another car. They had eleven people in the three vehicles, one of which was the wounded Meeks. His wound wasn't too serious, just painful. Pain medication would be helpful, and some rest. That would have to come later.

They followed the convoy of thirty vehicles, which were of various sizes. Three were transports, which held their friends prisoners.

As they approached Gary, Indiana, Taylor got on the radio. "Looks like this is where they're looking to get more fuel."

Scar grabbed the radio. "Are they exiting?"

"Yeah, let's give it a minute and see where they're going?"

Taylor pulled over and Bassett came up behind him. Everyone got out and watched the National Police convoy heading to the Gary airport.

"They must have a stash of fuel at the airport," said Taylor.

"I don't see us taking them on here," said Scar.

"There's no real advantage we can take," agreed Bassett.

Scar thought about what to do, remembering how they had stopped Major Green's convoy with just seven men. This area was too open with no real place to hide. Plus, there were a lot more vehicles and cops to deal with. He decided they would follow them to St. Paul and make the rescue there. That would give them a chance to gather whatever they could find of their scattered forces. He didn't like the idea of traveling so far to rescue the men. It meant killing precious time, time that left Winters with Mordulfah.

"Taylor, I want you and your men to follow the convoy to St. Paul. You're from there, so it should be easy for you to figure out where they'll be held."

"What about you?" asked Taylor.

"As soon, as this convoy leaves, we're going to go down there and get us some fuel, then we'll go to Paw Paw, see who shows up, and meet up with you in St. Paul."

Taylor nodded and signaled his men to go.

"Can you find someone in St. Paul to patch Meeks up?"

The news surprised Taylor and he walked over to Meeks, who still sat in the back of the car. "How bad is it, Meeks?"

"Just winged me, but man, it hurts like hell."

Taylor turned to Scar. "Yeah, I know someone, in fact we'll just go there right now. No sense in following this convoy, we know where it's going."

With that decided, Scar and Bassett helped Meeks out of the car. They moved him to Taylor's and put him in the backseat. One of the guys got him some water, which Meeks eagerly drank.

Scar turned to Amber. "You should go with them."

She agreed, and crawled in the back with Meeks where she could help him get comfortable.

Bassett, Scar and Hadley watched as the two vehicles pulled away. They got back in Hadley's car and drove across the other lanes and up on an over pass, which would give them a bird's eye view. They all got out of the car, walked to the side of the bridge, and waited.

While they waited, Bassett gave Scar a heads up on Major Green and what he was in charge of in Washington. Scar had let out a laugh after hearing, but then thought that perhaps Green could be in trouble if word got out Bassett was here with them. Basset had the same concerns, but figured Green would more than likely have a ready excuse. They also realized that now Hadley was with them, they would need to be careful who saw them together. It still wasn't too late for Hadley to feign ignorance and insert himself back in with the cops.

An hour later, they heard the trucks in the distance and watched as all the vehicles headed back to the interstate. They gave them a few minutes before they got back into the car and drove to the Gary Airport. They drove to the building Stiver's trucks had just vacated.

"Don't see anyone around," said Scar.

"Must be a secret storage place for them," said Bassett.

Bassett pulled up to the oversized garage door and parked the car. Hadley stayed in the car while the other two got out and walked up to the door. Scar twisted the doorknob and found it unlocked, which surprised him. He thought perhaps that they forgot to lock up. Scar peeked into the darkness, but didn't see or hear anyone. He turned back, shook his shoulders, and walked in. He found the garage door and gave it a push. It started to slide open spilling sunlight into the building. Bassett came up and helped give it a final shove.

Inside the building sat four gas tanker trailers. Scar looked at Bassett with a big smile on his face. The Shadow Patriots were always in need of fuel, and this would be a great place for them to fill up at will. His smile disappeared when he heard the bolt slide back on a rifle. The sound was familiar to both of them. Scar now knew why the door was unlocked. Knowing someone had the drop on them, they both stopped dead in their tracks and raised their arms in surrender.

A voice spoke out and told them to drop their guns, which they both slowly did. The light from outside blinded them and they couldn't see how many they had to contend with. Scar put his hand up to his face to block the sun and saw just one man. He wondered if Hadley knew what was happening.

"Who are you?" asked the man.

"Who are we, who the hell are you?" answered Scar.

"I'm the one with the rifle, so again, I ask, who are you?"

"We're just a couple of guys wanting some fuel is all, saw some of your buddies getting some over here and didn't think you'd mind if we filled our car up."

"Just a couple of guys, huh?"

"You got it, man."

"You're not part of the Shadow Patriots? You know, like the ones in the back of those three transports you just happened to follow in here."

"Shadow who?"

"You think I'm stupid or something?"

Scar was about to reply when he saw Hadley sneaking up on the man and decided to wait another second before he answered. Hadley approached carrying his bad ass Colt M-4 Carbine. He shuffled in a little closer and his foot scraped a small rock that lay on the ground. The man turned to Hadley, and squeezed the trigger before he had it pointed. The loud crackle of the gun threw Hadley off for a second, before he fired a three shot burst. The deadly projectiles ripped through the man's chest, splattering blood into the air.

Bassett and Scar had both fallen to the floor as soon as the man had started to turn toward Hadley. They jumped up, grabbed their weapons and pointed them at the downed man. Scar could see it wasn't necessary. The man was dead. A pool of blood seeped out in an ever-widening pattern. Scar looked over at Hadley who couldn't take his eyes off the dead man.

Scar walked over to him. "Don, it's okay. He's dead."

Hadley didn't respond.

"Is this your first time, Don?"

Hadley jerked his head up and down.

Scar took the M4 from Hadley and escorted him to the entrance, where he proceeded to throw up. Scar stayed with him while Bassett checked out the rest of the building for any more guards. A few minutes later, he came back and gave Scar a nod. He then drove the car inside and filled it up.

Scar left Hadley and came inside. "First time's always the toughest."

"Especially when it's up close, wouldn't have liked mine that close."

"Me either."

Bassett looked down at the dead man. "What about him?"

Scar gave it some thought and decided to go follow the old way of cleaning up the mess. Scar wanted to be able to come back for more fuel in the future and didn't want to give the bad guys a heads up that their place had been compromised.

Bassett agreed and told Scar how it had fooled Major Green for the longest time. Scar chuckled, remembering how much work it had been, but took satisfaction in knowing how well it had worked.

CHAPTER 46

DETROIT MICHIGAN

Cox's nose was throbbing in pain by the time they made it back to Detroit late in the afternoon. He ordered the prisoners taken downstairs to the cells then went to the doctor to get his nose fixed.

After the doc treated him, he looked into a mirror and thought the bandage made him look like an idiot. Mordulfah had better pay a pretty penny for the pain he was enduring. He would wait until morning to call him, after he had rested up.

When he got back to the station, his men informed him that Bassett was gone. Cox told them to find out who released him. He wondered if Bassett had flown back to Washington. He'd have to make an inquiry in the morning and find out if there had been any flights to D.C. yesterday. If not, perhaps he was still snooping around here. Then a thought occurred to him, something that Stiver said about a leak. Could Bassett actually be helping the rebels? Why else would he not insist on coming with them? Bassett only asked once and then dropped the subject. Getting more fuel was the issue he kept pushing. If Bassett was involved then perhaps his boss, Major Green, was a traitor as well. Cox's thoughts turned to yet another reward for such a discovery. He smiled to himself satisfied with how things were working. He decided to pay his prisoners a visit.

Winters was, at least, glad to be in a cell next to Reese and Sadie, where he'd be able to keep an eye on them. Their journey was rough with the transport bouncing along the non-maintained road. Winters kept wondering about Scar and Meeks, and if they were still alive. He knew many of his men were now prisoners and some dead. What he didn't know, was if any of them would attempt a rescue. Winters wasn't sure if anyone even knew where they were.

Everything had happened so fast that his men hadn't had much time to do anything but save themselves. He was grateful Bassett had come to warn them. Had he not done so, then they'd all be either dead or taken prisoner. He wondered how Cox had found out where they were staying. Then it dawned on him. It must have been the last cop car from the sandpits. They must have followed them back to South Bend. Winters began to get angry for letting himself be followed, but he stopped second-guessing, when he remembered the crisis at the time. They had people with serious wounds in need of immediate medical attention.

He looked over at Reese and Sadie with sadness. He knew what was going to happen to him. They would kill him. He wouldn't have to experience what these two girls, would be going through. It was bad enough that Reese had already suffered such a terrible thing, but Sadie, she was just a child. He shivered at the thought.

At the top of the stairs, he heard the door open and heard footsteps coming down the steps. He hoped they would be bringing food. None of them had eaten all day.

He stood up as Captain Cox approached. He noticed the bandage on his nose. Winters held back a laugh because he wanted food from the man and didn't want to give him any more excuses to say no.

"Well, Mr. Winters, glad to see you locked up."

Winters didn't respond.

He turned to the girls. "And my two bonuses, how are you?"

Sadie looked up at him. "We're hungry."

"Yes, I'll bet you are. We might be able to rustle you up something in the morning," he said with a wicked smile on his face.

"I can't wait till morning, I've not eaten all day."

"Yes, well, we all have our problems now don't we."

Sadie got up and stared at Cox for a moment. "You can't get us something now?"

"I'm afraid the kitchen is closed."

Winters moved over closer to the door. "You know, just because you're pissed off at me, doesn't mean you should take it out on them."

"Don't know what you're talking about."

Sadie interrupted him. "I wonder how Mr. Mordulfah is going to feel when he finds out we were not given anything to eat."

The comment made Cox's smile disappear. He looked down at her. It seemed he didn't know how to respond.

Winters couldn't help but crack a smirk. She really did have a smart mouth on her, but more importantly, she knew how to use it. Cox was obviously afraid of Mordulfah and didn't want to take any chance on upsetting him. If Sadie were indeed a bonus, then she would be something Mordulfah would cherish and treat well, if only for his own deviant purposes.

Cox stormed back up the stairs and slammed the door. Winters didn't think it would be too long before they had their dinner. He moved over to Sadie's cell and put his hand in to give her a high five.

"Nice one, kiddo."

"Thanks, I just hope it works, cause I'm starving."

"Oh, I've no doubt that we'll get something, might not be much, but it'll be something."

Reese, who had been quiet, looked up at Winters. "Will they come rescue us?"

Winters didn't want to lie but he didn't want to give up hope either. "They'll come for us, don't worry. Believe me I've been in tighter spots than this."

"You have?" asked Reese.

"Tell her how you escaped into Canada," said Sadie excitedly.

For the next thirty minutes, Winters regaled Reese and Sadie with stories about what he and the Shadow Patriots had gone through. The more he told them, the better their morale became, which seemed to lift Winters' spirits as well. "Perhaps not all was lost," Winters thought. He finished up just as a cop came down stairs with a bag full of sandwiches.

CHAPTER 47

Bassett, Scar and Hadley arrived in Paw Paw, Michigan, and found nineteen men waiting. Scar was happy to see them, but had hoped more would have made it out. With his group, these nineteen, Taylor's six, and counting himself, Meeks, and Amber, it was only thirty. Scar figured there were roughly ten in each of the transports. Unless they weren't able to make it here, it would mean the cops killed thirty of their men. That was a devastating death toll.

Scar was considering what to do. He knew he needed to get word to Winters to let him know they were coming for him. He looked at Hadley. "Don, I wonder if you'd do us a big favor. We need to get word to Winters and you're the only one who can do that. Do you think you'd be able to go right now and do that?"

Hadley was still a little shaken up over his first kill, but he thought for a moment, and then nodded.

Scar went over to him and put his hand on his shoulder. "If you think it's too dangerous then don't do it. Don't be putting yourself at risk."

"No, it'll be alright. I can say I was sick today and couldn't make it in. Not that it'll matter much, they don't pay much attention to me anyways."

"What about Bassett missing?"

"I'll just act surprised and play stupid. They think I'm stupid anyways so it'll be okay."

"Whatever you do," said Bassett. "Don't offer any more info than you have to, otherwise, you'll look guilty."

Hadley nodded.

Scar and Bassett escorted Hadley to his car.

Bassett leaned on the door. "You did good here Don, you did real good."

Hadley smiled.

Scar crouched down. "If you see Winters, tell him we're coming for him. See what else you can find out."

Hadley gave them his home address so they'd know where to find him, and took off for Detroit.

"Think he'll be okay?" asked Scar.

"Kid's got courage, besides, he's a Texan."

"Okay then, let's get to St. Paul."

They all got in their vehicles and returned to Gary, Indiana to refuel before making the four hundred mile trip. They would be running on fumes by the time they got to their destination.

As the hours passed, Scar started to understand the stress Winters was under, constantly having to worry about the men. It was a burden, but one he could carry. Serving in the Marine Corps, he was taught how to think under pressure and how to survive. He was grateful for the skills that, albeit a bit rusty, never left you. He began formulating a game plan and was confident it was the right course.

First on his agenda was to get more men. He figured he would need at least twenty more shooters, depending on the intel Taylor would put together. He was sure Taylor would have the location where the cops were holding their men, and would be able to recruit some additional men.

St. Paul had one of the largest police forces in the Midwest and his thirty guys weren't going to be enough. So, he decided they would have to make a trip into Canada. He needed Nate and Burns back, hopefully Elliott too. He didn't hold out much hope for Murphy. Mr. Peterson should also have more men ready to return with them, plus the Canadians needed to know what was going on.

Scar had an idea what this Mordulfah character was going to do with Winters. He didn't think he'd kill him right away. However, he'd torture him and take his time doing it. So, time was still of the essence. He figured he had at least a day or two, maybe three. What bothered him the most were Sadie and Reese. How long would Mordulfah wait with them? Reese had already experienced a sex house once before and would have to go through that hell all over again. Sadie, on the other hand, had no idea of what could be in store. The question was how long she had before this monster would consume her soul with his perversions.

The more he thought about it, the more anxious he became. As soon as they hit St. Paul, he'd find Taylor, drop these guys off, and head for Canada. He'd find out if Meeks had gotten proper care and if not, he'd take him across the border too. He needed his right hand man in tiptop shape when they paid a visit to Mordulfah.

As dusk came, they rolled into St. Paul and found Taylor who informed him they had made it back ahead of the police.

Scar stood with Taylor and Bassett. "So those transports made it here then, right?"

"Oh yeah, pulled in a couple of hours ago," said Taylor.

"Where at?"

"Downtown at the county jail."

"Can you round up some more guys?"

"Shouldn't be a problem."

"Corporal, you up to going to Canada tonight?"

Bassett's left eyebrow lifted at the question. "What's on your mind?"

"Some of our guys are up there and we need them back."

"Yeah, why not."

"Taylor, you got a car fueled up for us?"

"Come on Scar, this is my town, of course I got what you need."

"If it's your town, then I'll rely on you for a rescue plan."

"They've got them locked up pretty tight, but I'll figure something out by the time you get back here."

Scar nodded his approval.

"You can take that beast over there, looks like hell but it'll get you there and it's good on gas."

"Where's Meeks at?"

"Inside doped up on painkillers. Why?"

"Think he needs to see a doctor?"

"No, not at all, my man did a bang up job on him."

Scar thanked Taylor. They walked over to the smaller car and Scar jumped in the passenger seat. "You don't mind do ya?"

"Gonna take a nap?" joked Bassett.

Scar let out a big laugh. "Oh, heck yeah, I am."

CHAPTER 48

Bassett drove the whole way to Canada while the older man took a much-needed nap. The day had taken a heavy toll on his body. From being woken up early in the morning, to escaping for their lives, chasing down the National Police and all the mileage he'd put on. He was more than happy to let the younger man drive. He had gotten to know Bassett, having made his acquaintance over the past two months through messages going back and forth between Winters and Major Green. The corporal was smart and confident and Scar felt safe having him at the wheel.

Their primary route was up Highway 59 but they would take a detour before reaching the border. This detour would take them through barren fields and right into Canada without anyone being able to spot them. After crossing, it was simply a matter of getting back onto 59, which would take them right into Winnipeg. Their destination was the James Armstrong Richardson International Airport. It was an expanded base, housing both British and Canadian air and ground forces.

Bassett reached the front gate. "We're here to see Colonel Brocket. He's not expecting us but it's urgent that we see him. I'm Bassett and this here is Scarborough. We're with the Shadow Patriots.

They waited a few minutes until the gate opened. "The Colonel will meet you in the mess hall. He's there now."

Scar looked at his watch. "Four in the morning, he must just be getting up."

They wound their way around the base and parked the car. Getting out of the car proved to be more of a challenge for Scar than it was for Bassett, who jumped right out. Scar's body had cramped up over the long drive and it took a moment to work out of the kinks. Bassett shot him a glance and started to laugh.

"You just wait buddy, someday you'll know how this feels," chided Scar.

"I hope not, I want to get old, but without the pains."

"Good luck on that."

The two of them entered the mess hall. The place was alive with men and women getting breakfast. Bassett felt comfortable in the setting, army mess halls were army mess halls, no matter the nationality. They found Colonel Brocket sitting with General Standish, the base commander.

"Colonel Brocket, it's good to see you, sir," said Scar as he extended his hand.

Both Brocket and Standish rose from their seats and shook hands. "It is indeed good to see you, Mr. Scarborough, but I have a feeling this isn't a social call," said Standish in his deep baritone voice.

"No, it's not. This here is Corporal Bassett, he works for Major Green, who is now in Washington."

"Yes, we're aware of that arrangement," said Brocket.

Scar gave him a slight smile. "Of course you are."

British intelligence had their spies all over Washington. It was essential for them to know what was going on with their American cousins. U.S. relations with Britain and Canada had deteriorated over the last decade to the point where, the U.S. didn't even request any assistance for the war with China. This was unheard of, and led them to believe something else was going on within the U.S. government. Having a long common border with America, it was imperative that Canada be in the loop. Many American refugees from the West Coast had fled to Canada. This was not a problem and they gladly took in all who came.

"Well, here's something you don't know. Captain Winters was captured yesterday morning."

The news startled Brocket and Standish.

Scar and Bassett gave them an account of yesterday's events. They sat entrenched by the story and nodded to each other.

"So, what are your plans?" asked Brocket.

"We mostly came here to get our guys back."

"Yes, I would imagine you'd want them now. They should be along here shortly. All but Mr. Murphy. He's in no shape to travel."

"Elliott?"

"He's still in some pain, but I've no doubt he'll be wanting to rejoin you."

"How are the girls we rescued?"

"Health wise, they're all going to be fine." Brocket paused for a moment. "Emotionally, well, that'll take longer to evaluate."

"We'll have to stop by and visit them before we go," said Scar.

Bassett nodded in agreement.

"Colonel, what can you tell us about this Mordulfah guy?"

"Yes, after Nate gave us the heads up, we've been looking into him. He's a Saudi Prince, but one of minor standing, which is probably why he's been trying to make a name for himself. He's into international banking and real estate and has holdings all over the world. The affairs of these businesses are where he's been making important connections, including Mr. Perozzi, the man behind the curtain in your government. We don't know the extent of their relationship, but it obviously concerns money and possibly real estate."

Scar didn't know what to say.

"As to why they're torching all those towns, it would seem it's a continuation of their mission to drive the current citizens out. Only they've moved their operations from Minnesota, to Michigan."

Scar thought about that. "Well, we did eliminate all their guys up in Minnesota, so it would make sense for them to start over in Michigan. There's a ready supply of Jijis around Detroit.

"Jijis?" asked Brocket.

Scar smiled. "It's our nickname for them. It's short for Jihadis."

Brocket nodded. "I like it."

"There's something else," said Standish. "Mordulfah also has some banking connections with the Chinese. We don't know with whom or how deep these connections are."

"It's just one big party in America," said Bassett.

"Yeah, including raping little girls," said Scar.

"Yes, that is a dreadful business," said Brocket.

"Mr. Scarborough, let us know whatever it is you need from us," said Standish.

"I could use a phone, I need to call Major Green," said Bassett.

"Come by my office, you can use mine," said Standish.

"I'll get your vehicles loaded, and will add a few more supplies than what Nate had requested," said Brocket.

Scar and Bassett took advantage of the buffet and devoured a pile of warm food. As they finished, a surprised Nate approached them with Burns following. They retold all that had happened. Afterwards Bassett left to call Major Green, while the other three found Elliott in his room. Emotions ran high during the conversations and no one wanted to waste another minute in Canada. They did find time to look in on the girls and Murphy, who was frustrated he couldn't join them. On the way out of the medical wing, they ran into Mr. Peterson, the man who had given them rest at his farm in Minnesota.

"Mr. Peterson," smiled Scar, giving the older man a bear hug.

"Scar, how the heck are you? What are you doing here?"

"Came to get these guys back, they've had enough R & R up here," said Scar, and then proceeded to tell him about Winters.

Shock and then anger came across Mr. Peterson's face. "I'm coming back with you."

"You sure about that?"

"As sure as I've ever been. I've been getting antsy up here anyway. I've never felt more alive than when I was with you guys."

"You mean on the run with us," said Nate.

"That was a helluva a day," said Mr. Peterson reminiscing about their escape from his farm to Canada.

"Luckiest day of my life," said Nate.

"Let's see if we can have another one of those," smiled Mr. Peterson.

CHAPTER 49

ALEXANDRIA VIRGINIA

Green got off the phone with Bassett, and started pacing the kitchen floor of his mother's home while trying to figure out what to do next. He could easily lie about Bassett's whereabouts and say he flew back to Washington. The first thing he wanted to do was find out more about Mordulfah, a person Green had never heard of before. He wondered if he should ask Reed directly. He had no doubt that Reed would lie to his face about his connections, but he could at least gage his response. Mordulfah must matter to the government, otherwise why would he be in Detroit and be able to get his hands on Winters. He wondered if Reed knew about it. He also wondered if Reed was aware of Cox going behind his back and not keeping him informed on their mission to capture Winters. Surely, it would be a better news story to have Winters brought to D.C. and put on trial. Of course, they would plaster his face all over the media, creating a spectacle for a show trial. The public would eat it up as well, since they believed Winters was a murderer of innocent women and children. The government almost needed Winters to be the boogieman, so they could keep blaming him for what they were doing. On the other hand, maybe the government wouldn't even bring him to trial. They might just pretend the man was still on the loose. Maybe this is why they allowed Mordulfah to retain him.

It was all speculation at this point. Until Green could get in to his office and start investigating who Mordulfah was and his connection to the government, he'd just have to be satisfied that Bassett and Scar were going after Winters.

After filling his mother in on the latest events, Green left for the office. He arrived earlier than usually and was there before his secretary. He had always liked being the first one in. This would give him peace and quiet before the start of what was shaping up to be a very hectic day.

He sat down at his desk, booted up the computer, and entered Mordulfah's name in the government's system. Nothing came up but a few newspaper articles on a couple of charities he was involved in, one of which was a children's hospital. "Like to be close to children, do ya?" he thought to himself.

He needed to inform Reed of what was happening, but before he did, he would call Cox and express interest in the capture. He would also have to convey his displeasure in the way Cox had treated Bassett.

He pulled up the number on his computer and clicked the auto dialer.

CHAPTER 50

DETROIT MICHIGAN

Captain Cox got up early, excited with anticipation as if it was Christmas morning. He couldn't wait to get on the phone to Mordulfah, and give him the good news. He looked in the mirror at his bandaged nose, which reminded him of his stupidity for letting Winters get close enough for the sucker punch. Had he not lost control of his temper, none of this would have happened.

He arrived at the station, and asked Millsap, the watchman for the night, for any updates.

"Everything was pretty quiet last night," said Millsap, who relished having tattoos inked on his body. He would have more if he could find someone capable of quality work, but with the war, finding a talented artist had become impossible.

"Any problem with the prisoners?"

"No. No problems at all, I checked on them regularly."

"And that's all you did, right?"

"I didn't touch them, if that's what you mean."

"You know that's exactly what I mean. Those girls are not for us. I'll kill anyone who goes near them."

"I know, I know," said Millsap. "I don't know what the big deal is with the older blonde. I heard some of the guys say she was at our Saline house."

"I don't care if she was the house mother. I don't want to upset the little one any more than she is right now. Last thing I need is for her to be hysterical when I bring her to Mordulfah. We'll let him decide what to do with the other one."

"Fine, whatever."

"What about Bassett? Did we find out who let him go?"

"No, not yet? I still need to ask Hadley."

"Hadley? Where is our little Texas hick?"

"He didn't come in yesterday?"

"He didn't? Well did it cross your little pea brain that he might have been the one to let Bassett go?"

Millsap shrugged his shoulders.

"Did you call the airport like I asked?"

"Yeah, they don't know anything about it."

Cox started toward his office. "There's something about Bassett that makes me think, he's not on our side."

Millsap whispered to himself. "Whatever, nose boy."

Cox sorted through some papers before going downstairs to check on his prisoners. He made a big production of descending the stairs to make a grand entrance as if he was going to be formally announced to an audience. He looked at each one of them. The older blonde had fire in her brown eyes as she stared Cox down, to the point where he was the first to turn away.

He stopped at Winters cell. "Well, how did our rebel killer sleep last night?"

Winters stretched himself out. "I haven't slept this good in quite sometime. How'd you sleep? Oh, I do hope you don't have sleep apnea. That mask would have been a bitch to wear."

Sadie let out a chuckle.

Cox caught himself before he lost his temper again. "So you slept well, on just a piece of plywood?"

"I usually sleep outside on the ground, so this was a real treat."

"Even knowing that we captured and killed some of your men?"

"Can't let that worry me," said Winters, who in fact worried all night.

"We even killed your friend Bassett," said Cox trying to trick Winters.

"I've got no man named Bassett, must be one of yours."

"No, I'm certain he's one of yours."

"Afraid not, sounds like you're not a very good administrator."

"I'm very good at my job."

"And yet you ask me if one of your guys belongs to me," said Winters in a condescending tone.

Cox didn't like his tone. "And yet I have you behind bars."

"For now you do."

"Oh, you think you're going to escape?"

"I said nothing of the sort, you're the one who brought it up."

"But you said for now."

"If I'm not mistaken, we're getting transferred out of here," said Winters who was enjoying his bantering with the weak minded Cox.

Cox's eye twitched. He then composed himself. "You'll be the guest of Prince Mordulfah." He turned to the two girls. "Don't worry, you two will be going with him."

Winters didn't respond.

Cox strutted back upstairs. Just as he made it to his office, the phone on his desk rang. He sat down and picked up the receiver.

"Captain Cox here."

"Captain Cox, this is Major Green with Homeland Security."

Cox straightened up. He hadn't expected this call and was caught off guard.

"What can I do you for, Major?"

"I understand you're to be congratulated."

Cox didn't know if Green knew about Winters. "Oh?"

"You've captured state enemy number one."

"Yes. Yes I did."

"That's great news. I'll be sure you're given an accommodation. This is a very big deal."

"Well thank you, Major. It was quite an undertaking, and sadly, I lost some men in the process. Regrettable for sure, but to be expected under such circumstances," he said not caring for his dead or regretting a thing.

"So, where are you holding him, and when can we have him?" asked Green, knowing this would throw the little bastard off.

Cox wasn't sure how to answer this. "We have him here, and until arrangements can be made, we'll keep him here."

"We'll arrange for it today. In fact, I'll have an escort fly in this afternoon."

Cox started to get nervous. "That won't be necessary. I need to check with my boss, he'll need to check with his, and so on up the line before I can let him go. You understand, I'm sure."

"I understand completely, I know all about bureaucracy and something tells me everyone is going to want a piece of this action."

"Yeah, you know how it goes."

"Regardless, I'll have our PR department put together a press release and have it ready to go. This is going to be big, Captain. You'll be famous before the day is out."

"I don't know if that's such a good idea," said Cox who was starting to worry that his prisoner might be too popular to hand over to Mordulfah.

"Don't you worry about anything," said Green, wanting to make Cox nervous. He needed to find out how much juice this guy had and how long it would take before someone contacted him. "You're a hero, and you know how the public loves heroes."

"Like I said, I need to talk to my boss and get everything squared away."

"Hey Captain, this has put me in such a good mood I'm even going to let that other thing go?"

"What other thing?"

"You know, that little stunt you pulled with my man, Bassett. He was pretty pissed off about it."

"Things got out of control is all. Didn't mean anything by it."

"I wouldn't worry too much about it. I'll calm him down as much as I can. His PTSD sometimes has a way of getting the best of him though."

"His PTSD?" asked Cox who was regretting picking up the phone.

"The man saw some crazy stuff when he was in Middle East. He told me about this one time when his squad came busting in on a harem of young girls. He said he just lost it and they killed everyone involved, including their family members." It was all Green could do to not laugh aloud. "Yeah, he said that really messed with his mind, still has nightmares about it."

Cox's hand started to shake. "That's uh, really too bad, like I said I didn't mean anything by it."

"Well, Captain, I'll be in touch later today, I've got a lot to do here to get ready for Cole Winters' delivery. Have a great day."

Cox hung up the phone. His mind was spinning a mile a minute. Not only did he not want to lose his prize possession but he also forgot to ask where Bassett was. If Millsap was correct, that no flights left last night, then Bassett might still be in Detroit.

He needed to stop this Major Green before he let the cat out of the bag and by telling the world about Winters. He picked up the phone, took a couple of deep breaths and dialed Mordulfah's number.

CHAPTER 51

ST. PAUL MINNESOTA

Scar was glad to be back in Minnesota and couldn't wait to talk to Bill Taylor. He was anxious to discuss the details of Taylor's plan to free the captured Patriots. He just hoped they had enough manpower to do the job. He felt more confident knowing he had Nate, Burns and Elliott back with him. Mr. Peterson had brought along six new men, two of whom were former military. People with military experience were hard to come by these days. They were either already fighting in the war, too old, or murdered by their own government, thanks to the Patriot Centers. Just thinking about the Patriot Centers made Scar's skin crawl. It was such a surreal thing that it didn't even seem conceivable. To take advantage of someone's patriotism was so underhanded and evil that he had difficulty understanding it. Did power and control mean so much that it justified the killing of innocent people to get what you want? It all boiled down to good versus evil.

Scar's thoughts turned to Colonel Brocket who had supplied them with more weapons and supplies, which was a blessing. He didn't know what they would be doing without their generosity and understanding. It re-instilled his faith in humanity to know there were still good people in the world who wanted to do the right thing.

They pulled into the outskirts of St. Paul and made their way to Taylor's place.

"Peterson, you old coot," greeted Taylor giving him a bear hug. "Couldn't keep away from all the fun, eh?"

"You know it, Bill. How the hell are you?" he asked his old friend.

"Ain't getting any younger and feeling it everyday, especially doing what we're doing."

"I hear ya. So you got a bead on the men."

Taylor looked at Mr. Peterson and the rest of them. "Told ya I'd come up with something before you came back."

"That's what I like to hear," said Scar.

"Found out that I've got a couple of old buddies of mine working at the jail, cleaning up after their messes. I'm meeting them later tonight. They say it's not going to be easy, but that it's doable."

"That's it?" asked Nate, annoyed with what he heard.

"Hey, I'm still working on it," said Taylor defensively.

"We ain't got a whole lot time to be waiting on a couple of garbage men to come and tell us it's doable. We need to storm the place, kill the bastards and get the hell out of here."

"Hey it's a fortified jail house."

Nate pointed his finger at Taylor. "I don't give a crap if it's Fort Knox, we can't wait till tonight to make plans. Time is running out. In case you've forgotten those pedophiles have Sadie and Reese."

Taylor didn't respond.

Scar looked at him. "Why don't you take us there and let us check it out."

"Fine, let's go," replied Taylor fuming. He glared at Nate as he walked away.

Scar, Bassett, Burns and Nate got in Taylor's car and headed downtown. They drove around the large building where their men were prisoners. It had no weak points, and looked impossible to storm.

"Like I said, the place is fortified real good," said Taylor.

"It'd take more than a frontal assault," said Bassett.

"Well, if you got a couple of guys inside, maybe they could sneak a few of us in," suggested Burns.

"Definitely give us an advantage, and if we do it late at night, won't be as many cops around," said Bassett.

Nate tried to contain himself as he listened to their ideas. He finally had enough and interjected. "Let's just go find the bastard in charge and make him an offer he can't refuse."

They all looked at each other and began to see the simplicity in his comment.

"Might not be a bad idea," said Scar. "Who's in charge?" he asked Taylor.

"Lieutenant Stiver."

"Where's the son-of-bitch live?" asked Nate

"Don't know but I can find out."

"Well, chop, chop, let's go," said Nate.

Scar put a hand on Nate's arm and gestured for him to settle down.

"Look, I'm just anxious, and don't like what might be happening to those girls."

"We're right with ya, Nate," said Scar. "Bill, get us out of here and let's find out about Stiver."

An hour later, Taylor came back with the information they needed. Stiver lived over in the same area they had found Commandant Boxer. An area that he normally wouldn't have been able to afford, but these days the tables were reversed. He who held government power dictated the rules, and Stiver, now a recipient of the times, obviously liked living in a well to do neighborhood.

Taylor drove them to Stiver's place and parked the car on the street. Bassett, who was the most clean-cut of the group walked up onto the wraparound porch and rang the bell.

A minute later a women came to the door.

"May I help you?" she asked through the screen door.

Bassett smiled. "Hi, is this where the Lieutenant lives?"

The woman hesitated, but Bassett kept smiling. "Yes it is."

"He isn't here, right?" he asked in a lowered voice.

"No, no he's not. What is this all about?"

"Well, the guys at the station want to give him a surprise party tonight for capturing the Shadow Patriots. We don't want to have it at the station so we got something set up at the Plaza. We want you to be there, of course, and I'm hoping you'll help us with our little subterfuge."

"Oh my, well, I don't know, I mean, I guess so, it sounds very exciting. Who did you say you were?"

"I'm Josh," he answered.

"I'm Carrie, his wife."

"Well, of course you are, I was told he had a pretty wife. I'm one of his newer guys and we're all just so excited by what he did."

She blushed at the compliment and instantly let her guard down. "Well, what do you want me to do?"

"Can I come in?"

She opened the screen door and they walked into the kitchen. "All we really need is for you to get him home early. Then some of us can also leave and set everything up. Plus, you should dress him in his best threads and get yourself all dolled up too."

Carrie was short and frumpy and had brown hair cut in a bob. She wore a headband, and it appeared she was trying to grow her hair longer. She was excited, and gushed about how much she loved parties, but hadn't been to one in such a long time. "I'll just tell him, I've got a special surprise at home, and he'll know what that means," she giggled. "Afterwards, I'll tell him I want to get dressed up and go out for dinner."

"Carrie you are a devilish little thing," said Bassett, pouring on the flattery to a rather pathetic little woman who was really a sucker for the attention.

She smiled and picked up the phone. "What time should he come home?"

"I'd say right away. It'll give us more time."

She nodded her head and dialed his number. "Hey honey, I was wondering if you could come home early." She looked up at Bassett and gave him a wink. "Well, it's just that I'm real lonely today and thought that, you know, we could spend some time together." She moved her head up and down. "How about right now, I'm just sitting in the bath tub, been reading some of my romance books. Okay, sweetie, I'll see you in just a bit."

She hung up the phone and jumped up and down. "This is so much fun. What time do you want him there?"

"Bring him over at six. That should be plenty of time."

"I'm so excited," she squealed.

"Well, you should be, he's a big hero. You just make sure you don't wear him out before he gets there."

She giggled and walked him to the door.

CHAPTER 52

DETROIT MICHIGAN

The conversation with Major Green had made Cox anxious and it was not helping that he couldn't get in touch with Mordulfah. He needed him to call off Major Green. It was lunchtime before Mordulfah called him back. Cox picked up the phone on the first ring.

"This is Captain Cox."

"Captain." said the voice on the other end.

"Your Excellency, I have good news for you."

There was silence on the line.

"I've got Winters locked up downstairs."

"This is good news, Captain. You're to be congratulated."

"Yes, well thank you," said Cox, thinking only about the payment.

"And, of course, you'll be rewarded greatly."

"Yes, well, thank you again, but the thing is, I have a problem."

"I'm listening."

"I received a phone call from Major Green. He's with Homeland Security and wants to transfer Winters to Washington today."

"What did you tell him?"

"I told him that I'd have to see what my boss wanted me to do."

"Which is the truth."

"He also said he was going to issue a press release today and assured me everyone would know who I was and what I did."

"This is not a problem. I'll take care of it."

"That's what I was hoping to hear. When do you want me to bring him to you?"

"I am not in town today, how about tomorrow?"

Cox thought about asking to bring him today but didn't want to leave and have to come back begging for his reward. "I can do that."

"How about first thing in the morning?"

"First thing it is.".

CHAPTER 53

G reen returned to his desk after investigating Mordulfah through a friend at the state department. His friend confirmed the stature of the Saudi prince. He had also discovered that not only was the prince in banking and real estate, he also had diplomatic credentials. This seemed rather odd. If he was a banker, what was he doing with diplomatic credentials?

Green sat pondering the situation when his assistant buzzed him. "Yes, Grace."

"Secretary Reed is here."

He had about given up on Reed ever calling him because of Cox.

He got up and greeted Reed. "Come in, sir. Have a seat."

Reed sat down and got right to the point. "Were you going to call me? Or were you just waiting on me to approve of this stunt?"

"Sir?"

"Let's not play games, Major."

Green was surprised by his attitude.

"You're not to worry about Winters, or his whereabouts, and you're not to make any press releases."

"Sir, I'm a little confused. I was under the impression it was my job to find him and bring him to Washington."

"Yes, well we found him, and you're not to worry about what we do with him. There are bigger things going on here, Major. Things that are way above your pay grade."

Green didn't like being talked down to this way. He put up with it from Colonel Nunn and now here he was taking it from this fat little man. "I'm sorry, sir but I wasn't made aware of these things."

"Well, now you are."

Green decided to go ahead and push him. "Does this have anything to do with Prince Mordulfah?"

Reed glared at Green. "What do you know of him?"

"Only that he's in Detroit, and has an interest in Winters."

"How do you know this?"

"Corporal Bassett told me. Captain Cox informed him."

"Where is Bassett now?"

"He flew in last night. He's taken a couple of days off, because of an altercation with Cox, who whacked him over the head and put him in jail."

Reed seemed surprised. "I wasn't aware that you even sent him there."

"I wanted him to check into the killings."

Reed didn't respond.

"So, what does Mordulfah want with Winters?"

Reed evaded the question. "Like I said, Major, these things are above your pay grade."

"So, if Winters is caught, what is it I'm suppose to be doing?" asked Green. He sensed Reed was losing his patience.

"Keep doing your job," said Reed, as he got up and started for the door. "I'm sure we don't have all the rebels rounded up yet, Major. We need them all."

Green stood up and watched Reed leave his office. He suspected Reed had just told him things he didn't want known and was now trying to cover himself. It was certainly an absolute priority for Reed to come here personally. He was glad he had brought up Mordulfah's name and had gotten to see the affect it had on him.

The conversation with Reed left Green with even more questions. There was an obvious connection between Mordulfah and Reed and by proxy, Perozzi. The testy manner in which Reed addressed him was confirmation of their association. So, this Saudi prince was important enough to keep him happy. The question wasn't necessarily why he was in Michigan, as there was definitely an overabundance of radical Muslims in the area. After losing the terrorist in Detroit Lakes, it seemed obvious they needed a closer supply of dedicated men. Though there was still a population of Muslim Somalis in Minneapolis, Green wondered if they were not to Mordulfah's liking. There was not as many as there had been before America's troubles began. Like a lot of the population, they too had pulled up roots and moved south. Regardless, all it would take to get the radicals riled up was a leader of substance, someone who could throw money around, and supply their Jihad with materiel and ordinance.

The bigger question was why was it so important to Perozzi and Reed, to hire someone to drive out the local population. What did they get out of this? That had been the central question for Green ever since he learned what they were up to. Yes, they wanted to control the country, but outsourcing to a bunch of Jihadist only created a bigger problem that they would have to deal with later. Once you struck a hornet's nest, it wasn't always easy to get away from it.

For now, Perozzi and Reed almost needed Winters to continue to be on the loose, in a manner of speaking. It made sense to blame Winters for the killings in Brainerd, Minnesota, and all the other places, because Reed wouldn't be able to keep a lid on the destruction there and in Michigan, much longer. At some point, word would get out and what could be better than to have a boogieman on a killing rampage. It was actually quite brilliant, and an easy thing to do with the media in your back pocket. Of course, not everyone will believe it, there would always be a few seeds of doubt.

Green knew he was dealing with some evil men. Men who would use any means at their disposal to get what they wanted, and they wouldn't hesitate a second to kill him. He would have to be more careful and watch his back. First thing he needed to do was find out exactly what he was up against and see if they had any weaknesses. He would have to gather all the information he could on Perozzi, Reed and Mordulfah. He knew he could rely on his friend, Sam, at the State Department.

CHAPTER 54

Reed met Perozzi at the Four Seasons for a late lunch. He plopped down in their usual booth and ordered a Scotch, neat. He waited for the waitress to get out of hearing range before he started in on Perozzi.

"We've got a problem."

"Oh, what might that be?"

"Well, besides that pig Mordulfah, which I'll get to in just a second, I think Green suspects something else is going on. He's not the dumb ass we thought he was. The little bastard played that other dumb ass, Captain Cox like a fiddle. How do I know Cox is a dumb ass? Cause I had to call him and he talked on and on about what happened."

"What happened?"

"Oh, Major Green called Cox and got him so worked up about being made out to be a hero in the press that he called Mordulfah, who in turn, ordered me to call Green off. Now, I don't know what Mordulfah promised Cox for Winters' head and I don't really give a crap, but I don't like being told what to do by that slimy pig of a pedophile, Mordulfah. I don't like being around him and I sure as hell don't like having to take his orders."

Perozzi chuckled at his friend as he watched him vent. The waitress arrived with their drinks. He picked his up and motioned for a toast. Their glasses met with a clink. Reed drank half of his in one swig.

"Here's to capturing Winters," said Perozzi.

"Yes, that is something to celebrate."

"Of course, no one is to know anything about that," said Perozzi taking another sip.

"Well, except Major Green. He's a little confused about that."

"How did he even find out?" asked Perozzi.

"He sent his man, Corporal Bassett, to Detroit to do some snooping around."

"Oh?"

"Yeah, well, I didn't know anything about it."

"It seems our Major is more capable than we suspected."

"Exactly. And Bassett just happened to be there when they got word on Winters' whereabouts."

"Well, we can't control coincidences."

"Cox told me another funny thing too. He said he locked Bassett up after getting into a scuffle with him over fuel for what Cox thought was to be used for another snooping trip. He told me when he got back with Winters, someone had let Bassett out, and coincidently the rebels knew they were coming. He thought it might have been Bassett and is now worried that he will be coming after him."

"Maybe he will."

"Green just told me that Bassett flew back to Washington."

"So then he won't."

"Yeah, but Cox insisted that no flights heading this way left Detroit."

Perozzi gave Reed a serious look before taking another sip of his Scotch. "You need to have Green followed. There are too many coincidences."

Reed nodded. "I was thinking the same thing. I'll use my regular man, he's quite good and won't pester me till he has something solid."

CHAPTER 55

ST PAUL MINNESOTA

Bassett sauntered down the walkway of the big Victorian home and took a left down the street. He burst out laughing when he got back to the car and began to explain what he had done.

Scar put his big hand on his shoulder. "I don't think I could have come up with anything better. You've done me proud."

"He'll be here in no time, something tells me he doesn't get an offer like that every day."

"How do you want to handle this?" Burns asked Scar.

"Besides putting a gun to his head," smirked Nate.

"I've been thinking about that," said Scar, who took the next few minutes to lay out his plan. When he finished they all sat back, impressed with what he'd come up with. It had an element of risk, like all operations of this nature, but nothing that couldn't be overcome by a little luck.

"The concept sounds solid to me," said Bassett.

"If we can pull this off right, Stiver won't even come after us," said Burns.

"That's the beauty of it," said Scar.

"Taylor, do you think you can get everything we need in a couple of hours?"

"Won't be a problem."

"Okay then, as soon as Stiver pulls in, you and Burns go and start scrounging the stuff up."

They didn't have to wait long for the Lieutenant to pull into his driveway. They watched from up the street as Stiver got out his car and hustle his out of shape body onto the porch. He was wearing his black assault uniform so his shiny baldhead was the only thing they could see as he disappeared into the shade of the porch.

"Should we give him a few minutes with his wife?" asked Bassett.

"Screw his wife, no pun intended, but let's go," said Nate.

Scar held his hand out. "Give him a few minutes. The more compromising position we catch him in, the easier he'll be to control. "

They got out of the car and watched as Taylor and Burns left the old Victorian neighborhood. The three of them traipsed up the drive and onto the porch, where they found the door unlocked. They pulled out their weapons and walked inside. They heard laughter coming from upstairs. "That didn't take long," said Scar. He led the way up the oversized wooden staircase and down the red-carpeted hall to the master bedroom. The voices came from the adjoining bathroom. Scar was the first to enter and see the two lovebirds splashing around in a big antique claw-foot bathtub. When he walked in with his gun pointed at them, it took a second before Stiver came to his senses.

He yelled out as his wife screamed and covered herself. "Who the hell are you, and what are you doing here?"

"Don't even get up, you're not something I want to see."

Bassett and Nate walked in the room.

"That man," screamed Carrie. "I know him."

Stiver looked at his wife. "How do you know him?"

"He was just here. He works for you."

"He what?" asked Stiver, as he turned back to Scar. "What are you doing in my house?"

"Is it your house, Stiver? Or are you squatting?"

Stiver didn't respond.

Scar grabbed a couple of towels, threw them over to Stiver, and motioned him to get up. Stiver covered himself as he got out of the tub. His wife followed suit. Scar led them into the bedroom. Nate checked Stiver's clothes for any weapons and then gave them to him to put on. Carrie put on a bathrobe.

"Now, do you mind telling me who you are, and what you want?"

"We want our men back, you know, the ones you took yesterday."

Stiver finally recognized the gravity of the situation. He had prisoners that would have put him back in the good graces of the National Police, but he was about to lose them. He would continue to be the laughing stock of the force.

"I can't let you have them," he tried to say bravely.

Nate lost his patience and wasn't in the mood to mess around. He walked up to Carrie, raised his gun to her head and glared at Stiver with his dark eyes. "I don't think you understand just how pissed off I am right now."

Carrie let out a sob. She looked at her husband who started to move toward her. Scar grabbed him. "I wouldn't be trying any heroics, Lieutenant. You see my friend here, is a cold hearted son-of-a-bitch and he won't think twice about pulling that trigger."

Stiver stopped moving. "Don't cry honey, I'll get us out of this."

"That's better," said Scar. "Now, you're going to help us get our men out of jail."

Stiver looked at Scar as if he couldn't believe what he was hearing. "You think you can just walk in there and expect me to turn the key."

"That's exactly what you're going to do, and if you behave yourself, we'll let you come back here tonight and finish your rendezvous with your wife. We'll even fix it so they still think you're the hero."

Stiver gave Scar a puzzled look.

A couple of hours later, Taylor and Burns returned. They carried a bag of clothes into Stiver's house and dropped them on the floor.

"Everything else ready?" Scar asked Burns.

Burns nodded. "Everyone's in place and ready to go."

The plan was a simple one. They would pose as government officials from Washington. Taylor had gathered a couple of business suits, and some fake ID's they hoped wouldn't be scrutinized too closely since they would be accompanied by Stiver. The rest would be in National Police uniforms that Taylor had gotten from a friend who was in the laundry business.

Basset would play himself, an agent of Homeland Security and would use, if needed, the documents Green had issued him. Everything depended on Stiver's demeanor, and he had a great motivator. They told him Nate would be guarding his wife. They made sure Stiver believed this, but in reality, they would bind and gag Carrie, and leave her by herself.

Scar had Stiver drive his own car downtown. He noticed beads of sweat running down Stivers temples. He didn't want him freaking out so he reached over and turn the air conditioner. He still looked nervous so Scar decided to give him a pep talk.

"Listen Stiver, you play nice with us and you'll get home safe and sound. We have no desire to hurt your wife, but know this for sure, if we don't make it out of there, Nate will kill her."

Stiver nodded. "I know. Believe me, I know."

"Just be cool."

"I'm going to look like a jack ass."

"No you won't. You're not looking at the big picture here. You're handing over the prisoners as directed by Homeland Security. No one will know you were forced into it." Scar didn't really care what happened to Stiver, but he could see saving face was important to him, so he played that card strongly.

"Yeah, but what happens when they do come for them?"

"You lie. Just say you executed them. No one is going to give a crap anyways. Winters is the one everyone wants."

As they arrived downtown, their transports pulled in and parked near the rear door of the jail where they would bring the prisoners out. The four of them got out of Stiver's SUV and headed to the entrance.

Stiver approached Corporal Gottlieb, the night desk clerk. "How's it going?"

"Hey Lieutenant, not too bad considering all the excitement from last night," said Gottlieb who looked like he was barely out of his teens and spoke with a heavy Minnesota accent. "Who have you got there?"

"These men are from Washington. Homeland Security and all."

"Oh really, from Washington, huh? You guys here because of our prisoners?"

"That's right son," said Scar, who at six four towered over the smaller corporal who still sat behind the desk.

"Gottlieb, these men are here to transfer the prisoners back to Washington."

"They are? I wasn't notified of any such thing."

"Maybe someone forgot?" said Stiver.

"I don't think someone would forget something like that," said Gottlieb.

Scar looked down on him. "You're absolutely right, Corporal. No one would forget something like that. The fact of the matter is, this is a classified mission. No one is supposed to know anything about it. Too much publicity surrounds these murdering bastards and there are too many loose lips. This is why we told no one. Just between you and me, it's also the reason why I had to leave my wife and kids to come to this godforsaken part of the country, and be sneaking around at night when I should be at home with my family."

Gottlieb didn't know what to say as Scar continued to stare at him. So, he got up and grabbed a set of keys. He got on the phone and ordered some help to release the prisoners. They all followed Gottlieb to the cells and watched as the cops pulled the men out and placed handcuff chains around their waist and shackles on their feet.

The cops escorted their prisoners down the hallway. The prisoners recognized what was happening, but thankfully didn't give any indication.

After filling out some paperwork releasing the thirty-four prisoners, Stiver walked Scar to the back door and down the set of cement stairs. The transports had already pulled out and Scar put his hand out to Stiver. "Nice work Stiver. That went better than expected."

"What about my wife?"

"She'll be at that closed down restaurant on Exit 207B off of 94. Give it ten minutes."

"She'll be alright?"

"Of course Stiver, unlike you guys, we don't like killing innocent people."

He didn't respond.

"Just remember, if you play it right and not spill the beans, then you'll still look like the hero."

Scar climbed into a waiting car.

Bassett looked over at him. "What did you tell him?"

"Told him he could find his wife west of here."

Bassett laughed. "That'll make him a little anxious."

"Yeah, but he'll be relieved when he sees her at home."

CHAPTER 56

WASHINGTON D.C.

Green left his office for the day, and planned to meet his friend, Sam, who worked at the State Department. Sam had the security clearance Green needed to access databases containing the information vital to his investigation. As he headed to the parking lot, he saw someone who seemed strangely out of place. The man had a massive receding hairline and wasn't dressed in business attire. This struck Green as odd. Everyone who worked in the building looked like a white-collar bureaucrat. The man was dressed in wrinkled khakis and wore a cheap pull over bright red polo shirt.

When Green made eye contact with the stranger, he turned his head and walked off in the opposite direction.

Green shrugged, continued to his car and drove to a shabbier part of town. He entered a restaurant and sat down at a booth in the bar area where Sam waited.

Sam was about the same age as Green, and kept himself in good shape. However, the stress from his government position had started to show on his face. Wrinkles were forming around his mouth and eyes, and premature gray hair crept into his sideburns. He was a career State Department employee and traveled extensively around the world to various embassies. They had met playing in a volleyball league at a local bar years ago, formed a friendship, and got together whenever they were both in town.

A waitress approached and took their orders. Green waited for her to leave and asked his friend if he had brought the information, he'd asked for.

"Got it right here, John. What's this all about?" asked Sam as he handed Green a high capacity flash drive.

Green stuck it in his laptop and skimmed over the data. He was pleased Sam had been able to dig up so much information. He would have plenty to do at home this evening.

"I'm not sure Sam, but something is going on, something that's big though."

"I was a little surprised when you asked for info on Perozzi and if he has any ties to Mordulfah. I'm a bit reluctant to give you this stuff."

"Oh?"

"You don't know do you?"

Green gave him a quizzical look.

"About Perozzi?"

"I don't even know what he looks like, all I know is he's got money. Lots of it."

"There's a picture of him in there. He's a billionaire many times over and he's a personal friend of the President."

"Close friends?" asked Green as he thumbed through the data to the photograph.

"Very close. That's him right there."

Green studied the picture. "I've seen this guy before."

"Where?"

"He was in Reed's office when I first met with him. I wasn't introduced, and he just sat in the corner not saying a word."

"That's weird."

"Yeah, it was, but I didn't really think too much about it, until now."

"Perozzi has his fingerprints on everything in the government. Word has it he runs the President. Plus, he definitely has business ties to Mordulfah, which include banking and real estate. I got you a small sample of their dealings."

"I figured he had connections to them, but it's good to see it confirmed," said Green, leaning back as the waitress came over with their beers. He picked up his glass and took a sip. "Now I know why they have an office in the Lafayette building. Place is crawling with bankers."

"Also, both Mordulfah and Perozzi have business dealings in China."

"I suppose if you're into international banking, you're going to have those types of contacts."

"Maybe, but we're at war with China, which makes it bit strange to have a Saudi Prince with diplomatic credentials in America who also has ties to the Chinese."

"What about Lawrence Reed, what's the deal on him?"

"Big time insider, he's got a lot of juice. Some say he orchestrated the resignation of the former president and set up the former VP in that bribery scandal."

Green looked surprised.

"It makes sense too, because he's a personal friend of the new President as well."

Green shook his head and let out an audible sigh.

"So, what are you going to do?"

"I don't know yet, do some more snooping around."

"John, you're not a spy. You're playing a dangerous game. These are the kind of people who don't bat an eye at killing anyone who dares to ask too many questions."

Green thought about that. Sam was right, he wasn't a spy and he was looking into things that could get him killed. "I know, I'll be careful."

"You damn well better be, because if they catch wind I gave you this info, then I'm as good as dead as well," said Sam in a nervous tone.

"I will, Sam."

After finishing their drinks, they left the restaurant and walked outside.

"Which way you headed?" asked Green.

"I'm parked over in the garage."

They shook hands, and Green assured his nervous friend he'd be careful.

Green started walking in the opposite direction deep in thought. Just as he reached his car, he remembered he had another question he wanted to ask Sam. He didn't want to wait until morning and decided to catch up to him. He turned around and hustled to the parking garage. As he entered the garage, he saw the stranger from earlier. He recognized the cheap red shirt right away.

Seeing this guy twice within a span of an hour couldn't be a coincidence, so he figured Reed was having him watched. The stranger must have wanted to find out who Sam was and decided to follow him.

Green kept ducking behind cars as he followed the stranger up a level. He heard a car start and thought it might be Sam. He waited and watched as the car came down the ramp, and recognized Sam as it went past. He knelt down to the cement, peeked under a car, and watched him drive out of the garage. He also noticed the stranger standing on the ramp. He had pulled out a piece of paper, and was writing down Sam's license plate number.

Green thought about confronting the man, but didn't want things to get out of hand. There were other people in the parking lot and the last thing he needed was a confrontation. The stranger walked to the stairs and out a side door. Green jumped up, thinking it prudent to follow. He sprinted to the exit and watched the man walk to the end of the block and turn left. Green tore after him, worried he might lose sight of him. He wasn't quite sure what he was going to do, but knew he had to find out who this person was.

The man jaywalked across the street to a decent old Porsche 911. The black car was jammed between two other vehicles and he struggled to get out of the spot. Green bolted to the other side and got close enough to read the license plate as the sports car finally tore away.

CHAPTER 57

DETROIT MICHIGAN

Winters didn't get much sleep and woke up feeling achy. Sleeping on plywood was not something he did well. He worked his way to the edge of the cot and grabbed onto the bars to stand up. He stretched his body a few times trying to work out all the kinks, and splashed cold water on his face. His face still hurt from the blow he'd received from Cox. He didn't think it was bruised too badly, otherwise Sadie would have said something.

All night, he had thought about his men and what they would do once they found out the cops had captured him. He wondered if Nate, Elliott and Burns were back from Canada and if they had met with any of the others. He figured they would come for him regardless of who might still be alive and able to join in the quest. Surly, someone must have seen the cops taking him away and made note of the direction. It wouldn't take much to know where he was if they knew the general direction. Of course, they could all be dead for all he knew. He shrugged the thought out of his mind.

Through the bars, he looked down at Reese and Sadie lying with their arms wrapped around each other. He formed a slight smile. It made

Winters pause for a moment, thinking that regardless of one's ominous situation, one could still find some joy, if only for a brief moment.

He thought about Reese's decision to stay with them and how brave it had been. She probably wasn't even aware of the latent courage she was able to muster when it was called for. That was the odd thing about dire circumstances. It forced one to discover what they were really made of, and often allowed greatness to surface. He had learned that from a conversation he had with General Standish. He had discovered that about himself after jumping out of the back of a truck to retrieve his hat. This one action put him into an impossible situation, forcing him to make hard choices, choices he didn't necessarily want to make. He learned he could lead men, which was something that surprised him since he had led the subservient life of a bookkeeper. He also didn't know he could unleash holy hell if needed. This characteristic actually scared him at first, as he felt like a different person, a modern day Mr. Hyde. He chuckled to himself thinking it better than being a coward.

Winters thought about Sadie and what lay ahead for her. He prayed to God to save the little thing from Mordulfah. Sadie came into his life and kept him from constantly dwelling on his own daughter. He was mad at himself for giving in and not insisting she go with Nate to Canada. She had played upon his emotions, but, in reality, he did it for his own selfish reasons, he simply liked having her around.

Winters heard the door unlock and footsteps coming down the stairs. It was Cox and Millsap. Winters wanted nothing more than to wrap his hands around Cox's neck.

"Well, Mr. Winters, today's the day you meet Mordulfah."

"You mean the man who holds your leash."

Cox let out a grunt.

"How's that nose of yours?"

Cox ignored the comment.

Pulling out his nightstick, Cox dragged it noisily across the bars. "Ladies, time to get up. You've got a big day ahead of you."

Reese and Sadie stood up.

Cox turned to Millsap. "I want you to take these two bedraggled looking creatures upstairs, get them to the showers and get them cleaned up. I want them to look their best."

"You got it, Captain," said an excited Millsap.

"Don't be getting any ideas."

"Wouldn't think of it, boss," he grumbled.

Cox turned back to Winters. "And you, Mr. Winters, well, you don't need to look good."

Millsap opened the cell door to let Reese and Sadie out of their cage. As Sadie walked out, she batted Millsap's hand off her shoulder.

"Don't be giving me any sass, little girl," yelled Millsap.

"Just get them upstairs," said Cox.

They marched the girls upstairs leaving Winters alone to ponder how they'd be treating them. He sat back down on his plywood bed and leaned back to wait.

Thirty minutes later Millsap escorted the girls back downstairs with their hair still wet. They carried some food with them, which they shared with Winters. As they ate, they heard yelling upstairs and wondered what was going on.

CHAPTER 58

Cox sat in his office thinking about his exciting day. He couldn't wait to deliver Winters and the two girls to Mordulfah. He had purposely not told him about the girls. He wanted it to be a pleasant enough surprise that Mordulfah would pay a more handsome reward. As he sat there, Millsap came in and reported that Hadley had just arrived for work. Cox sat up straight in his chair and ordered Millsap to bring the Texan to him.

Hadley walked in. "You wanted to see me, sir?"

"Where were you yesterday?"

"Huh, I wasn't feeling well and took the day off."

Cox raised an eyebrow. "Not feeling well, huh?"

"Yes sir."

"What was wrong with you?"

"Ate something bad is all, felt terrible all day."

"Your tummy feeling better today is it?"

"Yes sir, it is."

Cox stood up. "What I want to know is who let out that D.C. puke we had locked up?"

"I've no idea, sir. I didn't even know he was gone until just now."

"Well, he is, and there was no one around to let him out. No one but you, that is."

"I didn't do it, sir."

Cox gestured with his hands. "You must think that I'm an idiot. You were the only one who didn't come with us."

"Sir, I swear I didn't let him go, I was home, sick."

"I don't believe a damn word you say," yelled Cox. "Millsap, get in here."

Millsap walked into the office. "I want you take our Texas friend downstairs and keep him there till I get back."

Millsap stripped Hadley of his sidearm and shoved him up against the wall, where he proceeded to handcuff him. "Boy, you're in real trouble now," snickered Millsap.

"Bring me Winters on your way back up."

Cox wanted to blow off some steam and Winters seemed like just the person to do it on. He needed to pay him back for breaking his nose and all his smart mouthing. He wouldn't rough him up too much. The poor bastard would need his strength when he met Mordulfah.

Cox walked outside and waited as Millsap led Winters out with his hands cuffed behind him. Cox grabbed his nightstick from his belt and slammed it point first into Winters' stomach. Winters doubled over and fell to the ground trying to catch his breath.

"That's for busting my nose," snarled Cox as he swung the club down across his back.

Millsap grabbed Winters' arm and yanked him to his feet. He held onto him while Cox balled his fist and delivered a couple of blows to the face. Winters collapsed to the ground. Cox then kicked dirt in his face.

"There you go, Mr. Rebel, how's that dirt taste?"

Winters groaned.

"I'd do more to you old man, but I'm afraid you'd have a heart attack and die on me." He looked at Millsap. "Get him into my car."

"You got it, boss," said Millsap.

"You got everything else set up and ready?"

"Just as you told me, boss."

"Good. Make sure you keep your eyes peeled."

Hadley hadn't expected his colleagues to throw him in jail when he came to work. He didn't think they would suspect him. His desire to help Winters had blinded him to the dangers of showing up. As soon as Millsap went back upstairs, Sadie immediately began peppering him with questions about what happened. Hadley wasn't sure if he should tell them or wait for Winters.

"Why did you come back here?" asked Reese.

Hadley hesitated before answering. "They asked me to come back."

"Who?" asked Reese.

"Scar."

"He's alive?" asked an excited Sadie.

Hadley nodded.

"What about Meeks?" asked Reese.

"Yes, he's alive, he got shot though."

Reese cringed. "Is he alright?"

"Yes, don't worry, he's good."

"Are they going to rescue us?" asked Reese.

"Yes."

"I knew it," said Sadie, confidently.

"It's why I came back here. Scar wanted me to get word to Winters."

Reese reached through the bars and rested her hand on Hadley's arm. "That was so brave of you."

Hadley blushed a little. "I just wish I could do more, but now I'm stuck here."

"You've done more than you know," said Reese, as she looked down at Sadie. "We've been so worried that everyone was dead or caught and that no one was coming."

Their conversation ended abruptly when they heard the upstairs door unlock and squeaked as it opened. Heavy footfalls came stomping down the stairs.

Hadley moved up close to the bars separating them and whispered. "You girls just stay strong."

Reese moved in, gave Hadley a kiss, and whispered a thank you.

Hadley grinned as blood rushed to his cheeks. No girl had kissed him since he had left home and never such a pretty girl.

Millsap opened the cell door. "Alright girls, upstairs, it is time to go."

Sadie turned to look back at Hadley and smiled at him as she reached the stairs.

The cops escorted the girls outside to a waiting car. Winters was slumped in the backseat of another. Sadie saw they had beaten him up and shot him a worried glance. Winters gave her a half smile and a wink. Sadie returned the gesture as the cops put her in the back of the squad car. Sadie looked around and then at Winters and tried to mouth the words, "they are coming". Seeing him in a daze made her tear up.

The armed convoy pulled out and headed to Grosse Pointe, and Mordulfah. Cox was in the best of moods and couldn't wait to get his reward. Everything was falling into place nicely.

CHAPTER 59

ALEXANDRIA VIRGINIA

Green's head was spinning as he drove home last night. He had made a tactical error in underestimating his boss, Lawrence Reed's, paranoia. Discovering he was being followed was fortuitous, getting the man's license plate number was icing on the cake. He'd have to find someone to run the plates.

He had tried calling his friend Sam last night when he got home, but he hadn't picked up. He left a message to call him at home as soon as he checked the recording. Not having access to one of the few remaining cell phones, he decided he would try Sam at his office number right at 0800.

He didn't look forward to telling him they were being followed, but he owed it to Sam to inform him. Green imagined his head exploding when he told him. His friend had already been nervous about handing over the information.

Before heading to the office, Green wanted to go for a run to clear his mind. As he got ready the phone rang. He picked it up and heard Sam's voice on the other end.

"Oh, hell, John." said Sam, after Green gave him the news.

"I'm sorry. I feel like an idiot."

"I told you that you weren't a spy."

"I know."

"So what are you going to do?"

"I need to find out who he is, I got his plate number, just need to find someone to run it."

"Give it to me, I know someone. What are you going to do when you know who he is?"

"I'm not sure yet, confront him, maybe find out for sure who he's working for."

"Give me a couple of hours on this. You want me to call you at work?"

"No. I'm pretty sure my phone is tapped. Just meet me at the Duxbury Coffee shop at ten."

The conversation with Sam made Green too anxious to go for a run, so after a quick breakfast with his mother, he went straight to work. He didn't tell her what had happened, but knew he'd have to give her a heads up when he found out more about the situation.

He arrived at the office in a restless state and had trouble focusing enough to go through the pile of paperwork on his desk. He kept looking at the clock as the hands crawled toward ten o'clock.

Green turned in his chair and looked out the window at the D.C. landscape. He had a good view of Lafayette Park and watched the people go about their lives seemingly oblivious to what was taking place out West and the hardships many of their fellow Americans were going through just to survive another day. He wondered how many of them had relatives suffering those hardships.

The clock ticked away and finally made it to 9:40. He got up, walked to the opposite end of the building, and took the stairs to the back entrance. He wanted to make sure no one could follow him as he exited out onto 15th Street. He walked to I Street, turned against the traffic and went the long way looking for the man in the red golf shirt. Satisfied no one was tailing him he set off for the Duxbury Coffee Shop.

He walked into the shop, which had the usual coffee bar with comfortable seating off to the side. Small groups of patrons sat chatting quietly to each other. Green spotted his friend and gave him a nod. After ordering, he sat down and joined him.

"Hey, I'm sorry for the trouble."

"I'm not happy, John. I can't believe I'm having to help you again, but then I don't have much choice."

Green took the lid off and took a sip of his latte. "Did you have any luck?"

Sam nodded. He reached into his jacket, pulled out two sheets of paper, unfolded them, and laid the first one down on table. It was a police mug shot.

Green studied the picture. "That's him alright."

"This guy's a piece of work. His name is Bruce Pruitt. He's a two-time loser, got sent away twice for burglary and grand larceny. Served five years the first time and then the second time, after only serving two, got himself paroled. Doesn't look like he's ever had a regular job. Fancies himself a private detective now, but that's not official, seeing as he doesn't have a license."

"How the hell does he know Reed?"

"Oh, it gets better," said Sam, who then handed him Pruitt's address. "He's got a place over in Bethesda."

"Nice neighborhood for a two-time loser."

"That's what I thought too, so I did a little extra checking. Turns out the house is owned by Reed."

"Is that where Reed lives?"

"No, he's got a place over in Annapolis."

Green pondered the significance of that information.

"What are you going to do?"

"I'm not sure yet."

"Whatever you do, you need to do it quickly. Thankfully, I was using a car out of the motor pool. So, it may take a little while before they can track down who drove it, but sooner than later, they'll trace it back to me."

"I promise you, I'll take care of this."

"You damn well better, or we both might be dead."

Green left the coffee shop and started walking back to his office. He stopped in mid-stride and decided to go to Bethesda. He would turn the tables and stalk his stalker.

CHAPTER 60

GROSSE POINTE MICHIGAN

Cox and his men reached the estate of Edsel & Eleanor Ford located in Grosse Pointe. The mansion sat right on the shore of Lake St. Clair. It had been opened to the public since the seventies when she had gifted it to the city.

They drove up to the gate where guards waved his motorcade in, and they made their way to the main house. More guards came and ushered them through the small entryway.

Cox stood with Winters, Sadie and Reese in the hallway as Mordulfah came in.

"Captain Cox, you are to be congratulated," said Mordulfah as he approached. He took a look a Cox's nose. "Oh, my, you were wounded?"

"Yes, sir," said Cox, eyeballing Winters.

"Well, I hope you're not in too much pain."

Mordulfah then moved to Winters. "So, you're the man who's been giving us so much trouble. You're quite old to be playing a young man's game." He then moved over to Reese and Sadie. "Now, what do we have here?"

"These are my gifts to you. The tall one is Reese and the little one is Sadie."

"My, my, you two are quite beautiful," said Mordulfah as he reached for Sadie's dishwater blond hair.

Sadie jerked away from his touch.

"She's a bit on the sassy side," said Cox.

Mordulfah laughed. "I can see. We'll take care of that." He motioned to Wali, his trusted assistant. Wali led the two girls away.

Mordulfah moved back over to Winters. "Mr. Winters is it?"

Winters didn't respond.

"Mr. Winters, you're being quite rude. You're to be a guest here in my home. Now I'll ask you again. It's Mr. Winters?"

Winters nodded.

"Now, that wasn't so difficult." He then spoke in Arabic to another servant, who turned and left the room, returning in a few moments with a thick envelope, handing it to Mordulfah. "For your services, Captain Cox."

Cox smiled and took the envelope and bowed his head.

Mordulfah then spoke again in Arabic and a servant led Winters out of the room. He then turned back to Cox. "Captain Cox, what about the rest of his men?"

"Most of them were rounded up, but not all of them."

"I'm assuming they'll attempt some sort of rescue."

"Yes, I believe they will, but we're ready for them."

"Are you?"

"Yes,"

"Do they know where I am?"

"No, they wouldn't know that, which is why they'll have to come to my station in order to find out. We have the traitor who helped them, locked up downstairs. So, they'll have to come there in order to get him."

"Excellent work."

"Thank you, sir."

"That will be all then, Captain."

"Yes, thank you," said Cox who motioned his men to leave.

Wali came back into the room. "Everything is arranged your Excellency."

Mordulfah went to where he had Sadie prisoner and found her sitting on a bed. He walked in and noticed that she didn't look frightened, which amused him. He pulled a chair closer to the bed and sat down.

"Sadie, such an enchanting name and very appropriate for you."

She looked at him. "And why's that?"

Mordulfah smiled. "Because the meaning of your name is Princess and tonight you'll become my wife and become a real princess."

She faked a smile.

"Today is such a special day."

"Well, tomorrow's my birthday," she lied.

"Is it?"

She nodded with another fake smile.

"How wonderful. How old will you be?"

"Twelve," she lied again.

"A perfect age," he responded enthusiastically. "Then we shall wait until tomorrow and have a double celebration."

"Will you get me a present?" she asked trying to work him over.

"Of course, you shall have many presents."

She muscled up a smile to melt his heart.

Mordulfah was quite satisfied and told her that someone would be along to help her get settled in. He left the room and headed to where they were holding Winters.

CHAPTER 61

After rescuing thirty-four prisoners from St. Paul, Scar had led their band of warriors back to South Bend. Some of the rescued men wouldn't be able to continue because of injuries they'd received during the campus raid. Scar figured the cops would never suspect they'd go back to the campus and thought it would be a safe place for a couple of days. Amber volunteered to stay with them to tend to their needs.

The Shadow Patriots then drove through the night as they proceeded to Detroit. Once they reached the outskirts, they pulled over to draw up a game plan. Having dropped off a dozen men, they had only sixty, which included the wounded Meeks and Elliott. Both insisted they were in good enough shape to go and wouldn't back down.

They all disembarked from the vehicles and assembled near Scar's SUV. The men had automatically looked to him as next in charge. He again realized the burden Winters felt every time he had to make decisions that would put his men in harm's way.

"Guys, from what Corporal Bassett has told me there's a lot of Jijis and cops roaming around town, so we need to be careful not to stand out. The first thing we need to do is to find Hadley. He gave me his address so a couple of us can go check it out and see if he's there."

"What if he's not?" asked Elliott.

"Then we need to go see if he's at work."

"At work? Are you mad?" asked Bassett.

Meeks piped up. "Of course we're mad, how the hell you think we got this far."

Bassett gave him a puzzled look.

"Listen, ole Scar and me have walked into worse situations than this."

"Glad to see you've volunteered yourself," said Scar.

218

"Can't let you have all the fun," smiled Meeks.

"You sure you're up to it?"

"Got myself some great painkillers, and they don't make me too loopy."

Scar thought it best to let that one go and get back to business. "In case we can't find Hadley, we need a backup." He turned to Nate. "You think you can rustle us up some cops for a friendly chat?"

Nate's eyes opened wide, pleased with his assignment. "How many you want?"

"One cooperative one should do it." He turned to Bassett. "In case we have to go to the station, I'll need you to lead some of the men and back us up."

Bassett shook his head in disbelief. "You guys always operate like this?"

"Afraid so, we're just a ragtag bunch, don't have the luxury of big guns."

"Alright then."

Nate and his friend since childhood, Elliott, grabbed half the men and headed back to Saline, where they had busted up the party house four days ago. Nate thought if the place was still open, they could kill two birds with one stone, free more girls, and capture a couple of cops.

Scar instructed Bassett to have his men split up to travel, and then reassemble at a place of his choosing, somewhere close to the police station. Scar and Meeks then drove to Hadley's house in Southgate, a one-story ranch with an attached two-car garage. After finding it empty, they headed downtown.

Scar pulled into the police station's parking lot and noticed a few cops look up as they came down the concrete steps. The two of them got out and headed inside.

"What can I do for you?" asked the desk Sergeant, who looked annoyed that he was being bothered.

"We want to report a break-in," said Scar.

"A break-in?"

"Yes, someone broke into our home this morning."

"No offense or anything, but you do live in Detroit, these things happen all the time. There's not a whole lot we can do about that."

"Can't you come by and find some fingerprints or something?"

"You're kidding right?"

"Isn't that what your job is?"

"Look, I'm sorry, but we don't have the manpower or the time to investigate every single break-in."

"Is there someone else we can talk to? I've got a friend who works here, maybe he can help us."

"Who might that be?"

"Don Hadley."

The sergeant raised an eyebrow. "You know, Don, do ya?"

"Yeah, is he here?"

The sergeant smiled and said that he'd be right back with Hadley.

Scar turned to Meeks and shrugged his shoulders.

A minute later, five cops with weapons drawn, surrounded them, shouting to put their hands up.

"Hey, what are you doing?" Scar yelled out.

"Hadley doesn't have any friends," said the sergeant.

"Well, there's where you're wrong."

The cops rushed in and slapped handcuffs on them. They found the pistols stuffed in the back of their pants.

"You come in here armed, asking for Hadley? You're part of those rebels."

They protested as the cops led them downstairs and pushed them into a cell adjoining the one that housed Hadley.

"Here's your friend, Hadley," laughed the sergeant.

After the cops left, Scar looked at Meeks. "Well, at least we found him."

"Is this one of those lemon, lemonade things?" quipped Meeks.

Scar ignored the jibe and turned to Hadley. "So what happened? Where's the Captain?"

Hadley told them what had happened and that they had left an hour ago. Scar was frustrated, but he had needed to find a safe place for the injured men before coming to Detroit. He hadn't had a choice in the matter and figured it was just the way it was.

"So, now what?" asked Hadley.

"We wait," said Scar.

"For what?"

"The Cavalry," answered Meeks.

CHAPTER 62

BETHESDA MARYLAND

After leaving his meeting with Sam at the coffee shop, Green decided to go to Bethesda to check out where Pruitt lived. He wasn't sure what he would do when he got there, but felt the need to do something.

He tried to wrap his mind around the connection between Pruitt and Reed. Why would Reed need the services of a two-time con, and why would he be putting him up in a house that was way out of his league. Reed must use Pruitt for other things besides following people around.

As Green wove his way around the streets of Bethesda, he noticed the homes increased in size the closer he got to where Pruitt lived. The well-maintained lawns also expanded, and the trees provided ample shade.

He found the street, and slowed down as he looked to his left for house numbers, counting the homes as he went. His heart beat faster the closer he got to his destination. Then he found it. The large house sat way back from the street, and had a long driveway where a 911 was parked in front of the garage. As Green drove past, the garage door opened and a man walked out.

Green turned his head and saw it was Pruitt. His palms started to sweat when he saw Pruitt turn his way. He immediately grew nervous wondering if Pruitt had recognized his car. He kept his eyes darting between the road ahead and his rearview mirror. Pruitt pulled out of the driveway and turned in his direction. Green pressed his foot on the accelerator. He reached the end of the block, made a right turn, and picked up speed. He kept his eye on the mirror, expecting Pruitt to follow. He let out a big sigh of relief when Pruitt continued straight. He parked his car wondering what to do next, and after a few moments, came up with an idea.

After finding the items he wanted, Green walked out of a home improvement store carrying his purchases to his car. He stripped off his uniform jacket and shirt, leaving only his white t-shirt. He reached into the bag and pulled out a yellow florescent safety vest and hat. After putting them on, he drove back and parked his car on the street behind Pruitt's house.

He got out and took a clipboard from the bag along with some paper fliers he had picked up in the store. Finally, he tucked his gun in the small of his back, and nonchalantly walked down the street.

Anyone who wore a yellow vest and hat, carrying a clipboard, looked like a municipal worker and could go most anywhere without question. He remembered seeing them in his own neighborhood and didn't give it a second thought, because they looked like they belonged.

He reached Pruitt's house, paused at the end of the driveway and thumbed through the papers before walking up the long empty driveway. He proceeded around to the back. Trees and shrubbery filled the small backyard giving him cover from prying eyes.

Sweat started to bead on his forehead and nerves shot through his body as he approached the patio. He hoped to God no one else lived there, but then remembered his disguise. He was a public servant; he belonged there and was doing his job. He pretended to look for a meter as he looked in the windows for any signs of life. No lights were on and he didn't hear any sound. He found the meter, which sat near a window on the opposite side of the driveway. He casually looked around before pulling out his gun. He used the butt end to break the glass. The noise, though slight, sounded like a canon shot to Green. He waited a few moments to see if it had aroused any attention.

After he was satisfied he was still alone, he squeezed through the basement window into what appeared to be a bedroom. The room looked unused. "Hopefully a spare," thought Green. He quickly moved into the hallway and up the wooden staircase. If anyone was home, they would have heard the creaks a couple of the steps made as he traipsed up to the main floor.

The home had a modern décor. In the center of the living room sat a big gray leather couch, with white and black pillows resting on either end. A mirrored coffee table stood between the couch and a white marbled fireplace, which had black book shelves on either side of it. A big flat screen television hung above the mantel. Large black and white scenic photographs in black frames decorated the gray walls.

Green admired the room. "Definitely not Pruitt's style," he thought. Satisfied no one was home, he relaxed as he walked around looking for anything that might give him an idea of what to do next. He found a room with a computer and figured this was his office.

The room had a Spartan look, with just a desk and chair. A laptop and printer were on the desk. He sat down in front of stacks of papers and photographs of people. He started to rifle through the photos and recognized some of the subjects. There were pictures of Senators and Members of the House, all in compromising positions with women. "Blackmail," thought Green. Other photos were of numerous VIP's meeting in restaurants and bars. Those pictured were men and women who didn't necessarily agree with the new government.

"So, Reed has Pruitt spying on people. No wonder he lets him stay here," thought Green.

He finished going through the photos and started in on the stacks of papers. Right on top was a note with a license plate number. A note referring to the state department and a name scribbled next to it. He grabbed his clipboard and wrote down the name, and then continued going through the papers. Toward the bottom, he came across a list of names. He studied the names and recognized a few of them because these were names of power players in the district. Some of the names had check marks by them, with two crossed out. Panic shot through him when he recognized one of the names. He remembered the man had died in a car crash.

Green knew he'd stumbled onto something big and decided to make a copy of the list and some of the photos. Just as he had finished copying and was putting everything back, he heard the front door open. He froze momentarily, then put the copies on his clipboard and stepped into the hallway. He peeked around the corner. An older, heavyset Hispanic woman, walked into the kitchen. "Damn, a housekeeper," he thought. He waited until she reached the kitchen and quietly snuck back to the staircase. He slipped down the stairs, trying to remember which ones creaked. His fifth step was the one he forgot. It squeaked loudly enough for him to stop in mid-stride.

"Hola. Señor Pruitt, is that you?"

Green tried to lighten his weight on the step by grabbing onto the banister. He skipped the next two steps, and then two more, before reaching the carpeted floor. He made it around the corner just as she came to the steps asking again for Señor Pruitt. Green hurried back to the spare bedroom and climbed out the window. He ran across the lawn and tore through the trees to the neighboring house. His heart raced as if he were in combat. He realized he was walking too fast for a salaried worker, and forced himself to slow down as he made his way along the sidewalk to the end of the block. Relief came when he finally reached his car.

CHAPTER 63

DETROIT MICHIGAN

Bassett had been waiting in angst for the last forty-five minutes and figured something must be wrong. He tried raising Nate on the radio, but couldn't reach him. He didn't want to wait any longer. Bassett couldn't think of any other alternative, but to storm the place. The station didn't appear to be over-crowded with security and he thought he could do it with the men he had. After all, they had the element of surprise on their side. He asked Mr. Peterson to stay behind to keep trying to raise Nate. He got on the radio and ordered the men waiting around back to attack.

Two cars filled with Bassett and seven of his men drove into the front parking lot. Another car filled with four men entered through the back. They all jumped out carrying their weapons. Bassett held the Colt M4 Carbine Hadley had given him. As he raced up the stairs, all he could think of was Meeks' comment that they were a ragtag group.

He entered the building and the desk sergeant's eyes opened wide. The sergeant tried to go for his sidearm. Bassett let off a quick spurt of bullets that exploded into the man's chest. The force threw him back against the wall. The loud cracking of the guns alerted the cops in the building. Bassett's men spread out and stormed down the hall firing their weapons. The cops returned fire.

Chaos ensued as gunfire erupted all over the station. Bassett could hear it from the back of the building. A shot splintered a doorway he was using as cover. He crouched down and peered around the corner. The hall contained more cops than he had expected. He took more fire as he turned to find four of his guys lying dead in the hallway. His position was collapsing.

A bullhorn crackled. "You're surrounded Bassett. Your men around back have already surrendered. Give it up, now."

Bassett couldn't hear anymore gunfire in the background. He looked out the window. More cops were coming in through the front. They had him.

Bassett threw his weapon around the corner. He motioned the others to do the same.

"Lay down spread eagle," the bullhorn cracked again.

The cops came storming over them yelling at them not to move. They fell all over him as they bound his hands behind him with flex cuffs.

Cox came up to him. "You actually thought you could just waltz right on in here and take over my station? You dumb-ass puke."

Millsap snatched up the M4. "This is one of ours." He took it and slammed the butt end into Bassett stomach.

Cox turned to Millsap. "Get them all downstairs."

CHAPTER 64

GROSSE POINTE MICHIGAN

Winters sat alone in a locked, windowless room in the basement. The room had a bed with a comfortable mattress. Overall, this was better accommodations than he'd had the last couple of nights sitting in a jail cell. His head still throbbed in pain from the blows he'd received from Cox. He worried about what was happening to Reese and Sadie. He could see right away that Mordulfah was quite taken with Sadie, and had no doubts about his plans for her. He closed his eyes and asked God to save both the girls.

He then thought about what might happen to him. He supposed they would torture him for information. He didn't think he had anything of value to tell them, but then thought they would do it simply for revenge, because he had killed their men. Regardless, he knew he was in for a world of pain.

His door unlocked and Wali came in and motioned him to get up. The two of them walked upstairs and into a large room with a long table placed in the center. Mordulfah was sitting at the end of the table, eating.

"Come in, Mr. Winters. Sit here next to me. Would you care for some food?"

Winters turned slightly to show his hands still in flex cuffs.

"Wali, remove Mr. Winters restraints."

Winters rubbed his wrist and sat down.

"You must be hungry. Please, I don't like eating alone."

Winters stared at the strange food and wondered what it was.

"I'm afraid it's all we have here, but I promise you, it's very good."

Winters played it safe, grabbed some fruit, and started to devour it. He snickered to himself thinking that he probably looked like a movie cliché, shoving food into his mouth.

"Did they not feed you?"

"Not so much."

"Yes, well that Captain Cox is a brutish man, but he has his uses."

"I see you pay him well enough."

Mordulfah let out a laugh. "What do you Americans say, every man for himself."

"Not everyone," Winters responded curtly.

"And you would be the prime example of that. Tell me, Mr. Winters, what exactly motivates you?"

"Saving the innocent, of course." he answered quickly.

"Saving the innocent, but from whom are you saving them?"

Winters thought about that for a moment. "Besides you?"

Mordulfah gave him a small wicked laugh. "Yes, besides me."

"I know there are some in my own country that are involved."

"As has been your experience. I would imagine you'd like to know who's in charge."

Winters already knew the answer to this question. It was the billionaire puppeteer Gerald Perozzi, who held all the strings of power. Winters had learned this from James Boxer, the former commandant of the National Police, when they captured him in St. Paul, Minnesota, some weeks ago. Boxer had told Winters the government wanted to be in complete control of the country and they would use any means necessary, even if it meant hiring terrorists. Neither party cared how many died in the process or what might happen to innocent women and children. What Winters didn't know was the extent of the conspiracy. He had been fooling himself, thinking they would stop after he had shut down the Patriot

Centers. The only thing that did was to force them to come up with different strategies. This is where this Saudi prince came in. Winters knew the man had to be getting something out of the deal.

"What I'd really like to know is how much Perozzi is paying you?"

Mordulfah seemed surprised by the question. "You know about Mr. Perozzi?"

Winters nodded.

"It would appear you are more knowledgeable than I was led to believe."

"How much to be his lapdog?" asked Winters

"Quite the opposite, it is Mr. Perozzi who is the lapdog."

"Oh?"

"Yes, Perozzi thinks he has the upper hand in our deal, but rest assured, in the end, it is I who will come out on top."

"Must be one hell of a payout."

"My terms with Mr. Perozzi are not important."

"Then tell me."

Mordulfah gave Winters a cold stare. His dark black eyes looked right into Winters like an X-Ray. "They're not important. What is important are the next few days of your life. Tomorrow, after I wed Sadie, and celebrate her birthday, we will begin your punishment."

The words ran down Winters' spine like a cold shot of Novocain. The pedophile was going to marry Sadie first. "So, this is how you justify raping little girls," he thought. Winters did take a bit of satisfaction, knowing Sadie had lied to him about her birthday. This probably bought her an extra day. "An extra day for what though, a rescue?" Winters wasn't holding out much hope. He wondered what was happening to Reese, but decided it was probably better not to dwell on that.

"You, of course, will not be attending the wedding, but you will be part of the celebration. There is nothing quite like beating another man to get one excited for his conjugal delights."

The thought made Winters' stomach turn.

CHAPTER 65

Reed sat in his office thinking about the recent capture of Winters. The news pleased him, and he was glad the issue was off his plate. The band of rebels had been a thorn in his side these past couple of months. Winters actions had proved him right though. He had predicted there would be trouble from the population if their plans were exposed. Now, because of Winters, they had to make a deal with the devil himself and hire Mordulfah to further their efforts. It bothered Reed the deal Perozzi had made with the man though. He considered the price way to high. "Too much was being given away with this lopsided deal," thought Reed.

Reed turned his chair to the salt-water tank and admired his fish. He had owned a fish tank ever since he was a boy, and found it a great way to help him get his thoughts in order. He loved the way it soothed him as he watched the fish go about their business. Theirs was an uncomplicated world of eating and swimming from one end of the tank to the other, never seeming to care how small the world they lived in really was.

This was a stark contrast to the world of politics and dealing with different personalities. Some of whom were the total opposite of him. His friend Gerald Perozzi was a prime example of being an opposite. Despite Perozzi's enormous wealth and the wheeling and dealing with world players, he never seemed to let the bad deals bother him. Reed wished he would show more concern for the deal they had made with Mordulfah. The absurdities of the deal never fazed him, saying it was the cost of doing business with such a man. Of course, Perozzi didn't have to put up with the day-to-day crap that always popped up. "No, I'm the one who has to do all the dirty work," Reed thought.

Reed got up and selected some food for the fish. He sprinkled it across the tank and watched all the fish rush to the surface to grab their share. His thoughts turned to his next immediate problem, Major Green. There was just something a little unnerving about the way he had brought up Mordulfah. It seemed like Green was trying to get a reaction out of him and he didn't appreciate being played. It was why he decided to send Pruitt to follow him. He was probably being paranoid, but he didn't trust anyone, especially in light of their recent takeover of the government. Too many people were still positioning themselves for whatever power they could grab. Everyone wanted something and he had to be on the constant lookout for anyone who wasn't on his side. If Green did suspect things weren't as they appeared, then perhaps he'd want some power for himself, or worse yet, cause trouble by trying to topple him.

This was why Pruitt's services were invaluable to him. He had already proven himself many times over by getting compromising photos of power players. This had proved to be a valuable tool to keep people in line. For those who had ethics and morals, well, they didn't always survive accidents, though this was always a last resort. Too many accidental deaths encouraged gossip, which could upset the apple cart, as it were.

If Green wasn't on his side then he might have to use that card, which would be a costly card to play, because his mother was well respected in the district and knew many important people. Reed also couldn't transfer him out to the war if he knew what was really going on, because he'd be able to poison the minds of well-armed military men. They, in turn, might come back to Washington and stage a coup. This would create a much greater liability than having Green killed here.

Reed sat back down in his chair and continued watching the fish devour the food, some of which sank to the bottom, where the fish would find it later while they swam back and forth to nowhere.

CHAPTER 66

After breaking into Pruitt's house, Green headed back to his office. He'd been away too long and didn't want anyone to think something was wrong. The day had been nerve racking, having discovered that Pruitt was Reed's go to guy for nefarious activities. It was bad enough finding Sam's license plate number written down, but to find scandalous photos and the list of names. One of these people, he knew, had been killed in an auto accident, and this was more than just a little unsettling. Green's mind was reeling with all the information, and it would take considerable sorting to determine his next course of action.

He arrived at the Lafayette building, and tried to contain his nerves as he greeted his secretary, Grace, who seemed to have thought nothing was uncommon about his absence. This gave him a little more confidence and since she never mentioned it, he could assume Reed had not been by to question him. He sat at his desk and looked at his computer with full knowledge they were monitoring his activities. He wanted to research the two crossed out names on the list, but that would send up red flags.

He tapped his fingers on the desk, and in a short while, came up with an idea. He got up, walked out to his secretary's desk, and offered her the rest of the day off. She didn't hesitate one bit and gave him a big smile. He said it would be no problem as long as she didn't tell anyone. Grace zipped her fingers across her lips, grabbed her purse and left the office.

Green waited ten minutes before he jumped on her computer and typed in the first of the crossed out names. At the top of the results was a news story on the man's death by a hit and run driver. He had left a restaurant and was crossing the street when a car hit him. Witnesses had said the driver appeared to be drunk and didn't pull over after hitting him. No one was able to get a license plate number and the death was still under investigation. The victim was the former Director for the Department of Commerce under the past administration. He had been an outspoken critic of the new administration and had accused it of being unlawful.

Green sat back in his secretary's chair after reading the article and took a deep breath, knowing it had been Pruitt driving that car. He typed in the next name and read an article on his unfortunate death. A stolen vehicle had rammed into his car, which had rolled down an embankment and caught fire. The police never found the driver of the stolen car. The hairs on Green's arm rose as he finished reading the news article of former Senator Kelly from Florida. Green knew of him, and remembered him to be another harsh critic of the new government. He had been calling for new elections, and had been getting some traction from likeminded people before the war had begun. The war had changed everything. The American people had rallied around the present government, but Senator Kelly hadn't given up calling for new elections.

Green made notations on all the remaining names, who they were and what they did for a living. The names with the marks next to them had been critics but changed their tune after the war started and now supported the government. The names without the marks had always appeared to be supporters of the current administration. These names matched up with the pictures he had copied. "Already in their pockets," thought Green.

To ensure his secretary wouldn't realize he'd been using her computer, he erased the search history. He knew he couldn't get rid of it completely. It would still be on the servers, but he figured no one would be keeping track of her searches.

A couple of hours later, he met Sam in an Alexandria sports bar called Pub II. No one knew where Pub I was or if one ever existed. The bar had a wide-open floor plan. High tables sat in the center with smaller tables surrounding them. Banners of various professional teams, along with the local college teams hung on the walls. The televisions were playing soccer games from Europe. Because of the war, all the American professional sports teams were out of business.

The place had few patrons and they had their choice of tables. They grabbed beers at the bar before picking a table by the dartboards and decided to play a game. Sam had played darts throughout his college years at Georgetown. He had been good enough to compete in a couple of tournaments in Vegas during the summer breaks.

"So, what did you find out?" asked Sam

Green took a sip of his beer and filled him in on everything he had done and what he had found in Pruitt's house, including the name written by his license plate number. Sam shook his head and let out a sigh. He grabbed the darts and wildly threw them at the dartboard missing it completely. He raised his beer and gulped half of it down.

Green waited for him to finish. "I guess none of this is surprising, if you think about everything else they've been doing."

"No, I don't suppose it is. Question is, how long will it be before they figure out what I helped you with?"

"Do you know Pruitt's contact at the State Department?"

"Yeah, I know him. He's a bit of a weasel, but he doesn't have direct access to those log sheets. He'll have to find someone to bribe in order to take a look, which won't be too difficult for the right price."

"Can't you bribe someone and get your name removed?"

"He's had a full day already, I'm going to assume he already has my name."

Green took a sip. "Even so, if Pruitt knows who you are, he still doesn't have anything. He'd need to look at your computer records."

"I'm aware of that, but all it'll take is for that weasel to offer another bribe to get at them. We have a big IT department. I've no doubt someone there wouldn't mind making an extra buck."

"So that should buy us another day."

"Okay, so what are you going to do about it tomorrow?"

Green hesitated because he didn't have a good answer. Sam stared at him with a look of desperation. Green felt bad for getting him involved and owed him big time. Then it dawned on him that he was at a crossroad and had a choice to make. He was either all in or nothing. He decided to go all in. This decision allowed him to see his next move with perfect clarity.

CHAPTER 67

Nate saw a squad car parked alone in an abandoned parking lot, and he pointed it out to Elliott, who was driving their SUV. It appeared the cop was taking a nap, which made him an easy target. They still needed a cop after coming up empty in Saline, which remained closed since they had come through there like hell on wheels. Elliott pulled into the far side of the parking lot and drove slowly across it.

The squad car was parked with its nose toward the building. He moved up close behind it and Nate jumped out carrying a sawed off, double barrel shotgun. He moved quickly to the driver's side and found the window rolled down. He shoved the shotgun against the side of the man's head.

"Wakey wakey," he sneered.

It took a second for the startled cop to realize what was happening. He started to reach for his sidearm, but thought better of it, when Nate shoved the barrels into his skull.

"Get out," Nate ordered as he moved back and pulled on the door handle.

"Don't kill me, please," said the frightened man.

"I won't kill you, just so long as you play nice with me," said Nate as he questioned himself about that statement. He didn't care for these cops and what they were doing. It pissed him off to no end, and he had no problem killing them. All he needed was an excuse, no matter how small, to pull the trigger, but he didn't.

Nate had the cop remove his gun belt and drop it to the ground. He motioned Bill Taylor to handcuff him.

When Nate got back into the SUV, he heard the radio coming alive. "Nate, come in."

Nate grabbed the radio. "Nate, here. Who's this?"

"It's Peterson."

Nate thought it odd for Peterson to contact him, and suspected something was wrong. "What's up?"

Nate absorbed the information with a cool demeanor, and told Peterson to stay out of sight until they got there.

Nate attempted to control his anger. He couldn't believe Bassett had gone in with such a small force. Over the past couple of months, he had learned, to act more rational and to devise an unexpected game plan. Patience had never been a virtue of his, but he'd seen how effective it had been for Winters. Too bad Bassett hadn't learned that lesson. He just hoped he hadn't lost any men in the process.

Now, he would have to remain calm and come up with a plan to rescue everyone, and do it without storming the place. He first needed to interrogate the cop and find out what he knew.

Nate and Elliott took the prisoner in their SUV and Taylor followed with the squad car. An abandoned vehicle might have caused someone to question the absence of the driver.

They drove to a secluded spot, pulled into a meadow, and parked behind a weeping willow tree. After they stopped, Nate yanked the cop out of the truck and threw him to the ground. He retrieved the shotgun and pointed it at him. The cop immediately began to plead for his life.

Nate stared down at him. "I'm only going to tell you this one time. If you don't answer my questions, then I'm just going to shoot you. Then, I'll go find another cop who, while kneeling beside your bullet-ridden body, will be more cooperative. So, it doesn't really matter to me, which one of you it is. You understand?"

The cop began to simulate a bobble head doll. "I'm the one you want to ask."

"Do you know who we are?"

"Yes."

"So, you know what I'm going to ask ya then?"

"Yes."

"First off, where is Winters?"

"Mordulfah has him."

"And where is that?"

"At Grosse Pointe. I can give you directions."

Nate looked over at Elliott who stood off to the side and gave him a nod.

"What about the rest of my friends."

"We caught them trying to storm our station."

"How many got killed?"

"Four."

Nate wondered who they were.

"Where are they at?"

"Locked up downstairs."

"What's going to happened to them?"

"Cox is going execute them."

"He's in charge?"

The cop bobbled his head.

"When's he going to execute them?"

"In the morning, he wants to make it a spectacle."

"Does Cox think he has all of us?"

"Yes."

"You wouldn't be lying to me now would you?"

"No, with the ones we killed and captured in South Bend, he thinks he's got all of you."

After asking more questions, regarding manpower and schedules, he moved off the side to talk to Elliott. They discussed whether to get the guys before trying for Winters. It was an obvious choice. They needed the manpower before storming Mordulfah's place. It frustrated Nate that they had to wait another day to free the girls from Mordulfah.

They had hoped to get to Cox at home like they had done Stiver, but their prisoner said he was staying the night at the station.

Nate gave it some thought, and decided to stage a rescue later that night when there wouldn't be as many cops on duty. He shoved the handcuffed cop in the trunk of his own vehicle and cold-cocked him, knocking him out. They then took off to find Mr. Peterson, who was still keeping an eye on the place.

It was two o'clock in the morning, and the remaining Shadow Patriots prepared for their raid. Nate, Taylor and Elliott changed into the business attire they had used in St. Paul. They would again pose as Government agents wanting Corporal Bassett back. Taylor had worked on their identification, perfecting their ruse. It would take an attitude, and he had plenty of it.

The three of them walked into the station to the surprise of the night watchman.

Taylor flashed his ID. "Homeland Security, you in charge here tonight, son?" he asked gruffly.

Millsap came out of his chair quickly. "No, I'm not. Captain Cox, the station commander, is in charge."

"He's here at this ungodly hour?"

"Yes he is."

"Well?"

"Well, what?" asked the tired looking cop, who had thick bags under his eyes.

"Where's Captain Cox?"

"He's in his office resting," said Millsap.

"Well, show me the way," said Taylor in an annoyed tone.

"To his office?"

Taylor let out a long grunt.

The baggy eyed Millsap took them to Cox's office. He gave the door a soft knock and waited for an answer.

Taylor shoved the man to the side and pounded on the door as he opened it. They all went into the darkened room and found Cox leaning back in his chair with his eyes shut. The loud knocking woke up a discombobulated Captain Cox. He leaned forward and looked at the three older men who were staring down at him.

"What the hell? Who the hell are you?"

Taylor reached into his pocket, pulled out his ID, and flashed it to Cox, who, as planned, didn't get a good look at it in the dark office. "We're with Homeland Security."

"Homeland Security?" Cox looked at his watch. "It's two in the morning."

"Yes and I should be at home cuddling with my wife of thirty years, but instead I'm here talking to you. You think I want to be here talking to you?"

"What do you want?"

"I want my man back."

Cox looked dumbfounded. "What man?"

"Corporal Bassett."

"You're here for Bassett? I've got him locked up for killing some of my men."

"Yes, I know that, he's also a traitor to the United States of America, which means he's committed a national crime against the state. He needs to stand trial before we execute him."

"He's being executed here in just a few hours."

"We're aware of this."

"You are?" asked a bewildered Cox.

"We're the government, we know everything."

"You can't have him, he killed some of my men."

"Did he not have help?"

"Yes."

"And do you not have those men?"

"Yes."

"Well, there you go. You can take your revenge on those men. Now if you don't mind, I'd like to get my prisoner, so I can get the hell out of here."

Cox shook his head, and led them downstairs to the cells, as Millsap and one other officer followed them. The shuffling footsteps woke everyone up, and they stared out of the crowded jail cells. They weren't too surprised to see their fellow patriots dressed up in business attire.

Millsap approached the cell holding Bassett and ordered the prisoners to back up. Bassett stepped out smiling at Cox. This scared Cox and he yelled for his men to handcuff him. Millsap and another cop came over and put their hands on Bassett. He reacted immediately. He grabbed one of Millsap's hands, and twisted it around as he took ahold of the knife on the officer's belt and jammed it into his gut. Millsap screamed out in agony. The other cop's reaction was hesitant, and cost him the advantage. Bassett yanked the knife out of Millsap's gut and spun the dying man around as his body fell to the ground. Bassett leapt at the other cop, swung his knife hand around and sliced the man's throat. Cox's eyes turned into saucers as he reached for his gun. He nervously grabbed it and pulled it out. He raised his arm just as Bassett rushed him, shoving the knife upward into Cox's armpit. In one continuous motion, Bassett stabbed him in the neck, and then the chest. Cox dropped his gun and slumped to the ground. Bassett looked down at him and screamed, "you friggen child rapist."

Nate stood watching the whole thing unfold. He thought about helping, but Bassett was very quick and seemed determined to take them all on. He liked the young corporal's moves. After it was over, he bent down and took the keys off the dead Millsap, who was lying in a pool of his own blood.

"Hell's bells, Bassett," said Scar. "You been planning that move all day?"

"No, it just kind of came to me."

"Improv...I like it."

"What took you guys so long?" asked Meeks.

"We all went out for massages," said Taylor.

"Well, I hope you enjoyed yourselves," laughed Meeks.

Nate and Elliott pulled the pistols they had smuggled in and handed them to ready hands. Nate then told Bassett to put the cuffs on. The four of them went back upstairs, where they met a cop out in the hall.

Nate looked at him. "Captain Cox needs you downstairs."

As soon as the man passed by, Taylor grabbed him from behind, and with his knife wielding right hand, sliced his throat. The man went slump, and Taylor passed his carcass down the stairs. Nate didn't see anyone else around, so he signaled the coast was clear. The Shadow Patriots had come in through the front door and then left through the same one as they hustled to their waiting vehicles.

CHAPTER 68

ALEXANDRIA VIRGINIA

Green had gotten up early to go for a run. After meeting with Sam last night, he felt good having made the decision to go all in. He needed to take Pruitt out. It only made sense, he really didn't have a choice, and it actually made things clearer. With Bassett still in the Midwest helping the Shadow Patriots, and Winters being held captive, he needed to have more skin in the game and honor his commitment to protect his friends. He would also have to let his mother know just how deeply he was going to be committed. He worried about her safety and felt she needed a heads up.

Green came into the kitchen and found her at the stove frying bacon and eggs for their breakfast. He loved his mother, but he wished he had a wife cooking for him instead. It was something he had decided to put off, at least until the war ended. He'd had girlfriends in the past, but the Army always got in the way. He didn't want to have to leave a wife, go to war and possibly never come back.

His mother, holding the frying pan, turned around to face him, and motioned him to sit down.

"What's on your agenda today, John."

"Got some things to take care of."

"Still haven't heard from Corporal Bassett?"

"Not since he left Canada, and that was two days ago."

"What about this Captain Cox?"

"He wouldn't take my calls yesterday. I'm afraid something bad has happened to Bassett."

"Is that all?" she asked, giving her son the 'don't try to pull my leg' look she used when she knew there was more going on than he was telling her.

Green sighed, and proceeded to fill her in on everything he'd been doing.

She served their breakfast and sat down. "I knew both those men. Now that I know they were killed by this Pruitt fellow, my suspicions are confirmed."

"Oh?"

"Yes, and I'm not the only one who thought it a bit strange they were both killed in car accidents."

"Who else?"

"You mean besides most everyone in Washington? I have many important friends who strongly disagree with this new government. Some are on that list of yours. It doesn't surprise me in the least that they're being black-mailed. It would explain why some of them altered their opinion so quickly. They're all weaklings anyways. The ones killed, now those were strong men."

Green stared at his mother.

"You're worried about me?"

"Of course I am."

"I wouldn't worry too much. I've been reaching out to certain people."

"Don't feel like running I take it."

"Never was one to run, John."

"This is not helping me any."

Sarah shrugged her shoulders.

"Who have you reached out to?"

"Well, there's Senator Abby Seeley"

Green leaned back in surprise.

"She and I go way back."

"Wasn't she on the Senate Select Committee?"

"Yes, not that it means anything anymore, but she and her husband still have ties to a lot of disgruntled power players, all in secret of course.

"Like who?"

"There's Jacob Gibbs, the former Assistant Director of the FBI and John Osborne, he's high up in the State Dept."

Green was impressed, and a little surprised to hear their names. He thought they too had sold out to the new government.

"There are others, John. Believe it not, there are people who don't like what's going on and want to do something about it."

"I guess I shouldn't be surprised. It just seemed everyone was cowering and running for cover, when the federal government collapsed."

"Do you blame them? Look what happened to the ones who did take a stand."

"Which could happen to us," said Green in a worried tone.

"You need to talk to these people and tell them what is really happening in the Midwest."

"I don't know."

"They need hope and a spark. You could be that messenger, maybe even the one that brings them together. They need a leader, John."

What his mother was telling him weighed heavily on Green's mind, but he decided to take her advice to start reaching out to others. He needed allies and the more people they could bring together, the stronger they'd become. They would need to be better prepared for the coming days, because he knew, Perozzi, Reed, and everyone else who had a stake in the new government, including the puppet president, would not relinquish their power easily.

CHAPTER 69

GROSSE POINTE MICHIGAN

Winters opened his eyes after hearing several people moving around upstairs. Despite having a comfortable bed, he hadn't slept much, if at all. He mostly thought about his conversation with Mordulfah. What exactly did Perozzi offer him, and what did Mordulfah mean when he said that in the end he would come out on top? After he got what he wanted, would he then assassinate Perozzi and Reed? Surely, Perozzi was smarter than to let this man put one over on him. However, the thought of Mordulfah killing the two men actually provided Winters a pleasant fantasy. He'd love to be there when that happened.

Winters sat up in his bed and began wondering what all was going to happen today. He hoped Reese was holding on. Mordulfah hadn't mentioned her, which gave Winters pause. From what he had gathered, she was a bit too old for his taste. So, what would he do with her, sell her into slavery...again? The thought sent shivers down his spine. Despite his wishes, the poor girl had opted to stay with them to continue to seek her revenge. She had gotten a taste of it and wanted more.

Sadie, on the other hand, concerned him the most. He had put her in a terrible situation, a situation he was unable to fix. She had already gone through enough. She had lost her mother and didn't know if her dad, who was fighting in the war, was still alive. Now that bastard would take from her what remained of her childhood. Winters cringed at the thought.

The unlocking of his door pulled him away from his thoughts. He turned to see Wali at the doorway, who motioned him to follow. Winters left his room, trailed by two more Jijis.

They took him upstairs to the same large room where he had met with Mordulfah yesterday. The room was empty of people, but had a large spread of food waiting at the table. He was told to sit and wait.

Winters looked at the strange food and wondered if it was his last meal. He hoped Mordulfah would join him, because he wanted answers. If he was to die, he, at least, wanted to know what the prince's plans were.

He didn't have to wait long before Mordulfah came into the room, dressed in a white silk robe. The silk seem to do a dance around his body as he moved to the head of the table.

"Good morning, Mr. Winters."

Winters tilted his head.

"An excellent day, is it not?"

His graciousness sickened Winters. "For you, perhaps."

Mordulfah let out a laugh. "Will you not join me for breakfast?"

"My last meal?"

Mordulfah sat down. "Oh no, you will have many more meals. Perhaps not as elaborate as this one, but it's the least I can do before your big day."

"Can't wait to see what you've got in mind."

"You won't have to wait much longer. Please help yourself."

Winters didn't have much of an appetite, but he knew he would need his strength, so he picked up a banana and forced himself to eat. He thought about what to say as he took small bites of the fruit. "Seeing as how you're going to torture and kill me, could you at least answer some questions?"

Mordulfah eyed him for a moment.

Winters pressed the subject. "If I am to die, then what does it matter to you?"

Mordulfah smiled. "Mr. Winters, you've caught me in an excellent mood, so I will answer your questions."

"What are you getting out of all of this?"

"Mr. Winters, you surprise me. I would think you'd want to know what your government is getting out of this first."

Winters placed the banana peel on the table. "Okay."

"Control. Your government wants total control over its people."

Winters already knew this.

"You can't accomplish total control over a people who are not used to being told what to do, so in order to do that you have to get rid of those who will not conform."

Winters knew what was coming next. He had heard it before when he had interrogated Commandant Boxer.

"The Midwest is a vast area and much more difficult to control than say the East Coast, where the population is more condensed. Here, you have large pockets of people who would rebel. Take yourself, as an example, you saw something you shouldn't have and didn't like it. So, what did you do? You took up arms against the government. Now imagine if say only five thousand people, spread out all over the Midwest did the same thing. Why, the government wouldn't be able handle it, and would collapse. So what do you do? You divide the country up."

"You're going to kill everyone in the Midwest?"

"They are much too independent minded to leave them to their own devices."

Winters remembered his 20th century history. He knew Lenin and Stalin had done the same thing. They killed millions of their own people to gain control over the whole country.

"And this is where you come in?" asked Winters.

"They did try to do it themselves with their pathetic Patriot Program. It worked to a degree. It certainly has made my job easier, but it was more than they could handle."

"And those terrorists we killed in Minnesota?"

"Terrorists? No, they were not terrorists. Those were my men, some of whom were very dear to me. That is the reason you are here with me today."

"Your men?"

"Yes. Mr. Perozzi came to me wanting to hire some men. He paid me well, but after what happened to them, it was not enough. He had given me his assurance they would not have any problems, and they wouldn't have, had you not come along."

Winters took some satisfaction in knowing that. "Just protecting the innocent."

Mordulfah grunted. "Yes, well, thanks to you, I negotiated a much better deal than before."

Winters gave him a puzzled look.

"Mr. Winters, after that debacle, Perozzi came groveling to me for help. I relented, of course, but not before he surrendered to my terms."

"And what were those?"

"He gave me all of the upper Midwest."

Winters leaned back in his chair shocked at what he just heard, not sure, that he heard the man correctly. "Excuse me?"

"Yes, we are to be our own country."

Winters stared at the man in silence.

"When I said I would divide the country up, I meant that literally. I will control the upper Midwest from Michigan all the way to the Dakotas with its rich oil fields. I will import my people here and we will have a Sharia compliant country."

Winters took a few moments to take in what he had just heard. He didn't want to believe it, but then, considering everything that had happened to America in the past year, it wasn't much of a stretch. He felt like he was a pawn in a chess game, where just one sacrificial move had an overall consequence in a grander scheme. These people who had taken over the country were as evil as they came, and had probably been scheming for more than a decade, which would explain why the government had systematically cut the military in half. These were diabolical people, yet very patient.

"I see you're having a difficult time believing all of this, Mr. Winters."

Winters turned to him. "No, it's actually starting to make sense now."

"I've treated you to these meals for two reasons."

Winters was interested.

"First, as I said before, had it not been for you, I wouldn't be in this position."

"And the other reason?"

"I actually admire what you've done. You are much like our own freedom fighters. Fighting for something you believe in, and you've accomplished much with so few resources."

Winters didn't respond.

"But, unfortunately, I still must punish you for killing my men."

"I'm just curious about one more thing. Yesterday, you said you would come out on top of Perozzi."

"Yes, Mr. Perozzi and that fat little man, Mr. Reed, think they're going to remove me once I've completed my task."

"How do you know that?"

"He was too eager to agree to my terms, even after I came back and asked for North Dakota. No one in his right mind would give up something so valuable, that easily. So, it is obvious he intends to have me killed."

Winters had to give Mordulfah credit. He wasn't a stupid man.

"Little do they know that I have my own people within arm's reach of them and once I am established, they will be the ones eliminated."

"Knight takes King."

"Yes, indeed Mr. Winters, are you a chess player?"

"I've played."

"It's a shame we haven't the time to play a game. Though I suppose we've been playing each other for some time. Now, Mr. Winters, I think we've talked enough. I've much to do today. I would advise you to take what time you have left to finish your meal, for you too, have a big day ahead of you."

Mordulfah got up and paraded out of the room with his silk robe flowing behind him.

After eating, the guards led Winters back to his room downstairs, where he sat down on the bed. His mind was reeling from his conversation with Mordulfah. He shook his head as he realized he was, in some way, responsible for the man even being here. Yes, the government would still be forcing their dominant control over the Midwest, but they would be doing it without Mordulfah. Without him, Sadie would not presently have to submit to the degradation of having to marry the bastard. He hung his head, overwhelmed by what was happening.

Sadie sat on the floor of a large bedroom overflowing with pillows. Mordulfah's ladies, who were part of his inner circle, and charged with caring for his harem, surrounded her. They had dressed her in an all white Zaboun, a traditional wedding garment, which they fitted to her child's body.

She sat while the women put a covering on her head. She couldn't understand a thing they were saying and didn't really care. She felt as if she was floating in space, everything was so strange and seemed to be moving in slow motion.

The previous day they scrubbed her down and anointed her with oils before dousing her in perfumes. They spent the evening painting henna designs on her hands, which she hated. They smacked and scolded her when she tried to pull away from her caretakers.

Sadie wondered where Cole and Reese were, and if they were okay. She had not seen either of them since their arrival at the estate. She wished she could have given Cole the message Hadley told her in the jail cell at the police station. She wondered what was taking their rescuers so long, and hoped nothing bad had happened to them.

The older woman who was in charge offered her some food. She couldn't pronounce her name and silently called her Crappy, referring to her demeanor. The woman was quite unpleasant to her and to the other ladies, ordering them around and not doing much of anything else.

She picked a piece of flat bread and a small amount of cheese from the plate and nibbled on it. The bread was bland and the cheese tasted awful. Crappy placed some dates on her plate, for which Sadie pretended to be thankful.

After the ladies were done and everyone had eaten, Crappy motioned her to leave the room. "This is it," thought Sadie. She rose and one of the ladies straightened her dress and headscarf. She bravely followed them from the room.

All eyes were on Sadie as she entered another large room with glass windows that stood as tall as the ceiling, which was where Mordulfah stood waiting for her to arrive. Sadie raised her eyebrows in angst when everyone turned their heads as she walked across the room.

Mordulfah was dressed in a white gown that was covered by a sheer black robe with gold piping. On his head was a white scarf with a black headband.

Sadie thought he looked weird wearing what she considered a woman's dress. She could smell a spicy aroma given off by the incenses burning off to the side. The smoke wafted throughout the large room.

Wali stood next to Mordulfah, and she figured he was to officiate the ceremony. As she reached them, Mordulfah looked down at her and smiled, showing his bright white teeth. His eyes were as black as she had remembered.

Wali started the ceremony.

Sadie stood, scared, while her mind was in a fog listening to the recitation of the Fatihah, which Wali spoke in Arabic. She didn't understand the words. All she was thinking about was what would happen afterward. She could smell Mordulfah who reeked of a foul spice mixed in with body odor. She had never smelled anything like it. She turned her head to the side and sucked in a couple of breaths of fresh air. Crappy shot her a glare that meant she should pay attention. She quickly looked back at Wali who was still speaking gibberish.

CHAPTER 70

Scar led the Shadow Patriots to the vast estate where Edsel & Eleanor Ford had once resided and had now been taken over by Mordulfah for his personal residence. The estate of over eighty acres, sat on the shore of Lake St. Clair and had many outlying buildings.

Hadley had picked up some maps and pictures of the grounds, which were easily obtained because of its status as an historical site. The obvious way in was not through the front, but from the side, through a cluster of trees that would provide cover. This meant they needed to be certain of the occupancy of the house adjacent to the grounds.

Bassett and Hadley, being the youngest of the group, dressed in National Police uniforms to lend an air of authority, drove boldly into the neighboring driveway. They stepped out of a squad car they had appropriated, walked up, and knocked on the door.

A young Middle Eastern man answered the door. "May I help you?"

"I hope so," answered Bassett. "We got a call there was a prowler around here, and we're just checking it out."

"I've seen no such prowler," answered the man annoyed.

"If it's all the same to you, we need to make sure. We don't want Prince Mordulfah getting upset and chew out our boss, Captain Cox, if you know what I mean."

"Yes, but of course."

"Mind if we check around back?"

"No, of course not."

"Will we run into anyone back there? I mean are there others who are here right now?"

"No one else is here, they are all next door making preparations."

"For what?"

"Mordulfah's wedding."

"Oh, yes, of course, he's getting married again," said Bassett with a grin.

"Yes, he is once again adding to his wonderful family," he returned the smile.

"Must be nice, though, to be honest with ya, I can hardly deal with one wife."

"He is a man full of energy."

Bassett smiled to the man, and acted as if he was leaving. He turned and pulled a knife from inside his jacket, and then turned back around and slammed it into the man's stomach, pulled it out and shoved it in again. The dying man held his stomach as he buckled to his knees before falling sideways.

Bassett and Hadley dragged him inside. They closed the door, pulled their side arms and methodically checked the house to make sure the dead man had not lied to them.

After clearing the way, Bassett pulled out his radio and gave Scar the okay.

The Shadow Patriots, after losing four members in the rescue attempt at the police station, now numbering only fifty-six men, stormed up the driveway. Scar had divided the men into three groups. He would lead twenty men through the back of the house, while Bassett would take another twenty in through the front. He assigned Burns to stay off to the side with the remaining sixteen men to cover any attempt for reinforcements from the outlying buildings.

The assault was problematic. They were approaching from the side of the house where the wedding was most likely to be held. They would have to use the shrubbery as cover to maintain the element of surprise.

Having served in the Marines and seen combat in Grenada, Scar's training kicked into high gear as he ordered the men to move out.

Scar led his men through the trees to the far side, which extended to shoreline. The closer they got to the house the trees became less dense, and there was open ground in which guards could easily spot them. The men darted from tree to tree in small groups.

They were almost there. The sun was to the southeast, beaming bright rays through the windows. Scar could see they were having a wedding. He could see Sadie, in a white dress, standing next to a man in black and white ceremonial robes. Another had his back toward them. Meeks looked and whispered to Scar, "wedding crashers." Scar rolled his eyes.

They got down low and moved across the lawn using the shrubbery for cover. Scar peeked around the corner. A lone guard, armed with an AK-47 was looking out over the water, not expecting any trouble. Complacency was always the downfall of the overconfident.

Scar held up one finger, handed Meeks his rifle and pulled a knife. The big man sprang up, covered the twenty yards in mere seconds, and overpowered the guard. He sank his knife into the guard's gut, and grabbed him around the head to take him to the ground. Meeks rushed over and helped Scar pull the man into the bushes.

The rest of the men then gathered forward.

Scar pulled out the floor plan Hadley had given him. They were by the library, which was adjacent to the drawing room where the wedding was taking place. He pointed to a back door that would provide them entry to the main hall.

Scar grabbed the radio. "Bassett, they're in the drawing room, copy."

"I copy. We saw them as we approached. We're in front of the gallery. Got Jijis guarding the main entrance, over."

Scar thought about that. "As soon as the shooting starts they'll rush inside, over."

"Copy. We'll be right behind them. "

"We're entering now," said Scar putting the radio back in his jacket.

He turned the door handle and entered.

Voices were coming from around the corner. He held up five fingers and motioned to his right, signaling the men to go in that direction.

Scar and Meeks padded across the floor, and turned the corner into the main hall. Four Jijis stood with their backs toward them looking into the drawing room.

They both raised their M4 rifles. Pulled the triggers and dropped the guards where they stood.

Chaos ensued within the wedding party. Women started screaming as men pushed them aside while grabbing hold of their weapons and returning fire. Scar took aim and dropped another. Two Jijis ran to the groom and shielded him as they pushed him up the hallway into the gallery. Several other Jijis started to return fire. Bullets ripped into the woodwork by

Meeks, who ducked behind a couch. He peered over the couch and took careful aim, not wanting to shoot near Sadie.

Sadie tried to pull away from a man who had put his arm around her and was picking her up. She pulled on the Jiji's thumb and took a bite. The man yelled in pain and dropped her. Scar took aim and shot him before he could grab her again. The impact threw him against wall. Scar motioned her to get down.

With Sadie on the ground, Scar and Meeks sprayed the room emptying their mags, shooting at everyone including the women. They weren't going to take any chances the women might pick up a gun. Rounds shattered the windows. The wounded knocked over tables as they fell to the ground. Screams and gunfire echoed throughout the room.

Meeks yelled at Scar. "I'll get her." He crouched down and made his way to Sadie who wrapped her arms around his neck. Scar slammed in another magazine, and started picking off more Jijis.

Basset heard the gunfire coming from inside and peeked around the corner. As expected, the guards ran inside. Bassett and his men ran toward the entrance and found the six men huddled in the hallway taking fire from some of Scar's men. He and Nate kept to the side of the doorway. Nate pointed his shotgun through the entrance and pulled both triggers letting loose two charges of Number 4 buckshot. All six bad guys were down. Nate nodded to Scar's men at the far end of the hallway. He gave Bassett a half smile, but then noticed through a side window, Jijis were running down the hallway to the gallery.

He pointed it out to Bassett.

Nate hurried to the window and peeked in. A Jiji let loose a hail of gunfire shattering the window. Nate reloaded his shotgun. He took another look and immediately discovered they had not given up on him. He threw himself down as bullets whizzed by his head. He took a couple of deep breaths and jumped up, leading the way with his shotgun, firing as he moved.

Bassett stormed toward Nate's position, firing his M4 at the window.

They stood there for a moment, leaning against the building.

Nate took another look and saw a Jiji lying on the floor. He stole another glance inside and saw more Jijis in the gallery.

"They're making a stand in there," he said to Bassett.

Jijis began racing up the driveway. Bassett knew their position was exposed and vulnerable. He grabbed his radio. "Burns. We've got them coming up the drive."

"We see them. Where are you at?"

"Still by the entrance."

"Copy. We're moving in now."

"We got Jijis in the gallery. They'll spot you," said Bassett. Then he heard gunfire shattering the gallery windows.

Bassett yelled for everyone to get inside.

He turned to Nate. "Burns is running into trouble."

Nate understood the problem. "Get him out of there then."

Bassett took ahold of the radio. "Burns, abort your approach, abort."

It took a moment before he responded. "I've got three down. We're back in the trees."

Bassett drew in a deep breath. "Copy that."

He told Nate to hold their position at all cost. He then ran down the hallway and met Meeks holding onto Sadie. "What's your situation here, Meeks?"

"Everyone is dead or dying in there, and we got the rest of them pinned down in the gallery."

Scar hurried up to them.

Bassett looked at him. "Those guys in the gallery are stopping Burns cold. He's got three down and if we don't hurry, they'll have us pinned down in no time."

Scar understood the priority. "Let's go find the Captain and Reese, and get the hell out of here."

Bassett nodded, grabbed Hadley and ran upstairs. Scar scooted down the basement stairs. As soon as he reached the last step, a Jiji fired at him. Scar jerked back. He raised his M-4 and poured rounds into the wall where the Jiji hid. He ran over to it and found him lying in a pool of blood.

CHAPTER 71

Winters was at his lowest point emotionally since he had watched his friends die in front of him at the train station. He was about to give up when he heard gunfire abrupt outside. He sprang from his bed knowing the cause of the ruckus was his men making a rescue attempt.

He knelt down on the floor and waited. He couldn't help but smile at the thought of Mordulfah being killed.

He listened as the gunfire rang out from multiple places above him. He could make out the sound of AK47's mixed in with various other calibers, some of which were familiar to him as ones used by the Patriots. Then the gunfire slowed and became sporadic off to the side and more faint outside. It sounded like a standstill.

A few moments later, he heard shots fired immediately outside his room. He crawled on the floor to his bed, took hold of it and threw it over on its side to provide cover. Seconds later, he heard the door open. He looked up to see Scar enter the room.

"Captain, you alright?"

Winters got up off the floor. "I am now. What's happening? Where are the girls?"

"Meeks has got Sadie. We're still looking for Reese. We need to get going."

The two of them bounded up the stairs where they met Meeks and Sadie. Sadie ran to Winters and threw her arms around him.

He looked down at her. "You alright?"

She nodded.

The sound of footsteps stomping through the hall upstairs diverted their attention. Everyone turned to see Basset and Hadley bringing ten young girls, including Reese, down the staircase.

Reese was the first to hit the ground floor giving Winters a hug.

Winters was shocked to see so many young girls. He looked at Bassett. "Are there anymore?"

He shook his head. "We cleared all the rooms."

"Captain, we're going out the back," said Scar who got on the radio to Burns. "Burns get your men going." He then yelled down the hallway. "Nate, we're leaving out the back. Can you cover our backsides?"

Nate yelled back. "We're right behind you."

The Shadow Patriots stormed out the backdoor and headed in the direction from which they had come. Bassett led the way firing a volley into the gallery. Everyone kept low, running through the trees to their waiting vehicles as bullets whizzed overhead.

Nate's men brought up the rear, laying down more cover fire.

Winters held Sadie's hand tightly as they ran across the lawn. Elliott waved him over to his SUV. He helped Sadie into the back and then jumped in the front seat.

"Good to have you back, Captain," said Elliott.

"Glad you guys showed up."

Elliott started the truck and after confirming everyone was loaded up, peeled out down the driveway.

Winters grabbed the AR-15 sitting on the floor and lowered the side glass. He twisted sideways in the seat and pointed his weapon out the window. Jijis were cutting across the backyard of an outlying building, which sat parallel to their escape. He opened fire, taking two down. The rest dropped to the ground for cover.

"Up ahead, Captain," yelled Elliott.

Winters shifted his aim and pulled the trigger laying down a blanket of fire at more approaching Jijis.

The SUV made it to the end of the driveway. Elliott yanked the steering wheel hard to the left and stomped on the gas pedal.

Winters looked in the passenger side mirror at the rest of their trailing vehicles.

The convoy barreled down Lakeshore Dr.

Winters got on the radio. "Scar, how's it looking back there?"

"We got a couple of cars following us. They're keeping their distance though."

"Looks like they want to see where we're going."

"That's what I'm figuring."

He turned to Elliott. "Do we have an escape route?"

Elliott shook his head. "We were hoping to have killed them all."

"This road takes us right into Detroit, doesn't it?"

"Yep."

Winters spoke into the radio. "Scar, we can't go into the city. They're going to be waiting for us. We'll take a right and go west."

"We need to lose the bad guys following us," responded Scar.

"Elliott, who's driving the car behind us?"

"Burns."

Winters got back on the radio. "Listen up, everyone. Those Jijis and cops are not going to let us out of the city. More than likely, they're setting up roadblocks right now. First thing, we need to do is lose our tail. We'll make a right up ahead, and then I want Burns and whoever is right behind him to speed up and get ahead of our convoy. We'll pull over somewhere, while the rest of you keep going straight. We'll wait for the tail and take them out."

"Burns here, and copy that."

"I'm right behind Burns," said Nate.

"Sounds good, Captain. We'll wait for you a little up the way," said Scar.

Winters turned in his seat and saw Mr. Peterson sitting across from Sadie. "Mr. Peterson, I didn't even see you, what are you doing here?

"I was getting a little bored up north," he said.

"You've come to the right place," said Winters who then turned to Sadie, "You alright, hon?"

She nodded her head and gave him a half-hearted smile.

"Don't worry, okay, we'll get out of here," said Winters in a reassuring tone. He hoped he sounded convincing. He wasn't too sure, whether they would get out of there alive, or not. With Canada to the east and the interstate to the west, they were boxed in. There was no way they'd be able to get to the interstate without running into the cops. No doubt, Mordulfah had already called them.

For now, his spirits were soaring as he drove away from his impending torture. The prospect of being tortured had not been pleasant. He was glad to have Sadie back with him. Knowing she wouldn't have to experience what the other girls had gone through was a relief. If they didn't make it out of here, at least they would go down fighting, and on their own terms.

Elliott swung the SUV onto Marlborough St. and sped up leaving the rest of the convoy behind on the tree-lined street, which had no houses on either side.

"Was hoping for more houses," said Winters.

"I'll keep going."

They flew across Kercheval Ave.

"There's some up ahead."

Elliott slowed the vehicle down, drove it onto an overgrown lawn, and backed in behind the house. Burns and Nate followed suit across the street.

"This isn't ideal," said Winters.

"That tail will just blow right by us," said Elliott.

Winters picked the radio up. "Scar, I need you to stop when you go by us. We need to slow them down."

"You got it. Just let me know where you're at."

Winters, Elliott and Mr. Peterson got out and leaned up against the house. Winters looked across the street. Burns and Nate were both ready with their men. Winters held the radio in his hand and waited for his men to arrive.

Moments later they came.

"Scar, everyone is passing us now, so get ready."

The last vehicle came by him. Meeks stared right at Winters and give him a nod as they passed by. Another seventy-five yards, Scar slowed down and came to a dead stop.

Winters crouched low behind some shrubbery as two black cars slowed down, and then stopped right in front of them. Winters looked across the street, Burns and Nate had their men rushing the cars. He reacted the same, got up with his AR-15 raised to his shoulders and began firing.

Bullets ripped through both of the vehicles, cracking windows, and flattening the tires. Nate was the first to charge and he led with his shotgun. Burns and his men, keeping up the onslaught, followed him.

Winters approached the car. He opened the door and a bloodied Jiji fell out of the car. Nate's men kept firing into the second car. He then turned to Winters and nodded his head in satisfaction.

"I think we're done here, guys," said Winters.

They all hopped back in their vehicles and joined the rest of the men, who had pulled over up ahead. Winters looked forward to seeing the men and telling them everything, he had learned from Mordulfah. He knew the reunion would be short lived though, because they still had to get out of the city and he didn't think it would be a Sunday walk in the park.

CHAPTER 72

Green was late getting to his office after spending more time with his mother, discussing the people he needed to contact. He felt renewed after organizing what they should do. It never ceased to amaze him, just how strong and capable she was. He'd always known that about her, but never realized how deep it ran, since neither of them had ever been in the position they found themselves in now.

As Green entered the parking lot to the Lafayette building he thought about his personal commitment to his friend, Sam, and the decision he had made on what needed to done. It was a decision reinforced by the conversation he had with his mother and their plans to take down Perozzi and Reed. He thought about how careful he would have to be though, knowing there were few he would be able to trust, especially with Pruitt running around town gathering dirt to keep people in line. Green figured there were more people who had already been turned, than not, on the list he'd found. He wondered how much information Reed already possessed.

The first thing he needed to do today was to check into the office and find out if Reed had been asking for him. He didn't have much day-to-day contact with his boss and knew something was up if he had been looking for him. More importantly, he wanted to check for any messages from Bassett. He hadn't received any word since the corporal had called from Canada, and was worried because he knew he'd be involved in trying to rescue Winters. He hadn't heard any news from Detroit either, and wondered if today was the day they would attempt the rescue.

He greeted his secretary and collected messages from various people in the task force he was heading. He spent the next couple of hours returning calls and handling their requests. It was noon before he received word the

Shadow Patriots had raided the police station during the night. Details were few, but he did learn they had killed Captain Cox. Green leaned back in his chair with a satisfied grin on his face. He had no doubt the Shadow Patriots were now on their way to Mordulfah's to get Winters.

He decided to call Reed to see what his reaction would be to this new development. He picked up the phone and dialed his number.

"What can I do for you, Major?" asked Reed

"Sir, have you heard about what happened in Detroit?"

"Yes, I just heard."

"The details are a little sketchy, and they don't mention Winters."

"He wasn't there," said Reed in harsh tone.

"Well, that's good news then," said Green pretending to be happy.

"Maybe not, because I haven't been able to get a hold of Mordulfah, which is unusual."

"Do you think the rebels were aware he was holding Winters at his place?"

"I'm not sure, but most likely."

"Do you think the rebels will attempt a rescue?"

"That would be my guess, and since I can't reach Mordulfah, I would say it's a damn good possibility it's happening right now."

"What do you want me to do?"

"There's not a whole hell of a lot we can do but wait."

"I understand."

Reed hung up on Green.

He couldn't help but smile after talking to Reed. He could hear the anger in his voice. Green knew Winters represented everything Reed was fighting. Winters was all about the American people yearning to be free. Reed's mind had to be spinning, knowing he wasn't as invisible as he thought he was. Winters was nothing but a fly in the ointment, but he was certainly making quite an impact with only a small complement of men. If there were more Winters' out there and they took the same steps, then there would be such a force it would be impossible to reckon with. Green had taken great pleasure in his conversation with Reed.

Green decided to excuse himself for lunch, but his main objective was to find Pruitt. He hoped the man would be outside waiting to follow him, making his task that much easier.

CHAPTER 73

DETROIT MICHIGAN

Everyone got out and crowded around Winters, shook his hand, and welcomed him back. He thanked each of one of them and exchanged words of gratitude for risking their lives to come for him and the girls. Winters basked in the moment as everyone stood around and talked about what they had just done. The triumph overshadowed the three men they lost. Although sad as it was, they were lucky to have lost only three and have no others wounded.

"That Mordulfah guy sure liked to keep busy," said Meeks gesturing over to the young girls.

"I had no idea they were even there," said Winters.

"What now, Captain?" asked Scar, who was more than happy to shift the burden of command back to Winters.

"If you were them, what would you be doing?"

"I'd be boxing us in," said Scar.

"Here we go again," said Nate.

"Nate, ye of little faith," laughed Meeks putting his arm around his shoulder. "We've been in much deeper doo-doo."

"Yeah, and I'm getting sick of it."

Winters gave Elliott a half smile. "Anyone got a Detroit map?"

Hadley came forward. "Right here."

Winters looked at him and recognized him from South Bend. "What's your name?"

"I'm Don Hadley, I'm a cop, or was a cop."

Winters heard his accent. "You from the South?"

"Waco, Texas, sir."

"Well, glad to have a Texan on our side," he said, unfolding the map. "Now, where are we, Don?"

Hadley pointed out their location.

"Okay, so we've got Canada behind us and I-94 up ahead and downtown to our south."

"Be nice to jump into Canada," said Meeks.

"They have the border closed down," said Hadley.

Winters kept looking at the map. "We need to check out the interstate, see if it's being patrolled."

Elliott, Burns and Taylor volunteered and took Hadley with them.

Winters looked around the decrepit neighborhood. "We might have to find an abandoned house we can hole up in."

"That won't be too difficult," chuckled Meeks, looking around.

Winters watched Elliott drive away, and then ordered the guys to hide the vehicles behind the empty houses. Afterward, they gathered in groups and talked amongst themselves.

Winters walked over to Sadie and Reese, who were sitting on the back porch with the other girls. They were making small talk with the girls, trying to comfort them. They were scared and yet relieved to be away from Mordulfah.

Sadie stood up and grabbed Winters' hand when he approached the group. "This is Cole, and he's going to get us all out of here."

Winters waved to them. "You girls are safe now, alright, and we'll get you out of here in no time, okay?"

Their expressions brightened some and they nodded their heads.

"Will you take us home?" one of them asked.

Winters didn't want to disappoint them, but felt it better to whitewash their true situation for now. "We will at some point, but for now we need to get out of here and then see what happens."

He sat down and put his arm around Sadie.

"That's some dress you've got on there."

"I can't wait to get it off, and wash this stuff off my hands."

Reese reached for her hand. "It's a dye so you won't be able to wash it off right away."

"I won't?"

"No, but it'll fade, and if we can find some salt and olive oil, we can get it off faster."

"How long will it take?" she asked rubbing her hands.

"Maybe a week."

"Ugh."

Winters laughed to himself. "I hope you guys weren't too scared."

Sadie looked at Reese. "We knew they were coming."

"Yeah, but we didn't know when," said Reese.

"Oh?"

"Don told us," said Sadie. "We wanted to tell you, but they took you upstairs before we found out and then…" she stopped.

"Then, what?"

"I saw that they beat you up and you didn't look too good."

"It's okay, it all worked out." He looked at Reese, wanting to know if they'd hurt her, but wasn't sure she'd tell him the truth.

She seemed to know what he wanted to ask. "No one touched me. They threw me in a room, and pretty much ignored me."

A sense of relief came over Winters. "So glad to hear it."

Scar and Meeks came over and joined them.

Again, Sadie introduced them to the new arrivals.

"This is Meeks and Scar and they're both pretty funny."

"I'm the funny one," said Meeks. "This one, not so much, he's more of a goof ball, if you ask me."

Scar wrapped his arm around Meeks head. "Don't listen to a thing he says, he only wishes he was me."

"See, I told you," laughed Sadie.

Winters stood up. "So what happened to you guys back at South Bend?"

Scar told Winters everything that happened to them, and how they managed to get up to Canada to pick up Nate and the guys.

"How's the leg?" Winters asked Meeks.

"Not too bad, got painkillers in me that don't make me loopy."

"Not any more than usual," smiled Scar. "My boy here is definitely slowing down."

"I can still outrun you," said Meeks. He turned to Sadie. "Oh, I've got something of yours."

She looked at him, full of curiosity.

Meeks pulled out the Ruger .22 he had given her. "You dropped this, and thank goodness you did."

She took the gun. "Why was it a good thing?"

"It's how we knew you guys had been captured. I knew you wouldn't lose it. As soon as I found it, we dashed over to where they were holding you. That's how we found out where they were taking you."

Sadie broke into a prideful smile, knowing she had been of some help.

Winters gave her a friendly bump and then looked back up at Scar. "So, Amber is taking care of the others back in South Bend. How bad are they?"

"Not too bad, they're just banged up a little."

Winters was impressed with everything they had done. He couldn't have asked for better men than these and only wished he had more. He knew he would have to gather a lot more if they were to take down this enemy. From what he had learned from Mordulfah, he knew the man had unlimited resources. There were also enough radical Islamic men in the Detroit area he could call upon. All they needed was a leader and a cause. Ironically, it was all the American people needed as well. Winters believed once the truth was out, citizens would have the courage to come out of the shadows and stand tall.

After Scar finished his story, Winters relayed all he had learned from Mordulfah. As he was telling them, the rest of the Shadow Patriots gathered around and listened to the shocking revelation. Not a single one of them was left without a stunned look on his face that soon turned to anger.

"Makes you wonder what else the government has been up to," said Scar.

"It's like they set up everything that's gone down," observed Meeks.

"They probably even set the former President up, so they could get their man in there," said Mr. Peterson. "It's happened throughout history, so why not here."

Everyone nodded their heads.

"Well, it sure as hell isn't going to happen on my watch," said an angry Nate. "I'm going to personally kill this Mordulfah son-of-a-bitch."

The guys all gave a hearty cheer.

"Ain't nobody gonna sell off my country," he added.

"Yeah, but what about the war out west?" asked Meeks.

"Them damn Chinese will get what's coming to them," he finished.

"Hopefully, if we can get our house in order, then we can drive them into the Pacific Ocean," said Winters.

More cheers among the men.

"That'll be way down the road, though. First things first, when we get out of here, we've got to gather a larger force and drive these terrorists out of Michigan," said Winters.

"Yeah, but then what?" asked Meeks.

"Washington," said Winters. "Somehow we need to expose Perozzi and Reed."

Bassett spoke up. "Major Green might be able to help."

Winters turned to him. "How's that?"

Everyone turned to Bassett. "He's stationed in Washington now."

This was news to Winters. "Since when?"

"Couple of weeks ago. Believe it or not, he works for Reed. It's why I was able to come and warn you. Major Green wanted to know about the cops you killed, and sent me here to find out what was really going on. I happened to get here just before Cox found out where you were"

"Wow, I was a little surprised to see you in South Bend. So have you talked to the Major?"

"Yes, and I told him all about Mordulfah. He said he'd look into it."

Winters was pleased, but his euphoria didn't last long because he knew that even though they had escaped the National Police before, they now had a more motivated enemy. This one would want his head on a platter and would stop at nothing to get Sadie and the other girls back.

CHAPTER 74

G reen had gone to a deli to grab some take out and then headed over to Lafayette Park to eat. He sat on a bench eating a ham and cheese sandwich, all the while keeping his eyes peeled for Pruitt. The day had warmed up since the early morning, which had been cloudy and brisk. The park was a favorite of the Washington crowd to walk around during their lunch hour. The cherry trees were past full bloom and had littered the ground with their pink and white blossoms. The air still carried their sweet aroma. Squirrels chased each other around the grounds shaking out their legs from the long winter. Any tourists that had come to D.C. had already gone home after the full bloom. There weren't as many tourists because business had dried up once the war started. Most everyone enjoying the park these days, worked in the surrounding offices.

He stared at the White House, wondering if the President was up to speed on what was happening in Detroit. Green figured the man didn't even know who the Shadow Patriots were. It would seem the President only did Perozzi's bidding while enjoying the trappings of the office. Pretending to care about what was going on in the country while golfing, holding parties, and meeting with foreign dignitaries, making them promises he would never keep.

Thirty minutes passed as he sat on the bench in Lafayette Park and there had been no sight of Pruitt. He finished his sandwich and decided to head to Bethesda to see if Pruitt might be at home.

He drove past the house, but didn't see the Porsche in the driveway or any lights on inside. He parked his car up the street and decided to wait.

ALEXANDRIA VIRGINIA

Pruitt found Sarah Green's address and headed for Alexandria. He had learned everything he needed to know regarding Sam White and his searches on Perozzi and Reed. He was elated when he learned Green was a troublemaker who needed to be taken out. It didn't take a genius to figure out Green was involved with the rebels, and plotting against Perozzi and Reed. He had just received the evidence from his man at the State Department. The information had cost him a pretty penny, but it was worth much more than the price he'd had to pay. Once he took care of Green, and his friend, Sam White, he'd report to Reed and collect his expenses, and then some.

After seeing his house had been broken into yesterday, he figured it had to have been Green. Nothing of value had been taken and the only things disturbed were the photos he'd had been stupid enough to leave out in the open. Green, no doubt, had made copies from his printer. He'd get those photos back even if it meant roughing up the mother, which was no problem for him.

He arrived at her home and noticed only one car in the driveway. He figured Mrs. Green was at home alone. He continued for another block and parked on the side of the street. He grabbed his gun, stuffed it in his waistband, got out of his car and looked up and down the quiet street. Not seeing anyone, he sauntered up the street, reached the door and rang the bell.

CHAPTER 75

DETROIT MICHIGAN

Winters worried about the girls. They were all tired and were now sleeping in the SUV's. He would do everything he could to protect these girls. They had all been through a lot and had endured things they never should have seen. Of course, it was a different world now, a world where evil prevailed over the land. Winters found it heartbreaking to discover this evil included using children for sexual pleasure. He had a difficult time wrapping his mind around it when the discovery was first made. After meeting Mordulfah and seeing what kind of scum he and his kind really were, it became clear. To them, women were nothing but property. The more he thought about it, the angrier he became. He needed to get off the subject and consider their current situation.

Elliott and company, had returned from reconnoitering the interstate. As expected, the cops had been smart and positioned vehicles at intervals up and down the freeway to maximize the patrolling of the road. The cops weren't taking any chances, and were hoping to box in the Shadow Patriots. Winters knew it would only be a matter of time before the cops, and Jijis, would start going street-to-street looking for them. His options were few, and he knew they would have to discover the holes in their enemy's lines to make their escape. Thanks to Colonel Brocket, Scar had come back from Canada with plenty of supplies and ammunition. Winters had decided to wait for the cover of darkness to escape, and nighttime couldn't come fast enough.

He thought about what they could do, and decided to use Bassett's recent combat experience, fighting house to house in the Middle East.

He approached Bassett. "Corporal, you have more experience in this type of setting, what do you think of our options to escape."

"Already been thinking about it, Captain."

"Glad to hear it, because I'm open to suggestions."

Bassett laid out his plan and Winters concluded it had an excellent chance for success.

Winters then got everyone's attention. "Guys, I'm going to have Corporal Basset brief you on our strategy."

Everyone nodded and moved over to the makeshift table they had put together, and looked down at the map.

"First thing we need is reconnaissance," said Bassett. "We need to find their weak points and then exploit them. The things we're looking for is their quantity and the quality of that manpower. We need to stay away from the battle hardened men. The Jijis will be the most experienced, but not all of them are trained soldiers either. You'll be able to tell by how they walk, how they carry themselves, are their weapons "at the ready", meaning are the weapons at a forty-five degree angle. My first choice would be to go through the cops. These guys won't have any combat experience, otherwise they'd be out West fighting."

Everyone nodded.

"We need to be ghosts out there, no contact what so ever, we don't want them to even know we were there. Radio communications at a minimum, keep the volume down, and whisper into the mics."

The men listened intently to what Bassett was telling them. When he was satisfied everyone was on the same page, he formed them into six, two-man teams.

CHAPTER 76

BETHESDA MARYLAND

Major Green had been waiting for Pruitt to show up for the last couple of hours. When he was a no-show, Green decided to go back to his office. He had a growing concern for what was happening while he'd been waiting for Pruitt. He would check in with his secretary and then come back to see if there was any activity in Bethesda.

As soon as he arrived, Grace gave him a stack of messages. He took his jacket off and thumbed through them ignoring the ones that could be put off till tomorrow. Toward the end of the pile was the one he was looking for. It was his contact at the National Police here in the district. He gave the man a call and learned the rebels had attacked Mordulfah's compound and freed Winters.

They killed over twenty of his men and some women as well, but Mordulfah had escaped unharmed. Green also learned they were still in pursuit of Winters and assumed he had not escaped the city. The local cops were going street-to-street looking for him. Green thanked his contact for the update.

He put the phone down and tried to contain his delight in the news, but couldn't help himself and threw his arms up with clenched fists. It was good news and he reveled in it for a few minutes. He just hoped they made it out of the city.

He continued to go through the stack of notes and decided he could put everything off until tomorrow. He grabbed his jacket and headed back to Pruitt's house. He purchased some takeout to tide him over in case he would have to wait for a while.

Green had parked the car up the street after seeing no lights on inside. After a few hours had passed, he grew restless and bored. He wondered how cops could sit hour after hour in a car during a stakeout. He had long ago finished eating his take out and wished he smoked cigarettes just to have something to do. He thought about breaking into the house again, but decided it wasn't such a good idea, especially if Pruitt didn't come home. Darkness had consumed the landscape and homes up and down the street were awash with light.

He looked at his watch. He decided he had waited long enough and headed home.

Green walked into his mother's home expecting the smell of dinner wafting through the air, but instead saw his mother sitting in a chair in the living room. She looked panic stricken. He stopped cold when he heard the cocking of a revolver. He found Pruitt pointing a Smith and Wesson .357 in his direction. He was wearing yet another golf shirt, only this one was a multiple colored stripped one.

"What are you doing here?" yelled Green.

"So, you do know me then, that's a start. Now, be a good soldier boy and slowly remove your jacket."

Green was pissed at himself for allowing Pruitt to learn he knew him. He removed his jacket and let it fall to the floor.

"Thought you might be carrying. Now, don't get any funny ideas, cause I'm quite a good shot, but even at this range it wouldn't take an expert to put a rather large hole in you."

Green removed his Army issued Beretta M9 pistol and dropped it on top of his jacket.

"Now move over to the couch."

Pruitt waited until Green sat down before picking up his pistol. He released the mag and tucked it in his pocket along with the round he removed from the chamber.

Green shot daggers at Pruitt. "Now, you mind telling me what you want."

"What I want, are all the copies you made yesterday."

"I don't know what you're talking about."

Pruitt moved over to Green's mother, and slapped her across the face.

She let out a yelp, but recovered quickly and glared at him as if to say, "Is that all you got."

273

Green stood up, but stopped in mid stride when Pruitt put his .357 to her head.

"Don't think I won't do it. Now sit back down," yelled Pruitt.

Green hesitated for a moment and then relented.

"I know it was you who broke into my place yesterday."

"Is it your place, Pruitt, or are you just a house pet for Reed."

Pruitt let out a laugh. "You think you're a bad ass, eh Major?"

Green didn't respond.

"Talk about amateur hour, you break in through a window but don't take anything. Hell, I had a wad of cash sitting in my room, so much that even my housekeeper is afraid to take it. She told me she thought she had heard someone sneaking around. I knew it had to be you. I'll give you credit for finding out who I was."

"It wasn't hard to spot someone wearing an ugly bright red golf shirt. It was about as bad as the one you have on now, but not quite."

"Oh, you made me the first night, touché. You're not as dumb as I thought. Now tell me, where are the copies?"

Green thought about his options, and decided they were few. He figured Pruitt would kill them as soon as he got the copies. Desperately wanting to get this man away from his mother, he began to lie. "They're not here."

"Where then?" asked Pruitt.

"I have them at my office?"

Pruitt slapped his hand across her face again.

This time the impact knocked her out of her chair. She landed on the carpeted floor where she curled up in pain. Green stood again, but Pruitt aimed the revolver in his face.

"You like hitting women, you piece of crap."

"If it gets the job done, what do I care? Now, Major, I know you're not stupid enough to have left 'em at your office."

Green looked down at his mother and back at Pruitt. "They're in the car."

"Well, let's go get them."

Pruitt waved his gun at Green motioning him outside. They both turned and headed toward the door. Just as Green pulled it opened, Pruitt heard the soft shuffle of approaching feet on the carpet.

CHAPTER 77

DETROIT MICHIGAN

Night had fallen over the city, and the sky was cloudy and moonless. Streetlights remained standing tall, but with no power, stood without purpose. The darkness only veiled the despair, that permeated the streets. There was an uneasy creepiness in the dilapidated neighborhoods, which had overgrown lawns, and boarded up houses, some with the roofs caving in. Trash littered the streets.

Bassett had led the six teams out on foot, disappearing into the darkness. Rather than go closer to downtown Detroit, which the cops had blockaded on I-75, they decided to try their luck a little further north along I-94. They would move the vehicles block by block through the dark streets.

Because of their injuries, Elliott and Meeks stayed behind with Winters who would coordinate with the recon teams and get everyone else ready to move out.

Winters had them all loaded up in vehicles and ready to go. All the drivers stayed huddled around the first truck. The atmosphere was tense, and everyone remained silent, waiting for word to move out.

A quiet breeze swirled around the men, and was a welcomed respite for Winters who felt beads of sweat run down the sides of his face. He took his hat off so he could feel the cool air. He was nervous and could hear his heart beating. He looked at the men, who stood like statues, staring down at the radio that was sitting on the hood of Elliott's SUV.

They listened to the whispering chatter go back and forth between the teams. They spotted their hunters driving through the neighborhoods to the east. As they announced the streets, Meeks would turn his military flashlight, equipped with a red lens, onto the map. Under the soft red glow, he marked all the occupied locations. It was easy to see that the cops were methodically closing in on their position.

Finally, Bassett announced he had located a safe place for them to move. "We're clear on Warren Ave," whispered Bassett. "Up to Yorkshire Rd."

Winters picked up the radio. "Copy."

Meeks found the intersection. "Few blocks over, and about a mile up."

Everyone scrambled to their vehicles.

Winters got in the passenger seat and glanced at Elliott behind the wheel. He gave him a reaffirming nod. Elliott turned the key and eased back out onto the street.

Maneuvering through the dark streets, without using the headlights, was not an easy task. Winters hunched forward, over the dashboard, trying get a better view. The group of vehicles stayed close together. Winters counted the number of streets they passed and soon came to Warren Ave. Elliott turned right onto the six-lane road. He was able to pick up a little speed on the wider road.

Slowly they made it to Yorkshire Road and parked between the boarded up businesses lining the street.

Winters picked the radio up. "Bassett, we're here."

"Copy, I'm just a few blocks away."

"Captain, you've got two coming your way on Outer Drive," said Scar.

Winters quickly look down at the map. "Elliott, we just passed that street, go, go, go."

Elliott let off the brake and pulled forward.

Winters kept his eye on the passing buildings. "Pull into this parking lot and go around back."

The sixteen-vehicle convoy followed suit.

Winters got out and ran back to the street. Meeks and Elliott joined him as they made their way to the curb. Two cop cars stopped in the intersection, and then started coming toward them at a snail's pace. Both cars had spotlights pointed at the buildings, searching, as they passed.

Winters, Elliott and Meeks scrambled back to their vehicles and waited for the two cars to pass them.

"Bassett, those two are headed up Warren," said Winters in a low voice.

"I'm watching them."

The two cops reached the intersection of Cadieux Rd and Chandler Park Dr. and stopped. Burns reported that squad cars were all over Mack Ave. Winters looked at the map, and noted the cops surrounded them more tightly than before. He figured they would not be able to sneak out of this one.

Thirty minutes later, all the recon teams came back to report.

Bassett and Hadley were the lasts ones to return. "We humped it past Cadieux, and saw that they're posted at all the major intersections."

"They're all up and down Mack Ave," said Burns, pointing to the map, "and, as you can see, Mack Ave runs closer to the interstate, which narrows our escape."

"Funny thing is, I didn't see any Jijis," said Scar.

"Nor did we," said Bassett.

The others acknowledged the same thing.

"That seems strange," said Winters.

"Jackasses must still be licking their wounds," said Nate.

"Regardless, they seem to have plenty enough looking for us," said Winters. "And we're back to square one, without an escape."

"Can't we keep snaking through the neighborhoods?" asked Elliott.

"Be sunup before we could finish," offered Bassett.

"We're going to have to blast our way through, Captain," said Nate.

"They're not at all alert, Captain," said Bassett. "We noticed the cops on Cadieux looking bored and goofing around."

"Then let's take the suckers out one at a time," said Nate.

Winters listened to the men go back and forth with different suggestions. He looked back down at the map and noticed a high school a few blocks away on Cadieux. Then an idea struck him and a wily smile came across his face. "Guys, I've got an idea."

Everyone stopped talking and looked at Winters.

Nate let out a snicker.

"Whatcha you got, Captain," asked Scar eagerly.

He pointed at the map. "There's a high school right over here."

Everyone looked at the map.

"Bassett, you said those cops, just up the street from the school, are not paying much attention."

Bassett nodded.

"Think you can take them out quietly?"

"How quiet?"

"No gunfire."

"Won't be easy, but yeah, it's doable," Bassett replied.

"Okay, so once we do that, we'll drive their cars over to the high school."

"Then what, Captain?" asked Meeks.

"Nate, you think you could set the school on fire, and I mean the whole thing?"

"Oh, hell yeah, I could."

"Once it's up and going, we'll get on their radios and tell everyone we're trapped in the school. Hadley, you can help with that, right?"

Hadley nodded.

"I like it, Captain," said Scar. "Should draw enough of them in."

Bassett looked doubtful. "You think this will work?"

Scar patted him on the shoulder. "I told you before, we didn't get this far by being careful."

"When we pull out we'll take one of their cars so we can monitor their communications," said Winters.

Bassett led a small team consisting of Scar, Hadley and Nate through the backyards up to Cadieux and circled around behind the four cops. They were out of their cars leaning against the fenders talking to one and another.

Bassett thought about what to do. "We need to get their attention directed away from us," he whispered. He turned to Nate, "you crazy enough to do something?"

Nate gave him a half smile.

"Can you get back around and approach them looking drunk?"

Nate let loose a small laugh and took off while the others waited in the shadows.

A few moments later, Nate came stumbling up the street. The cops looked his way and started moving toward him.

"You there! Who are you?" shouted the tallest of the four.

"Who me?" slurred Nate.

"This guy is plastered," said the tall cop.

Bassett watched as Nate fell to the pavement and struggled to get back up. Bassett withdrew his knife and waited until the cops were ten yards away from Nate. He gave a signal to Hadley and Scar. The three of them sprang toward the cops.

The cops' backs were toward them as Bassett closed in. When he reached the first cop, he thrust his knife into the man's side. He immediately withdrew it and went for the one next to him. The first cop screamed as he dropped to the ground in pain. The second one grabbed Bassett's arm as the knife penetrated him. Scar jumped on top of him, his big frame took the second cop to the ground. Scar grabbed his head, jerked it up, and then slammed it into the asphalt. Hadley threw himself into the third cop. The two of them fell into a roll. Hadley found himself at a disadvantage as the cop rolled over on top of him, and started punching him in the face.

Nate leapt up, faced the approaching tall cop, and kicked him in the groin. He sliced his knife through the cop's throat while he was kneeling in pain. Nate then lunged over to the cop who was on top of Hadley. He grabbed the man's hair and pulled him back. Nate kicked him in the face until he stopped moving.

Nate helped Hadley up. "You alright?"

"I'm good."

The four of them breathed heavily as they recovered from their efforts. They dragged the dead cops behind a house and signaled Winters to meet them at the school. Finally, they moved the patrol cars to the school parking lot, where Nate proceeded to break into the boarded up building. He found a couple of five gallon buckets, and went back to one of the cars, punched a hole in the fuel tank, and collected the gasoline.

Winters arrived at the school just as Nate was putting the final touches on the trail of fuel he had sloshed up and down the hallways.

"We're all set, Captain," said Scar.

Winters looked at him. "You and Bassett grab the cop car. Hadley, once we're a few blocks up, you let Corporal Bassett handle the call, you tell him what to say."

"Oh?"

"Your Texas drawl might be a dead giveaway, besides, Bassett has experience with this type of thing too."

Hadley shrugged.

Nate came outside and walked up to them. "Got it already, Captain. I even planted ammo in some adjoining rooms. Should throw them off a bit more."

"Nice touch, Nate."

"Well, I figure it worked once, why not again."

Winters gave him the go ahead.

Nate and Scar walked inside and down a long hallway before turning down another. They could smell the gasoline fumes rising from the floor before they reached it. Nate had spilled the fuel towards the back of the school. He had chosen a few classrooms, and drizzled the gas out into the hallway.

Nate stopped and looked down at the small puddle that had gathered and hesitated.

"What's the matter?" asked Scar.

"Gasoline is not the best accelerant to be using. If we're not careful, this will blow up in our faces."

"What do you do want to do?"

Nate looked around, found some paper, and crumpled it up. He then lit it, stepped back from the puddle, and threw it in.

The gasoline exploded and fire swooshed into the classrooms, instantaneously engulfing them. The two men hurried back up the hallway and out the door.

"It's looking good, guys," said Nate.

Meeks turned to Scar, "Every kid's fantasy at one time or another."

Scar gave him a sideways glance. "Uh, not every kid. I'm not quite sure I even know who you are anymore."

Meeks rolled his eyes. "Whatever."

The Shadow Patriots rolled out of the parking lot and picked their way through the neighborhood to the back parking lot of what looked like an old car dealership on Mack Ave.

Winters got out and walked over to the cop car. "Okay, you know what to do, Corporal."

Bassett nodded and turned his attention to the police radio. He started breathing heavily and worked himself up. "10-99 10-99, shots fired,"

"What's your twenty?"

"I'm at the old high school at Cadieux. It's the rebels, we've chased them inside the school."

"All units, all units, shots fired at Cadieux and Warren. All units respond."

"My partner's in the building, I'm going in."

Bassett put the mic down. "That should keep them busy."

The Shadow Patriots watched as dozens of cop cars, with their lights flashing and sirens screaming, rushed past them on Mack Ave. Winters wondered how long they had before their ruse was discovered.

The radio was abuzz with chatter as the cops arrived, shouting that the place was on fire and they couldn't locate the cops on scene. After a few moments, the cops reported gunfire inside the school.

Winters ordered Bassett up Mack Ave. After the all clear, they moved their convoy across Mack Ave and onto Chalfonte Ave and traveled through the neighborhood. A few more turns and they finally returned to Mack Ave. Bassett kept the lead in the squad car as they made their way north to Interstate 69.

Winters was satisfied with the distance they were putting between them and the burning school. He followed their progress on the map. He studied the map and noticed that Mack Ave came close to where Mordulfah had held him prisoner. The close proximity worried him. He wondered if Jijis would be patrolling the area to protect Mordulfah. The more he thought about it the more he wanted to get to the interstate as soon as they could.

He got on the radio and asked Bassett to check out the interstate at Vernier Rd. A few minutes later, Bassett gave them the all clear. They were no more than a mile away. A sense of relief came over Winters, but was short lived when Scar came on the radio.

"We've got trouble, guys."

CHAPTER 78

BETHESDA MARYLAND

Major Green reached the door and started to open it, turning his body slightly to the right toward Pruitt who was close behind him. Green had the door halfway open when his mother came rushing toward them. Green made his move. He spun to his right grabbing Pruitt's pistol with one hand and his wrist with the other. The gun moved away from his body as a bullet spat into the door just as his mother slammed into Pruitt. The three of them stumbled into the dining room. Mrs. Green fell to the floor, hitting her head. Major Green threw his weight into Pruitt as he tried to fight for control of the gun. Green could feel the heat of the barrel as he tightened his grip around it. He threw a haymaker into Pruitt's right cheek. The blow sent them to the floor. Green twisted around to get on top. He then tried to wrench the gun free by slamming it on the hardwood floor. Pruitt broke free from Green's grip and swung his arm arcing it from one side to the other. Green met it halfway and grabbed Pruitt's forearm. The gun went flying across the room. Green jumped off him and scrambled across the floor to retrieve it. He reached for the revolver, picked it up, and turned around to find Pruitt holding Mrs. Green around her chest with a knife to her throat.

Green raised the .357 aiming it right at Pruitt's head. "Let go of her."

"Or what, Major?" demanded Pruitt as he broke Mrs. Green's skin. Blood started to trickle down her throat. "Go ahead Major, let's see how good a shot you are."

Green watched Pruitt get on his feet, dragging his mother with him as a shield. Her eyes didn't give a hint of giving up.

"Now, your mom and I are going to walk to the door, and I'm going to walk out of here."

"I don't think so," said a defiant Green.

Pruitt pressed the knife in a little further, causing more blood to seep down her chest. "You get any closer and it goes in all the way."

Pruitt pulled Sarah back into the foyer. Green kept his gun aimed at Pruitt's head, but the man kept weaving back and forth, using his mother's head as a shield. Green kept following Pruitt's bobbing head waiting for the right moment. They made it to the entrance. Pruitt kicked the door open and took another step backwards. He stumbled slightly over the jacket Green had dropped when he first came in. Mrs. Green used the opportunity to grab Pruitt's pinkie and twist it in an unnatural way. Pruitt let out a scream and tried to jerk his hand from her. Green fired the gun twice, hitting him in the head. Brain matter plastered the wall as Pruitt collapsed to the floor.

CHAPTER 79

DETROIT MICHIGAN

W inters felt the blood rush to his face when Scar had yelled his warning of trouble into the radio. He grabbed his radio. "Whatcha got Scar?"

"Got three cars on my tail."

"Are they cops?"

"Don't look like it. I think they're Jijis."

Winters shot a glance at Elliott. "Step on it." He looked at the map. They had just passed Cook Rd. He got back on the radio. "Let's try and outrun them."

As Elliott step on the gas, Winters tightened his grip on his AR-15.

A few moments later, Bassett's frantic warning lit up the radio. "I've got multiple cars coming down Vernier Rd from the east."

Winters instantly knew they were Jijis coming from Mordulfah's compound.

Elliott kept his foot on the gas pedal.

Bassett came back. "There's three of them and they're turning onto Mack. They're headed right toward you."

Winters looked ahead and saw the headlights coming at them. Off to his right was an empty field. "Go right," he yelled.

Elliott threw the vehicle into a hard right and crashed through a fence, onto what looked like a baseball field. The bouncing SUV fishtailed through the overgrown grass. The rest of the convoy followed him.

Elliott jumped the SUV across a paved road and onto another field. It was a golf course and they were fishtailing across the greens, causing extensive damage to the still maintained fairways.

"Everyone's going in separate directions," exclaimed Elliott.

Winters got on the radio. "Scar, what's happening back there?"

"We're taking fire. We pulled into a parking lot to the right of the field. We got nowhere to go."

"Who's with you?"

"Burns."

"Bassett where are you?"

"We're coming down Mack now."

"Get over to Scar."

Elliott kept maneuvering around the well-tended greens trying to lose a car that was following and now shooting at them. Winters turned to Elliott. "Pull around those trees and let us out." Winters twisted in his seat and looked at Mr. Peterson. "You up for it?"

"It's what I'm here for."

Winters went to give Sadie and Reese a reassuring look, but noticed both were chambering a round in their pistols. Their faces were in rapt attention as Reese pushed the button down to lower the window. She twisted in her seat to line up a shot. Winters silently thanked Meeks for their training.

Elliott circled around the trees and stopped. Winters and Mr. Peterson jumped out. Elliott stepped on the gas as soon as the doors shut.

They both raced for the cover of the trees.

Winters breathed heavily and raised his rifle to his shoulder. "Aim for the tires first and then give them everything we got."

A black Mercedes roared around the end of the trees heading toward them. The two men rushed out from their cover and squeezed off long bursts. Bullets pelted the car. The left front tire blew out immediately. Winters dashed forward as the black car swerved toward them. He shot at the windshield. Cracks raced across it. The car came to a stop and the doors flew open. The front passenger rolled out firing. Mr. Peterson dropped to the ground, blasted the man, and then took out another as he tried to exit the rear door. Winters jumped in front of the car. Two Jijis leapt out. He took aim and fired through the glass. He held his rifle tightly and swung around the open doors. Both Jijis were floundering on the grass. Winters felt his Mr. Hyde personality taking hold as he emptied the magazine.

Scar and Burns crashed their SUV's through another fence and into a parking lot, with office buildings to either side. Burns lost control of his big SUV as he tried to make a tight turn into an alley at the back of the lot. The SUV slid into a cement wall and stalled. Scar came up behind him, bringing two cars full of Jijis on his tail. The Jijis stopped short and got out of their cars firing at the trapped vehicles. Bullets battered the vehicles taking out the glass. Scar's men spilled out, took cover and returned fire. The gunfire echoed off the two buildings, and was non-stop.

Meeks grabbed Scar's shoulder. "What's our game plan?"

"Bassett should be here in any second. Take a couple of guys and get into this building." He turned and shouted. "Burns, make sure no one is trying to flank us."

Burns nodded, and grabbed a couple of men, crawled around the crashed SUV and ran down the alley.

Meeks followed Burns' lead and ran around the corner with them.

"We're going all the way around," said Burns.

Meeks acknowledged and then found a window. He pulled his M4 up and shot the window out. He and his men climbed in and ran through the hallway. They arrived at the front entrance and discovered they had the advantage. The Jiji's rear was exposed.

Meeks sent one of the men down the hall to locate Burns. Moments later he came back. "He's coming around now."

"Did he see you?"

"Yeah, I tapped on the window," he chuckled.

"Nice," responded Meeks.

They all loaded fresh magazines. Meeks unlocked the door and stepped outside just as Burns came around the corner. He gave him a nod. The six Shadow Patriots lined up behind the Jijis and began firing, taking them all down.

Meeks saw the flashing lights of a police car coming across the field, but knew it was Bassett.

Bassett pulled in and got out of the squad car.

Scar hustled over to them. He could hear more gunfire in the distance. He got on the radio. "Captain, you there?"

"He's not," replied Elliott. "I dropped him and Peterson off somewhere and now I can't find them."

Scar gave Meeks a concerned look as he lifted the radio back to his mouth. "Nate, where you at?"

"I've got two of them on my tail. I can't shake them."

Scar looked at Bassett.

"Get him back this way," said Bassett.

"Nate, can you get back over here?"

"Hell, I'm so friggen lost on this damn golf course, I don't know where I'm at."

"Bassett's got the cop lights flashing on. Can you see them?"

There was silence for a few moments. "I see him."

"We'll be ready. Anyone else out there, come toward the flashing lights. We'll take out your tails as you pass us."

Bassett scanned the area and pointed to the golf course. "Let's get over to those trees."

They quickly relocated and got ready.

As soon as they were set up, more of their friends came rushing in from the field. Scar got on the radio and told them to block off the exit to Mack Ave. Gunfire erupted as Nate yelled into the radio that he was coming through now.

Nate flew across the road and into the field. Right behind him were two black Mercedes. The Jijis broke off the chase when they began taking fire. Their two cars didn't get far as tires were blown out and glass was shattered. The Shadow Patriots charged the vehicles and chased the Jijis across the field as they tried to escape. The cars had come to an immediate halt as the Shadow Patriots encircled them in rapid gunfire.

Elliott came across the field and stopped at the sight of the mayhem. Scar and Basset ran to him. Scar looked in the back and saw Sadie and Reese holding their pistols. "Where's the Captain?"

"I don't know. I dropped him and Peterson off and lost track of them."

"Bassett, how many cars did you see?" asked Scar.

"Three."

"Okay, and there were three chasing us. How many did we take out?"

"There's two back there, and two here," said Meeks.

"Elliott how many were chasing you?"

"I think only one."

"Okay, we've got at least one more out there, maybe two," said Scar in a concerned voice. "Let's get back to the other side of the golf course and find them."

As the men headed across the course, they broke through the trees and heard Winters yelling across a green. Relief washed over the men when Winters and Peterson came walking toward them.

Then they all heard the roar of an engine come out of nowhere.

CHAPTER 80

S car turned toward the sound. A car with no lights came racing down the fairway headed towards Winters and Peterson.

They turned as the car came barreling toward them.

Mr. Peterson reacted first and shoved Winters out of the way just as the car plowed into him. The impact threw him onto the hood. He bounced off the windshield and over the top.

The rest of the Shadow Patriots came running at the car and opened fire. The car spun around and came to a stop.

Nate rushed the car by himself carrying an M4 he had taken from the tall cop he had kicked in the groin. He emptied the magazine. Threw in another and kept firing. He forced his deadly weapon into the driver's smashed window and finished him off. He dropped his rifle, grabbed his Mark 23, reached for the rear door, opened it and dragged the bloodied passenger out. He fired directly into the man's face. The bullets came exploding out of the back of his head.

Winters got up and hurried over to Mr. Peterson. He could see he was already dead before he reached him. A cold sweat poured out as he bent down and embraced the broken body. He looked into the face of the old man, and watched the blood run down his forehead. Guilt overwhelmed him as he cradled the body. He wanted it to be him. It would be easier than having to grieve for this sweet man, who did nothing, but help them in their time of need.

All the men surrounded Winters and stood over him. A silence of mourning swept over them.

Winters felt a small pair of arms wrap around his neck. Sadie sat down and snuggled up next to him. Winters collected his thoughts, and let go of Mr. Peterson. He picked Sadie up off the ground. He looked at Scar and motioned him to bring the body with them. Scar put his hand on Winters' back and gave him a sorrowful nod.

Winters carried Sadie across the field in silence.

EPILOGUE

After tending to his mother's wounds, Major Green found Pruitt's Porsche and dumped his body in it. He then drove the car to Pruitt's house and put it in the garage. Green decided to set the house on fire, but not before grabbing all the files and photos that Pruitt had in his office. He also took the man's laptop and the wad of cash from the bedroom. He stuffed everything into a leather bag, walked out the backdoor, and over to the next block where his friend Sam waited for him.

The Shadow Patriots, after reuniting with Amber and the others back in South Bend made their way to Canada to nurse their wounds. The past ten days had been both devastating and triumphant. They had liberated Reese, and many other girls, from having to continue to endure the living nightmare of being sex slaves. They had rescued Amber before she became one of the pleasure objects, found Sadie and took her in. They had killed dirty cops and Jijis, and discovered Perozzi was conspiring with Mordulfah. They had also lost many men during the past ten days, which put a damper on any celebration.

Winters sat in his room playing Cat's Cradle with Sadie, and relishing his down time. General Standish had, once again, seen to their needs, and had even gotten Sadie a couple of new outfits. The henna dye on her hands was starting to fade and she was her perky self again. Winters admired her resiliency and wished he could bounce back as quickly. The past ten days weighed heavily on his shoulders. His thoughts were on the lives they'd lost and how Mr. Peterson had sacrificed his own life to protect him. He hoped to honor these sacrifices and be able to continue in the long coming days.

Sadie laughed at him. "You can't keep making the same lame moves."

A slight smile formed on his face. "I'm just not as good as you."

"Finally," she giggled.

"What?"

"You smiled. It's the first one I've seen since we got here."

Winters thought about that. "Is it really?"

"Yes, and I'm glad. I like it when you smile."

Winters gave her another one.

There was a knock on the door. They both turned to see it open and Colonel Brocket peering through. "Hope I'm not interrupting anything."

"Not at all Colonel, come in. Sadie is just schooling me in a game of Cat's Cradle."

"Why, I haven't played that since I was a boy."

"You can have the next turn," said Sadie.

"Can I take a rain check on that?"

She looked puzzled.

"He means, can he play later," said Winters. "What can we do for you, Colonel?"

"General Standish and I would like a word with you, if you don't mind."

Winters looked at Sadie. "We'll pick this up later. Why don't you go see what the other girls are up to?"

Winters walked to the conference room where General Standish was waiting. It was the same room he had taken tea with them a few weeks ago. He noticed they were using the same tea set as before. He sat down in the same blue swivel chair.

"Captain, thanks for coming. Can I assume you have everything you need?"

"Yes sir, and thank you, everyone has been more than gracious."

"Well Captain, everyone here, and I mean everyone, are in awe of what you and your men have accomplished."

As before, Winters was humbled, never being comfortable with compliments.

"We interrogated Commandant Boxer again, asking him specific questions about Mordulfah, and he confirmed the info you provided. It all fits nicely with what our contacts in Washington were able to ascertain. We do know, of course, Perozzi's ultimate goal is to be in complete control of the United States, but with such a vast country, that will take considerable time. How many different ways they're going about it is still a mystery, but we'll piece it together. We think Mordulfah is only a small part of the overall plan. While the war out West isn't going well for your military, it's certainly being used as an excuse for Perozzi to gather more power."

Winters listened to the chilling words as if they were spoken in a dream. With everything that had been happening to the country in the past year, none of this came at much of a surprise, but hearing it from Standish's deep voice, seemed to give it more credence.

"Corporal Bassett was able to get us in contact with Major Green."

This caught Winters' attention.

Standish filled him in on what was happening with Major Green, and about Green's mother being held hostage.

Winters was shocked by the news, but now had more appreciation of the danger Major Green had put himself in by working for Reed.

Standish continued telling Winters that Green was committed to stay in Washington, and had already made some important contacts with like-minded power players. People who were willing to support the cause and bring Perozzi down.

The news reached deep into his soul and gave Winters much needed encouragement. He leaned back in his chair, and slowly formed his third smile of the day. He was pleased with the knowledge, that for the first time since losing his friends at the train station, the Shadow Patriots were not alone in their struggle.

Thanks, to all my Shadow Patriots fans for your support. I've had the pleasure of meeting many of you and have enjoyed interacting with you and reading your comments on facebook.

Reviews, good or bad are important to any author, so if you have the time, please leave a review. Also, visit my fan page on facebook, under The Shadow Patriots.

The third book, Dark Maneuvers, will be available in the fall of 2015. It will involve more characters, plenty of action, more political intrigue, and I'll reveal all the secret dealings of Gerald Perozzi and Lawrence Reed.

I had hoped to finish the series on the third book, but because this story took a left turn in order to meet Amber, Reese and Sadie, it will be a four book series.

Stay strong my fellow patriots, no matter what country you live in, do not be afraid to stand tall, we all have much at stake.